CU00660579

INTO THE ABYSS

She knew that to get the answers, she would have to descend further. She would have to enter the abyss itself. She would have to risk not coming back. No safety net. Nothing to pull her back toward consciousness, save her own determination to live, save whatever she encountered at the bottom of the bottomless pit. And that was bound to be hostile . . . wasn't it?

She teetered at the very edge. She felt the cord that connected her to the material world. It was fraying . . . weakening.

Beneath her, the black maelstrom churned.

Then the perspective shifted. It was as if the whirling chasm had become a scrying bowl. She knelt at the edge. The wind was more powerful now, and the shrieks of the maddened birds more dissonant. But in the chaos she could see images . . . pieces of the real world. The bottomless pit was also a window into the world . . . a sort of two-way mirror between realities.

She saw a graveyard. She saw a woman. She saw a crow.

LOOK FOR MORE *THE CROW* BOOKS
PUBLISHED BY HARPERCOLLINS:

The Crow: Quoth the Crow
by David Bischoff

The Crow: Clash by Night
by Chet Williamson

The Crow: The Lazarus Heart
by Poppy Z. Brite

The Crow: Wicked Prayer
by Norman Partridge

ATTENTION: ORGANIZATIONS AND CORPORATIONS
Most HarperEntertainment books are available at special
discounts for bulk purchases for sales promotions, premi-
ums, or fund-raising. For information please call or write:
Special Markets Department, HarperCollins Publishers Inc.,
10 East 53rd Street, New York, NY 10022.
Telephone: (212) 207-7528. Fax: (212) 207-7222.

THE CROW™

Temple of Night

S. P. SOMTOW

INSPIRED BY THE SERIES CREATED BY

JAMES O'BARR

HarperEntertainment
An Imprint of HarperCollinsPublishers

 HarperEntertainment
An Imprint of HarperCollins*Publishers*

If you purchased this book without a cover, you should
be aware that this book is stolen property. It was reported as
"unsold and destroyed" to the publisher and neither
the author nor the publisher has received any
payment for this "stripped book."

This is a work of fiction. The characters, incidents, and
dialogues are products of the author's imagination and are not
to be construed as real. Any resemblance to actual events or
persons, living or dead, is entirely coincidental.

Copyright © 1999 by Edward R. Pressman Film Corporation.
All rights reserved. Printed in the United States of America.
No part of this book may be used or reproduced in any manner
whatsoever without written permission except in the case of
brief quotations embodied in critical articles and reviews.
For information address HarperCollins Publishers Inc.,
10 East 53rd Street, New York, NY 10022.

HarperCollins®, ♠®, and HarperEntertainment™ are
trademarks of HarperCollins Publishers Inc.

The Crow™ is a trademark of
Edward R. Pressman Film Corporation.

A trade paperback edition of this book was published in 1999.

Cover illustration © 1999 by Cliff Nielsen

ISBN 0-06-105993-5

First mass-market edition printing: November 2000

Printed in the United States of America

Visit HarperEntertainment on the World Wide Web at
www.harpercollins.com

00 01 02 03 04 ❖ 10 9 8 7 6 5 4 3 2 1

To Jerbear & Ste

ACKNOWLEDGMENTS
AND DISCLAIMERS

This novel is a work of fiction. It takes place in a Universe similar to, yet subtly different from our own. Any similarity between the characters, persons, events, places, and circumstances herein and characters, persons, events, places, and circumstances in the world the reader inhabits are purelycoincidental, unintentional, and accidental; they are merely the result of this author's perfervid imagination. None of these things ever happened. I made it up. It isn't true. Thank you for your attention.

I would like to thank John Douglas, Jeff Conner, and of course the visionary James O'Barr for allowing me to make a guest appearance in his Universe. I'd also like to thank Eleanor Wood, my determined agent, Bob Villard, my flagellating manager, P. D. Cacek for making wise comments about my initial premise for this novel, and a Thai shamaness (who must remain nameless) for her insights into how the spirit world works.

contents

Temple of Night

prologue
THE DREAM

EYES. EYES. EYES.

Staring. Accusing. Recriminating. Derisive. Mocking. Infuriated. Raging. Eyes. Eyes. Eyes. Eyes, nothing but eyes, all eyes on him, all eyes turned to him, singling him out. Eyes in the shadows, eyes behind pillars, eyes in the sky.

He hastens. It is night. Has to be night, for the only light comes from the eyes. It is maybe a forest. The chittering of wild animals, the distant trumpeting of an elephant . . . yeah . . . a jungle. Dark, exotic, full of primal terror. Or the back streets of a huge bustling city. Yeah. City. It has to be a city. The jangling cacophony in the background is resolving into sounds of a city: sirens, snarling traffic, shouts and cries . . . but he can't make out the language. Or the odors. He doesn't recognize some of them. Flowers and fruits he's never smelled before all mingling with smells that he knows too well: rotting fish, gasoline, old Dumpsters. He keeps walking. Still can't see anything but the eyes. He walks faster, faster. Doesn't know why he needs to get away. Maybe someone chasing him. Maybe . . . he doesn't know.

A strange ache in his groin, equally compounded of desire and pain. He wants . . . needs . . . he cannot say. And then, rounding a corner, retreating into an alley even more dark than before—

A doorway.

Light. And the light disperses the staring eyes. Now there's only one pair of eyes: eyes full of solemn serenity . . . childlike yet infinitely ancient.

A woman in the doorway. Perfect woman. China-doll features—complexion porcelain-clear, hair long and jet-black and billowing in a wind that seems only to blow around the woman. And a smile that seems to be the source of the sourceless light.

A dark diaphanous robe is all she wears. The robe, too, flutters in the wind that seems to blow for her alone, for the air around him is sultry, dripping with dark moisture, preternaturally still.

Come, she whispers, *come, come, come . . .*

"How did you pick me?" he whispers. "How is it that I deserve you?"

You paid for me, she says softly. *You paid the price in blood and suffering.*

He follows.

Up a staircase . . . rickety wooden steps . . . decaying walls . . . the light from the woman's eyes still the only light, the twin shafts of pale radiance falling on images etched into the walls, images of unspeakable acts . . . sketchily painted, like cave drawings. Hearts being ripped from the chests of still-living victims, arms and legs being severed by huge wheeled machines with rotating blades, eyeless faces, skull-like, feasting on the amputated breasts of screaming women.

How can this woman be in this place? He cannot tell. He follows. The staircase turns, turns, turns . . . becomes a spiral. The walls reel with images of horror, flames that seem alive, licking through gutted cages where chained children wait to be consumed, their sunken eyes set into hollow cheeks. He holds in his terror. He follows. She beckons always, beckons him above . . . beckons him toward an L-shaped room at the pinnacle of the infinite stairwell. Doors open for him, doors within doors within doors . . . and finally she is there, inside the room, a room that glows with the red light of passion.

I am yours, she says, *if you can find the way within.*

"Yes!" he cries. And moves toward her. Wants her. Wants to feel the warmth of her flesh against his cold, rejected body . . . the moisture of her mouth against his desiccated lips.

Slowly she is peeling away the sheer black fabric that envelops her.

You want me, don't you? she whispers. *Come closer. Feel. Touch.*

He stretches out his hand. She smiles. The smile, the eyes, all suffused with warmth and light. His hand touches flesh. But it's not flesh. His hand follows the delicate curve of her bosom, tears at the remnants of the cloth that cover her. She arches her back, seductively licks her lips. But there's something wrong with the skin . . . it's not skin at all, it's slippery, spongy, like the texture of ground beef wrapped in Saran Wrap.

What is wrong with her? He pulls her to him. He grabs her flesh, which gives like Silly Putty and springs back when he lets go. His hand roves down to her vulva now, seeking a lubricious opening, and encounters only . . . more skin, more latexlike covering.

What's the matter with you? Don't you want to fuck me?

"There's . . . nothing to . . . no opening . . ."

He's panicking. The woman is writhing in his arms. He realizes that there are no openings at all . . . even her lips are covered with a translucent sheath. Her whole body seems like a silicone doll, retaining the impression of his fingers before it slowly springs back into shape. There's nothing inside her but some viscous gelatinous fluid, no bones, no muscle, no structure. . . . *What is she?*

I am the Ur-Woman, she says. *All women are in me. Conquer me, and you conquer the very earth herself.*

"But how can I—"

She screams now, the cackle of an evil witch, laced with the silvery laughter of a siren. *I am the virgin of all virgins. I am she who has never been breached, and you are the one who comes before all the others. If you want to fuck me*, she cries, *you'll have to cut your own opening!*

And she spins away from him—and suddenly—in his hands—there is a knife—a glassy, black knife—obsidian—like the knives that used to cut out human hearts in the Aztec city of Tenochtitlan—a knife to rip open the wall between worlds, a knife to divide the darkness from the light . . .

and he feels greater than himself . . . his penis is rampant, all-powerful, godlike. He wants to, needs to, rive the rubber flesh, to slide his human weapon down the avenue of blood.

He slashes her! Rips her abdomen! Clutches her to him, and penetrates her! Oh, the warm blood that sluices about his penis . . . the warm, slick, oily life force! Oh, the—

Are you all right? We can go on later. If you want.
No. No. I have to.
Yes. Go back inside. Pull out the memory. Uproot the trauma.
Yes. Yes.
I'm taking notes.
Am I sick, am I really really sick?
Perhaps . . . perhaps . . . now . . . go back into the dream.
But it's the bad part now. The part that really scares me. The part that makes me afraid to go to sleep at night.
It's all right. I'm there with you. I'll face the darkness with you. Afterward . . . you'll sleep. And if you don't, I'll write you a prescription.
Thank you.

—feel of the innards, slipping and sliding . . . the living intestines wrapping and raveling about him, tightening around his flesh and squeezing him in powerful, rhythmic pulses . . . and then, just in the moment when he is about to burst forth in unbearable ecstasy, he—

• • •

Go on. It's all right.

—suddenly—a sharp intolerable pain—like a shard of glass being rammed into the glans and—

—inside the woman—something living—something sharp, tearing at him—a beak—within the woman's rubber womb—a tangle of raspy feathers—slicing at him—jabbing into his flesh—he feels his blood oozing out, mingling with the bubbling, seething blood within the woman—blood that boils like lava—and, as he backs away, the woman's abdomen—

—bursts open—two creatures with onyx feathers, intertwined, creatures with crimson eyes and beaks and claws of serrated steel—opening their wings—wings that tinkle as though they were stitched together from infinitesimal fragments of broken glass—the eyes—burning—hellish—the beaks full of razor-sharp teeth—splitting the woman in two as the twin birds explode out of the bloody womb—

He is screaming now, backing away as the woman detonates, pieces of charred flesh flying, bone fragments riddling the walls, the eyeballs melting into balls of liquid fire, the tongue coiling and uncoiling like a dying serpent—and he runs, he runs, runs—

—but the room is a circle, a treadmill, a Möbius strip that meets itself in the middle and there is no escape as the crystal ravens, one on either side, pursue him, dart down, dive down onto his shoulders to rip out strips of bloody flesh, and still he runs, even though he's trapped, even though there can be no possible escape—

—and now he's being slammed against the wall and the whole room is spinning, spinning, spinning—the world is a circle—a catherine wheel— a chariot of fire—agony as his arms are pushed against the wall, as the twin ravens bore through his palms with their beaks, as they pin him against the wall in a grotesque crucifixion—and he cries out, to the whirling mass of flesh at the center of the room, the tornado of bloody tissue that was once the Ur-Woman—*Why have you forsaken me?*—and there comes no answer, only the searing pain as the crows' beaks rip through flesh, bone, and skin and down into stucco and brick—

—and then you wake up?

Yeah. I wake up.

You have to try to stay asleep. Tell yourself it's a dream. Tell yourself, "This is a problem, a monstrous darkness within me, and I will confront it, and I will be victorious." Face the horror. Overcome. Find out what the dream is trying to tell you—and learn from it.

Only one problem with that, Doc.

What?

It's not a dream.

CONFIDENTIAL REPORT

TO: Amelia Steinbrunner
        Personnel Review,
        State Department

FROM: Dr. Ezekiel Melendez
SUBJECT: Dirk Temple

The subject appears to suffer from delusional thinking, megalomania, a messiah complex, and fear of sexual contact. Despite these problems, however, there seems to be nothing that can't be controlled with a judicious regimen of Xanax.

My recommendation is that he be cautiously assigned to noncrucial duties—rubber stamping documents, that sort of thing. You know the routine. A back office in some third world country. Asia's good, they're more tolerant of weirdoes. I don't suppose he'll do much harm—he's an ineffectual little guy.

His dreams are pretty interesting, in a low-budget-horror-movie kind of way. They do tap into the Joseph Campbell–Carl Jung "big picture"—you know, the vision of the anima—the doorway—the symbolic use of twin ravens or crows as harbingers of death. Wonder if he knows anything about Norse mythology? And the Jesus thing with the crows' beaks in the palms . . . there's a new twist on stigmata.

Well—keep him under control. Lunch at Honi Soit next week? And send me some more interesting subjects—I'm collecting dreams for a new academic treatise. . . .

part one

The City That Never Sleeps

Four faces hath Great Brahma:
That's known throughout the land:
But a thousand times more two-faced
Are the people of Siam.
    —Sunthorn Phu,
    18th-century Thai poet

one

THE COFFINMAKER

WHEN SHE WAS A CHILD THEY USED TO CALL IT THE
Venice of the East, an emerald city quilted with
canals and studded with temples. Stilted houses
backed out over the city's waterways. Stoneware jars,
tall as a twelve-year-old, captured the monsoon; the
rains were pure and sweet to the taste. Her friends
leaped naked from rickety wooden bridges into clear
water that teemed with catfish and river shrimp as
big as your fist.

At night, huddled under mosquito nets, you listened to the whispering of spirits. There were a thousand spirits with a thousand names, and all as familiar
to her as the boy next door, who never spoke, and the
ducks who scavenged under the house.

But now it was the eve of the millennium, and
Linda Dusit's childhood home on the canal was part of
a seven-story shopping mall. The banana and mango
orchard was a parking structure, and the canal itself,
the *klong* as they called it, was an on ramp. There
weren't many *klongs* left. The few that remained were
stagnant, piled high with garbage. Mosquito factories.

There were no stilted houses either. Condominiums and apartment complexes towered above a congested expressway. Without zoning, building styles clashed: here a slablike, primary-colored building like a monstrous Mondrian, there a Greek colonnade athwart a deco skyscraper; there again an untouched temple, its pointed eaves and pastel pagodas drowning in a sea of architectural discord; and everywhere neon. Neon that screamed out world-class name brands: Coke and Versace and Tag Heuer and Sony. Neon for massage parlors, transvestite clubs, live sex shows, gay bars, and fortunetellers. The concrete supports of an uncompleted L-train threading through the chaos, symbolizing both bureaucratic bungling and eternal optimism: all these things were Bangkok, a city both futuristic and feudalistic, a city where the first and the third worlds were in endless collision.

One thing, however, had not changed in fifty years. For all its multitudes, Bangkok still had more spirits than people. You didn't have to be a shaman to sense that.

Then again, Linda Dusit was, indeed, a shaman, on weekends at least. She tried not to let it show, but in a place like Bangkok, people just knew.

Like that morning. The morning it all began. The morning she was on her way to the airport to pick up her grandson, Stephen, who was flying in from Los Angeles, and she decided to make a brief detour to pick out her coffin for the month.

She liked to buy a coffin the second week of every month—she had a thing about allowing a week for her paycheck from the university to clear—but today was only the second of March. Linda was a creature of habit, and this disruption bothered her. She tried to tell herself that it was only because, with the traffic, this longer route to the airport had to pass the Alley of the Coffinmakers anyway, that this was saving her a half day in traffic next week, that she wanted to clear more time to spend with her grandson . . . but she knew these were all rationalizations after the fact.

It wasn't logic that brought her there. It was one of those pesky spirits—probably, Linda was thinking, the coffin's prospective occupant, impatiently awaiting the start of his journey toward his next life.

She told her chauffeur to let her off at the corner, and to bring the Mercedes around to the other end of the alley. It was early and many of the coffin shops were still shuttered. That annoyed her a little. She was a creature of habit. She couldn't go to her favorite coffin shop, the only one where they knew to bring her a cold can of Diet Pepsi, a rare commodity in the downscale side of town. Any coffin shop would have done perfectly well, of course. You didn't shop for them like you'd shop for a designer dress. It was different in America, where you could go to a showroom and pick out a pretty coffin for yourself, velvet-lined, perhaps, or engraved with a flowery gold monogram, and even get it on credit or layaway.

Like many well-to-do people in Thailand, Linda bought coffins not for herself, but for the poor. To provide a vessel for a pauper to travel toward his next incarnation is an act that greases the wheel of karma, and can ease your own suffering in a future life. If it is for a stranger, all the better, for then there is no emotional attachment to taint the act of charity with self-interest. Some of Linda's friends bought coffins once a year, getting a quantity discount, reasoning that one could purchase the same amount of karmic merit for less money; the karmic equivalent of buying stocks on margin, she supposed. But Linda always did it one at a time, and put as much thought into it as if she was paying for the funeral of someone she loved.

It was getting into the height of the dry-hot season, and even at this hour she was sweating. The coffins on display were simple things, with very little carving, made of cheap woods for the most part. Linda was becoming annoyed with herself for having given in to one of her hunches.

The white Mercedes waited at the other end of the alley. The motor was running. She was sure the air-conditioning would be crisp and chill. She started to flag the driver, but before she could do so, she was drawn to the window of the last coffin shop on her left. There was something in the window . . . a coiling mist, a shimmering of the sunlight in the glass . . . a cold, staring eye, some creature, perhaps a bird. The pit of her stomach was knotting again. *What do you want from me?* she thought. *Who are you?* No answer, only a sound like the beating of great wings . . . the churning of a dark wind. She had to fight it. Visions were annoying if you couldn't keep them under control. She opened her eyes. For a fraction of a second she had been away from her body. Warily, she looked around. Shamans are a dime a dozen in Bangkok, but Linda did not believe in advertising.

The aluminum shutters were being cranked up by a shirtless old Chinese man. Linda suddenly felt a stabbing pain in her abdomen. She clutched her side, had to grit her teeth to avoid an unseemly cry of agony. Those pesky spirits again! She murmured a hasty pacifying mantra. *Who is this?* she thought. *What soul's need is so dire that it could force me from my rigid routine and compel me to buy it a coffin out of turn?*

"You come inside now, elder sister," said the *thaokae* as he finished rolling up the shutter. "You see what you want." He spoke Thai with a decidedly Chinese accent, though his family had probably not been to the motherland in generations. One of his incisors had the glint of twenty-four-karat gold. He seemed to know who she was, had even been expecting her.

Of course, he probably made every customer feel that way—a salesman's trick, she thought. He stepped into his shop, pausing in the doorway to beckon her with a strange half smile.

She looked back at the window.

There was a coffin there, a double coffin. It wasn't like the others on the alley. It was teakwood, and intricately carved in high relief with celestial beings—*apsaras*—strumming on ancient instruments. On the lid, done in a dark mahogany and inlaid into the teak, was a crow. Its wings were spread out so the wing tips wrapped around the coffin's sides. A single ruby eye glared from its profile. Though the heavenly creatures were depicted very naturalistically, indeed, alluringly bare-breasted, the crow was carved in a more stylized, abstract way—it seemed almost an afterthought. But the eye demanded attention: it smoldered; it seemed like a little piece of Hell.

Resolutely, she looked away and followed the old man into the coffin shop. It was dark inside, and the

air-conditioning was struggling; bare concrete walls
sweated. Propped against them were the plain cheap
wooden boxes that you could buy in any shop in the
alley. On the floor, a shrine to a Chinese luck deity,
painted a garish red; behind the counter, on a shelf,
the traditional bronze Nang Kwak, the beckoning
goddess, held out her arm to draw in customers. Ten-
drils of incense wafted from both shrines.

"The distinguished lady is from America?" said
the *thaokae*. "It is rare for overseas Thais to visit the
homeland during the hot season; most can't stand the
weather."

There was nothing supernatural about his seem-
ing to know where she was from. Linda Dusit owned
a Thai restaurant in Los Angeles and taught one
semester a year at Chulalongkorn University in
Bangkok; and when you establish a home away from
Bangkok, everything changes: your body language,
the way you dress; most of all, there's a rhythm of
social intercourse, a hierarchical way of thinking, and
if you're not around it every day, you get careless, you
start to treat inferiors with too much familiarity, you
start to contradict superiors instead of dropping subtle hints, you forget the appropriate formula of
politeness—or impoliteness—that you're supposed
to use on people. Linda ignored him for a while; he
was probably trying to figure out whether she was
going to bargain.

"I want a coffin," she said at last. "I buy them
every month, so don't treat me like a tourist."

"Most assuredly, distinguished elder sister," said
the storekeeper. "It's for the poor, isn't it? We make a
line of coffins for charity-seekers. They are shoddy

work, but the poor don't seem to mind." He waved at the coffins that lined one wall; they were little more than packing crates. "A thousand baht each; six for five thousand." She paused, waiting for him to go on. "Well, eight hundred," he said. "Seven-fifty even. A distinguished lady like you shouldn't need to haggle. In fact, an arrangement could be made, perhaps; she need not even come to the Alley of the Coffinmakers at all, in future. She could perhaps just send her driver, and we do take American Express, MasterCard, and Visa."

But Linda Dusit wasn't there. She had left her body again.

She found herself in a gray wasteland . . . like a black-and-white movie . . . a desert . . . craters . . . more like the moon than the earth . . . a tempest seemed to be raging around her . . . a bracing wind whistling . . . her white hair flying about her . . . but the landscape itself preternaturally still . . . as though divorced from the storm that swirled over it. She knelt down, emptied the vessel of her mind by reciting a mantra of ultimate nothingness . . . she clasped her hands in a *wai* of obeisance then touched her hands and forehead to the ground . . . the ground was wood. Hard, heavy, black wood. The pits, fissures, and craters were the knots and surface features of a vast slab of wood. In the distance she could see something red . . . fiery . . . spheroid . . . hugging the gray horizon like a sunset.

I'm on the coffin, she thought. *I'm walking across the surface of the crow carving . . . and that glaring red sun is the eye of the crow.*

The wind howled. And now she could hear voices in the wind. Calling out names. Her own name among them. "Who are you?" she screamed. "What are you?"

The wind was not just any wind. It was the beating of great wings. And the eye wasn't any deep crimson ruby cabochon. It concealed a gateway to some unearthly realm. Linda had traveled to many otherworldly kingdoms . . . had visited the dreams of many who consulted her . . . had spoken to higher consciousnesses . . . but this was a darker realm than any she had encountered. She was afraid. Of course she was afraid. This was Narok, the dark domain ruled over by Yama, Lord of the Dead. It had to be. Narok, the nine-leveled Hell spoken of in the Buddhist scriptures, and in the writings of ancient Christians.

She tried to make light of it. She whispered a mantra to dispel fear, then resolutely began to walk in the direction of the fiery sunset. No, she did not walk exactly . . . her feet had left the surface of the mahogany world and she was slicing through the dense air . . . accelerating as she neared the vortex . . . the eye growing . . . filling her field of vision . . . the iris a whirlwind, the still center of the whirlwind, the pupil of the crow's eye, a bottomless abyss . . . a circle of ultimate darkness. And now, her flimsy floral print summer dress flapping about her, her arms outstretched as though they were wings, she could feel herself swooping down into that pit. . . .

"I'll buy it," she said abruptly, snapping awake. "I'll have my driver come by to pay the bill in a day or two."

"But . . . the distinguished elder sister isn't even going to bargain?" said the *thaokae*, incredulous.

"That crow coffin is a very fine piece of work, and as you can see . . . it is built for two. Unless, of course, the occupant is particularly . . . wide." He chuckled, then stopped abruptly.

"Don't worry," she said, "I'll watch my weight."

He nodded. "I'll have it sent along to your family temple," he said.

It was only later, interminably stuck in traffic on the expressway, with Don Muang Airport as visible and as unattainable as the promised land, that it occurred to her that she had not told the *thaokae* her identity . . . yet he must clearly have known.

Oh well, she thought, *all those coffinmakers gossip. They must have known I'm a regular.*

When was this traffic jam going to end? Outside her Mercedes the sun blazed, although it was not yet noon. Inside, the air was cold and sterile, and the sound system was playing a *Lion King* medley, and Yom, her taciturn driver, sat rigid and expressionless as a robot.

"How far are we?" she said. "Will we make it in time?"

"I don't know, *Khunpuying*," he said deferentially. "Perhaps a half hour. But it's less than a kilometer . . . as the crow flies."

And Linda Dusit knew that she had but to close her eyes, take a deep breath, and murmur a few magical words to be hurled once more into the whirlwind, to pass through the crimson eye into the desolate kingdom of the dead.

Something is about to happen, she told herself.

Every now and then—call it a conjoining of the stars, call it serendipity, call it happenstance—there comes a time when people and events that have no business being together are juxtaposed into some hypercosmic nexus. It is in those moments that magic is real . . . that the dead truly speak to the living . . . that the doors between worlds are opened for a few moments . . . only moments. But in those moments one can live centuries.

Is it my death that all this portends? she thought. *Or many deaths? Or am I to be the lone survivor of some catastrophe?*

There was a break in the traffic. Yom stepped on the gas and began flying along the expressway, weaving in and out of slower cars with a virtuoso dexterity that Bangkok driving rarely afforded.

What was rarer? thought Linda Dusit. A grand cosmic conjunction such as she dreaded . . . or a break in the Bangkok traffic? Perhaps one was omen of the other. But which, and of which?

She closed her eyes in meditation once again.

A single syllable came spontaneously to her lips: *Ka.*

She wasn't sure what it meant.

An Egyptian word for soul.

A Thai word for a crow.

Now there was an arcane connection.

two

THE DIPLOMAT

FRIDAY NIGHT AT THE CULTURAL AFFAIRS OFFICE. Everyone was clearing out as quickly as they could, even Porntip, the floor receptionist. When Dirk Temple looked up from his desk, she was putting away the last of the files, and she had already turned on the answering machine.

She put her head in the doorway.

"I'm leaving now, Mr. Temple . . . unless you have a last minute emergency."

"I don't think so, Porno," he said.

"Oh, stop calling me Porno, Mr. Temple," she said. But she giggled. That was the best thing about the girls in this country, Dirk thought. None of this sexual harassment bullshit. Anyway, with a name like Porntip, a Thai girl working for Americans needed to develop a good sense of humor. He had heard from Schwarz, down the hall, that the girl more than lived up to her name.

"Well, just remember," said Porntip, "you have eleven o'clock staff meeting Monday with ambassador, and lunch with journalist from the U.S. American-

Thai guy. Delicate situation. He's doing undercover piece for tabloid TV show in the States."

"Another exposé of the sex industry?" Dirk said. He tried not to appear alarmed. Nobody in the department knew about . . . what he did in his spare time. He adjusted his glasses.

"Yes, the sex industry," Porntip said. "Be careful with this one . . . he speaks Thai, doesn't scare too easy. His grandmother is *khon song*."

"What's that?"

"Oh, magic stuff. Go into trance, speak with the spirits. Crossing over into other worlds, taking messages. A lot of people believe in her. Linda Dusit."

"Linda? Doesn't sound very Thai."

"She owns a restaurant in Los Angeles. You see, she is used to going from world to world."

He glanced at the appointment sheet she had just handed him. "So what am I to do with this Stephen . . . Lelliott, is that the name? These yellow journalists are all the same. They come here with some high-minded notion of liberating the hookers and end up having their dicks sucked in some sleazy bordello and compromising their . . . ah, objectivity."

"Just be careful. They're always doing stories about the pervs of Bangkok . . . but they never send someone who speaks the lingo before. You just be very careful, Mr. Temple, watch your back. Ambassador's gonna tell you that, too. Politics important. Image important."

"You already know what the ambassadors going to talk to me about on Monday? You don't even have clearance!"

Porntip laughed. "But janitor in ambassador's

office my cousin," she said, and giggled again. "Okay, I go now. I got a two hour commute."

"Holy—two hours?"

"Traffic very bad tonight! Friday night."

She left. Dirk Temple was alone, a hunched, professorial, bespectacled man, deliberate of speech, a little socially awkward, wearing a suit two sizes too big. He was a second-string attaché in a second-string office in the cultural exchange division of the U.S. Information Agency, a minor diplomat whose position didn't even merit an office in the embassy proper, but in this annex on the grounds of the American University Alumni building. His days were spent rubber-stamping meaningless documents and entertaining second-tier cultural icons as they visited Thailand for the dubious purpose of promoting American culture.

Dirk Temple's colleagues didn't know about his other life.

He puttered about the office a little, making sure every pile of papers on his desk was completely straight. He was very meticulous about such things. He made sure all the paper clips were in the paper-clip holder, and sharpened all the pencils in the pencil box. Something was out of place . . . what was it? Oh yes. The stapler. Maddening, maddening! Then he went to the bookshelves behind his desk and nudged each book until its spine was exactly even with its neighbors. He looked about shiftily as he did those innocuous things. Perhaps he knew they were symptomatic of far darker obsessions.

Yes. Dirk's other life.

It wasn't much of an other life yet. But each

weekend the fantasy had crept closer to the edge of possibility.

Perhaps this weekend it would finally happen.

By the time Dirk Temple left the AUA compound, the place was practically deserted. His job came with a car and driver, and an apartment in an all-American suburb, but he never kept the driver weekends. Just as well! He didn't want anyone talking about his other place. The secret weekend place.

As he walked through the parking lot his gait began to straighten. He stopped glancing from side to side. He passed through the gate, accepted the guard's cursory salute, then took off his glasses.

I'm turning into a superhero, he thought. *Pity there's no fucking phone booth.*

No need for a phone booth. He held his head up. The street was crammed with cars. Sunset had brought no relief from the heat. But he was barely sweating. He hit his stride now. He didn't even mind stepping on the cracks in the pavement. He stood a head taller than the people who thronged the sidewalk, hawking flowers, begging, racing to catch their buses. Motorcycles whizzed like mosquitoes between stalled cars; fumes poured into the twilight air. He walked ever more briskly, shedding his mild-mannered bureaucrat persona as he neared the intersection he was looking for—a snarling five-way collision of streets with names like Suriwong, Sathorn, and Silom.

He walked on. On Silom, at sundown, hundreds of vendors set up stalls in the sidewalks, leaving barely enough room to squeeze past. Tourists were every-where. It was a feeding frenzy. You couldn't tell who was feeding on whom. Stacks of fake Armani shirts, fake software, fake Rolexes, fake computer games, and fake jewelry jostled with stalls piled high with antiques, curios, and genuine jewelry. Dirk loved it all. Every sense was on overload. The smells of rotting garbage and night-blooming jasmine laced the air. A noodle stand sprouted surreptitiously in the shadow of a McDonald's.

He turned a corner and was in Patpong, a tiny street that many believed to be the very hub of the sexual adventurer's universe. Bars lined both sides; their garish neon signs, in exotically fractured English, proclaimed a smorgasbord of sensual delights: Pussies Collection, Boy Bar Belle, Motorcycle Sex Queens Parlor, Delightful Vagina, Ping Pong Poo. The neon bounced off the plastic awnings of souvenir stands that glistened with the night air's ripe and rancid sweat; tourists and touts were squashed together, sourceless voices wafted in his ears: "This way, sir. Girl show, very nice, no cover charge. Boy show. Lesbian show. You like. Very cheap, you like. No cover charge." Now and then a hand tugged at his sleeve. They all wanted him. They needed his attention. He was powerful here, a god.

The crowd surged, swelled around him. The tourists, many of them curiously innocent; families with children and cameras thronging the stands to buy their embroidered T-shirts and pirated Play-Station games; two worlds intersecting really, swap meet and sex mart shoehorned into the same narrow street. Amid the tour groups and loud families, it was easy to figure out the seekers of sex; they were solitary; they glanced furtively about; now and then, one, seeing at last the tidbit that he craved, would sort of dart into one of those dim doorways and disappear.

Dirk, too, was looking for tidbits.

But this wasn't like cruising along some stateside boulevard. Here the whores were gregarious. They clustered at card tables. Many wore the uniforms of their establishments; here was a benchful of French maids, there a gaggle of leather sirens. Country girls mostly, sloe-eyed, wearing too much makeup, dusky—these girls did not appeal to Thai aesthetics, which favored an ethereal, almost Eurasian look, but to what was perceived as the more vulgar taste of the foreign visitor—blunt-nosed and in-your-face. Dirk didn't mind that at all. He liked vulgar girls.

He had tried most of the bars that faced the alley, but there were others, hidden ones, ones with inconspicuous back entrances. What would there be on the menu tonight?

Perhaps a buttock-pounding from the ample Miss Piggy? A blowjob from Marvin the Martian? Dirk had his little private nicknames for all the whores he'd purchased over the past year. Sometimes he'd be stuck on one thing for several weeks. He had really enjoyed the spankings administered by a withered crone he called Nurse Ratchett, for instance; for two months he'd kept her Ping-Pong paddle in his office, and he'd get hard just fiddling with it as he carefully rubber-stamped each grant proposal on his desk.

But there was one fantasy he had never dared to indulge.

He didn't even dare think of it too much. But he was thinking about it now. Not directly, of course—

he had kept the fantasy submerged in his unconscious, allowing only the most oblique allusions to reach his conscious thoughts—such as—

Water.

A carving knife.

A rare steak.

A severed head.

I'm going crazy, he thought.

On the other hand, I do have diplomatic immunity. I could get away with a lot. Maybe even—

And then he saw the woman.

—*a figure from a dream—the Ur-Woman—*

No. A thousand just like her on this very street. But . . . she wasn't congregating like the others. She was alone. She stood in a swath of lime-green neon, her face half obscured by the shadow of a doorway, and she had a strange half smile on her lips—not the usual smile of a hooker that says, *Here I am, come get me,* but rather, *You can't catch me.* Which made her irresistible to Dirk Temple.

Her hair was long, waist-length almost, and she didn't have much makeup on. You almost couldn't tell she was a prostitute. Except for what she wore. It was a clinging, silver-lamé halter top and miniskirt . . . the uniform of one particular establishment, the Cleopatra. The Cleo was notorious among the aficionados of this demimonde. It had a reputation . . . but no one was willing to say what that reputation really was. It was one of those bars whose name the ex-pats would invoke in nudge-nudge, yet mantra-like, tones; even more nebulous, and more sinister, was the reputation of the Cleo's owner, Ai Tong. A powerful man. A man who had everybody's number, whose closets housed the collective skeletons of Bangkok's high society. A man never seen in public without at least four bodyguards. The kind of man who might own a whore that refused to act like a whore.

How old was she? Twelve? Thirty? You could never tell with these creatures. This was a street of youthful faces and ancient eyes.

"Hey," he said. "What's your name?"

She merely shook her head. Then turned her back on him, dissolved into the shadows. It was almost supernatural. One moment a woman, the next a whorl of light specks, the flicker of a dying neon sign.

He went after her.

Turned another corner. The Cleo was tucked into a side alley, little wider than the open gutter that ran down the middle. It was quite void of tourists. The laughter, the clamor, the cacophony was muted here; there wasn't even a neon sign above the doorway; but a man-tall statue of Anubis stood guard, as though it were the entrance to an Egyptian tomb, and peeling hieroglyphs adorned the stucco.

The woman paused at the entrance.

A door opened. In the half-light she turned to him and smiled again, that maddening smile that said, *Look, but don't touch*. Didn't she know that she was breaking the rules, that there was nothing on this street that money couldn't buy?

She was such a slight thing. He could break her like a twig.

He had been thinking about violence lately. More

and more and more. Flashes. Disconnected images.

A knife.

A steak.

A woman with her arms outstretched, eyeless, and the blood spurting from the empty sockets . . . calling his name.

A severed head.

Making love in a Jacuzzi of blood.

Then, suddenly, another image—

The Ur-Woman. Leading him up the stairwell. Through the doorway. The woman with the death birds in her womb.

He hadn't had those dreams in a long time. But then again, he wasn't doing the Xanax regularly anymore. Anyway, they had never been dreams. More like prophecies.

He wondered if they would take American Express.

They did not.

He asked about the woman.

Sitting in the lounge—rattan chairs, incense, Egyptian murals—he sipped his drink—one drink was pretty much obligatory in such establishments—and saw nothing special. In a fish tank a bored, naked woman frolicked with a randy porpoise—why did they always have that in every girlie bar these days? What was so sexy about a fucking dolphin? On a platform ringed with flashing purple lights, two women expelled Ping-Pong balls from their pussies while another pulled a string of razor blades from her vagina. Nothing you couldn't see in a dozen other bars on the same street. The customers, too, seemed not to be out of the ordinary. But Dirk had the feeling he was missing something.

A bare-breasted girl—she had the silver lamé miniskirt but no halter top—sidled up to him, pleaded for a drink, and when he looked away, said, "Come on, sir, I miss my quota, you just buy me one drink, I no bother you again," and he almost relented.

But instead he said, "Tell me about the girl."

"What girl? Many girl here."

"No, no. The one who smiles funny."

"She not for you, sir."

"Why not?"

"Just buy me drink, sir, I no bother you no more."

He fished a thousand baht note from his wallet. "No drink," he said. "You sit here, you talk."

"Okay, I talk. My name Keo." There were a hundred Keos working this very strip. It was the Thai equivalent of a hillbilly name; it screamed *poor country girl*. Indentured, perhaps.

"I know what Keo means," he said.

"Oh! You know Thai?"

"It means jewel," he said. "And it also means glass." He drank. "That's so like you people . . . you use the same word for something priceless and something worthless that just gives you the illusion of something priceless. Something's wrong with you people. You don't believe in anything real. You don't have values. How can you? You're all Buddhists. The world is an illusion."

She smiled at him.

"Fuck, even that smile," said Dirk, "that universal smile . . . how does that tourist ad go? 'Land of a thousand smiles.' You smile when you're happy. And you smile when you're wracked with grief. And you smile when you give gifts. And you smile when you stick a knife in people."

She didn't understand a word he said. He didn't care. He kept looking around the room, hoping to catch a glimpse of that woman.

"You take me to hotel?" Keo said, smiling.

"No, no, no, damn it, just sit there and listen to me talk."

She sat there, on the rattan stool, scratching her breast and sipping the glass of tea for which Dirk would be charged the price of a double shot of Black Label. She was unremarkable—all the girls in this barroom were, and so were all the customers—and that lead Dirk to suspect—to *know*—that the Cleo must have other rooms, other mysteries, doors that only money could unlock. He got out another thousand baht. Her attention stopped wandering.

"I see you want me to feed the meter."

She smiled blankly and she stuffed the second thousand into a fold of her miniskirt.

"I don't know why I have to pay someone to just fucking listen to me," he said. "I ought to have you tied to that stool. Then you'd pay attention. And maybe you'd stop smiling."

"If you want tie me up, you have to talk Mr. Tong," she said.

"What if I wanted to cut you up a bit?"

She went on smiling. He drained his drink, and as he set it down he felt a hand on his shoulder. He didn't turn. The hand was not a tender hand. He heard a voice in his ear. A wet rasp tinged with garlic.

"Mr. Tong could not help overhearing your conversation," he said.

"Mr. Tong," said Dirk Temple, "isn't even in this room."

"No," said the voice, "but his ears are."

"So I see," said Dirk.

The girl went on smiling.

"So," said Dirk, "there's an inner sanctum of some kind? And somehow I've come up with the magic word that lets me in?"

"There are no magic words, Mr. Temple."

"You know who I am."

"Mr. Tong sees all, knows all."

"And why does he want to meet me now?"

"No reason," said the voice in his ear, "unless it is to ask you how he may be of service to you."

"I've heard a lot about your boss's services," said Dirk, though truth to tell he had heard only the reputation, which came without salacious details. "I've seen one of your boss's . . . special women."

"Dao," said the voice.

Which was the Thai word for star.

"How much?" said Dirk.

"You have money," said the voice. "You'll need it, of course. But for services of the highest quality, there is a price beyond money. I refer, of course, to your soul."

"Now you're talking," Dirk Temple said. A sense of unspeakable excitement was welling up in him. He hadn't felt it since he'd been a child . . . since he stopped believing in Santa Claus. He knew he was trembling. He gripped the side of the table to steady himself. *My soul!* he thought. *Since I don't even believe in the soul, why shouldn't I trade it in for a few moments of pleasure? My soul, my soul. If you want my soul, there's a bridge I can throw in, no extra cost.*

I am a chrysalis, he thought, *and inside me is something infinitely beautiful, strange, brightly colored, evanescent . . . a wholly new kind of creature. I am an Ugly Duckling,* he thought, *and the metamorphosis is long overdue.*

Perhaps, he thought, *perhaps it will be tonight.*

three

THE JOURNALIST

"REALLY, GRANDMA," SAID STEPHEN LELLIOTT, "YOU smother me sometimes."

"I'm just trying to make sure you get enough to eat," said Linda, as she directed Yom, the chauffeur, to pull up to a noodle stand. "What with the plane being four hours late, us being stuck in traffic for another two hours . . . and you're probably all jet-lagged. You shouldn't wear black all the time, all you L.A. boys do it, it's so depressing; I know they didn't feed you on the plane, a bowl of rice soup will calm your stomach, and you can have a proper bowel movement at the house."

It's strange, Stephen thought. *Back home, I'm the hot kid on the block at the network . . . they act like every opinion I utter is some hip new pearl of wisdom . . . because I understand the youth market or something . . . and I walk through the gate at Don Muang Airport and all of a sudden I'm this speechless little kid again, and Grandma knows best . . . when to eat, what to wear, and yeah, when to have bowel movements. In America, polite people don't talk about shitting; in Thailand, polite people don't talk about feet. That's biculturalism.*

"You know, Grandma," he said, instinctively straightening his shirt, but she was already casually doing so with one dainty hand, "maybe I ought to just sleep it off. No bowls of *khao tom.*"

"Nonsense, my grandson," said Linda. "We're already here."

The street corner was unprepossessing, but there were quite a few other Mercedes parked there; the midnight bowl of *khao tom* is one of Bangkok's great leveling rituals, where shipping magnates squat alongside paupers to wolf down steaming bowls of rice soup and piquant condiments at ad hoc open-air restaurants that sprout at dusk and disappear at dawn. Stephen was resigned to having his life micromanaged by his grandma for at least a day or two before taking off to do the research for his TV segment.

But you know, he thought, *Grandma does have a knack for being right.* When the bowl of steaming rice soup, with little bits of pork and a few diced kidneys and assorted un-American animal parts arrived on the rickety aluminum table, he realized it was just the right thing. He hated to admit it, but Linda Dusit usually had his number.

"So," she said, "this tabloid TV show that you're doing . . . why do they have to do the Bangkok sex industry?"

"It sells, Grandma." The night air was steamy with the boiling soup stock of a dozen food stalls. A little boy hawked jasmine garlands, squeezing his way discreetly through the packed sidewalk. Behind them, a pawnshop was doing a brisk business. The rest of the stores were shuttered up.

"But, my grandson," said Linda, "they've done the sex industry to death. There was that *20/20* segment ten years ago. And didn't *Hard Copy* do a piece? The tourist board didn't like it at all; it drove the director general into the arms of some transvestite. I had to exorcise his house. His wife always has that done, you know, whenever she finds he's been fooling around; she assumes the other woman's going to hire a shaman to send a few malevolent spirits to haunt her house and scare the servants; she always calls me in, calls it a preemptive strike. Well, that aside, I know why they've assigned you to this job. They can get away with more because you're Thai."

"Grandma, most people I work with aren't even consciously aware that I'm part Asian," Stephen said. "You know I take after the Irish side more."

"Yes," she said, "but management knows. You played the minority card to get that promotion. Now if anyone complains about the show—the Thai government, the Thai press—they'll just point to your twenty-five percent Thai DNA—and they'll be able to make hay on their integrity, while the Thai establishment has your Uncle Tom hide for breakfast."

"Grandma, you're seeing too much into everything," said Stephen. "This is an important subject, and yeah, it's racy and it's gonna sell a lot of Pampers, but that doesn't mean it's not a story worth telling. I mean, truth and justice and all that crap."

Linda smiled. Stephen was exasperated. Especially since he knew that once again she had it figured out. They'd appealed to his high-mindedness, his knee-jerk hatred of exploitation and corruption; but they were probably going to show as much skin as they could get away with, and reduce the liberal guilt to a couple of sound bites at the end of the show, maybe even while the credits were rolling. And they were going to sacrifice him on the altar of diversity.

"I'm still going to go through with it," he said. "I mean, they *are* paying my salary; they oughta get something."

"Of course you will, my dear," said Linda, "but first you'll finish your rice soup."

Maybe it was the jet lag, but Stephen couldn't sleep that night. Linda's house, though smack in the middle of the bustling Sathorn district, was a little piece of old Bangkok; though surrounded by shopping malls and high rises—on land she had once owned, but which she had sold off piece by piece to finance her Los Angeles restaurant business—she'd managed to recreate the teakwood houses of her childhood while installing all the modern amenities: air-conditioning, cable, Internet access.

Stephen's room was a shrine to his childhood; it contained every teddy bear, every Star Wars action figure, every baseball card he'd accumulated. He'd spent the 1970s with his grandmother—his parents had been troubled then—commuting between a snooty American private school in Bangkok and a drug-and-gang-infested middle school in the San Fernando Valley of Los Angeles. He'd clung to his toys, carting the whole trunkload back and forth across the Pacific every three months, until he decided to stop brooding about his cultural disorientation. He had to put down one set of roots, and he decided on California and a career in television.

After journalism and film school he'd gone straight

to work for the network, playing the ethnic card occasionally to get ahead—why not, "Asian" was just an anonymous check mark on a form, most of his friends had no idea. He'd shipped all his toys to Thailand; he had more expensive toys now: a laptop to drool over, a minidigital camcorder—toys that reeked of success. But now, just turning thirty, he was feeling shiftless again.

Was it because he couldn't seem to keep a relationship going for more than six months? Was it because, having surreptitiously played that ethnic card, he could never be entirely sure that his own talents had brought him to where he was?

A month ago he'd started having nightmares.

Tonight, in this familiar room, full of all the comforting reminders of childhood, he was afraid to go to sleep. Afraid that the nightmare would come back:

An empty room. Black walls. Black satin sheets on a bed. And on the bedpost, staring him in the eye, a crow: staring, staring. Eyes without a soul.

Sometimes that was the whole dream, because he would wake up in time, take a hit of Valium, knock himself out cold. Other times the crow was molting, morphing, metamorphosing . . . into the twisted, broken naked body of a woman.

And the woman said: "*Ka, ka, ka.*"

And he would run. Run! Through labyrinths of passageways, through streets thronging with the walking dead, through walls, through water, through whirlwinds, and always the woman, her arms outstretched toward him, a milky blood spurting from her nipples, blood running from her lifeless eyes, blood pouring from gaping holes in her palms . . . no matter where he ran, she was there.

Ka, ka, ka.

Why was it so frightening? He did not know. Dead bodies didn't frighten him in real life; he'd done a show on autopsies, a show on the mortician necrophilia scandal in Schenectady, he'd covered a serial killer. But there was something about this dream. What was the meaning of *ka, ka, ka?* The Egyptian word for the soul was *ka.* And in Thai the word *ka* means crow. Dreams often had a double meaning. Maybe there was an answer somewhere in his grandmother's mystic bullshit. He didn't buy any of it, but the woman lived by her conversations with spirits, and a lot of people took her seriously enough.

Fuck all this, he thought. *I just can't sleep. I'll have to go somewhere, do something.*

He sat up. Turned on the light.

In the distance, traffic and rock music. In Bangkok the background noise could never be turned off, though it was masked here by the thrum of the air conditioner, the mating calls of the frogs, crickets, and lizards that populated Linda Dusit's garden with its lotus pond and antique pavilion.

His open suitcase lay on the floor. There was a jumble of shirts—Stephen did not believe in packing neatly—and his minidigital camcorder, a device small enough to squeeze into a shirt pocket, yet powerful enough to deliver broadcast quality when transferred to Betacam back in the studio.

What the hell, he told himself. *Maybe I should just get started. I could run down to Patpong, get some B-roll down on tape, and be that much closer to the meat of my story.*

He threw on some clothes—a fake Armani shirt,

socks that didn't match—tucked the camcorder into a tote bag, and slipped out of the room. He didn't want to wake his grandmother, so he slipped past her open bedroom toward the carved teak staircase. A thick Chinese dragon carpet masked his footsteps. He made it to the living room, where gods of many religions stared down from niches, where candles burned all night long and incense tendriled from freshly lit joss sticks . . . all the way to the anteroom where you put on your shoes to go outside, when the voice of his grandmother startled him.

"Take some money," she said. "You're such a forgetful boy sometimes, I don't know *what* to do with you."

"Yes, Grandma," he said. But she wasn't really awake, he realized. She was sitting by the door in her robe, cross-legged, her hands folded in prayer. She was in a trance, on one of those shamanistic journeys she was so wont to take. Her lips were moving; now and then he could make out a whispered word in some alien tongue, perhaps Sanskrit.

Incense swirled about her. Her eyes had gone white; she was looking inward. Stephen didn't really care for all this hocus-pocus, but he had grown up with it; he knew she wouldn't remember a thing in the morning. He sat down on a stool to tie his shoes. Linda didn't even seem to be breathing; he was used to that, too.

"I'll be back in time for breakfast, Grandma," he said.

She didn't answer him. He opened the front door. The night breeze assailed him, that uniquely Bangkok mélange of night-blooming jasmine and industrial waste.

He slung the tote over his shoulder and started to step out into the garden.

Softly, Linda said, *"Ka, ka, ka."*

Stephen stumbled out of the house. He ran for the front gate, let himself out, walked alongside the stagnant canal until he reached the main road. A taxi appeared instantly. "Patpong," he said.

The driver launched into a tired description of the Patpong's delights.

"I don't have time for that," said Stephen in Thai, startling the driver. "Just get me there."

Ka, ka, ka, ka, ka . . .

What did it mean? And why was Stephen's dream leaking into the real world? When Linda went into her trances and visited distant universes, was she able to invade her grandson's very nightmares? *Forget about it,* he thought. *She was just mumbling. She's a deluded old woman who's not all there at the best of times. Let me spend the night disguised as a tourist, melting into the throng, just another white guy with a camcorder, and not have to think about my half-mad grandmother.*

But as he got out of the green and purple Toyota—taxis in Thailand were all Toyotas, and all garishly colored—and was about to plunge into the crowd, he saw someone.

A woman in a silver lamé miniskirt, sitting at a sidewalk noodle cafe, staring off into space. The pavement around her was packed—Patpong with its cacophony and color veered off behind her—on the street in front of her, taxis raced, *tuk-tuks* sputtered, motorcycles weaved—and an elephant in a pink tutu was holding up an intersection as camera-toting tourists hemmed it in. But the woman sat alone at a table for two. The crowd had parted to reveal her to him. She sat in a private pool of silence and soft light, as though she and the space around her were a fragment of some other universe.

"I—" he began. But surely she could not hear him; she was clear across the street. And yet she turned to him and smiled.

"I know you," he said.

He had seen her naked body, ripped asunder, twisted, tied into knots, broken, jigsawed, reassembled. He stood there, waiting for the dread to descend on him as it always did in the dream . . . waiting for the panic. It didn't happen. There was nothing supernatural about this woman. She was staring at him, too, as if she recognized him. And he found himself drawn to her, until he was gazing down at her. She was not some striking Miss Thailand type: Her features did not possess the pale, high-nosed Eurasian cast that generally found favor among the Thais. She was darker-skinned than was usually popular. Her thick, long hair was remarkable in its profusion, not its couture. And yet she was beautiful. It was all in her eyes. Terrible pain, he saw, and terrible strength. She said, "Howdy, pilgrim."

He laughed.

"Oh!" she said. "You making fun of me."

"No . . . no . . . God forbid. Can I sit down?"

She looked around warily. "Okay you sit," she said. "I off duty. But only talk."

"I didn't expect someone like you to quote John Wayne."

"Oh," she said, "daytime, I work in Blockbuster at Soi Six. I watch a lot of movies. I'm learning English.

But it very difficult. I always end up saying wrong thing. But still I watch movies. I think about being movie star sometimes. Hasta la vista, baby!"

"You work in Blockbuster," Stephen said. "But you also work in . . ."

"Yes. I have contract at the Cleo. But not do any work yet. Waiting for my special day. You see, I virgin. I can fetch big price. Maybe . . ." She looked at him with wide, earnest eyes. "Maybe you come to auction? I want handsome young American man. I don't want old wrinkled Chinese dope dealer, don't want Indian fabric millionaire. I want someone like you. You look like Keanu Reeves. You nice."

Stephen could only stare. This woman had all the makings of great television. That was clear. The vulnerability, the youth—how old could she be? Eighteen would be a stretch. The odd sort of self-assurance when she said, "I can fetch big price." And the insidious corruption of American culture that led her to believe that giving herself to an American was somehow less ignoble . . . almost redeeming. L.A. and New York might be blasé, but Peoria would weep. It was a lot easier to see her as a packageable commodity than to face the fact that this was the very woman in his dream, the woman whose twisted corpse had haunted his nights for months . . . the woman whose dead visage had made him flee his grandmother's house.

"Perhaps . . . you could be in a movie one day. At least a television documentary."

"Oh, video, video, they offer me video already. But first wait till after my big night."

"Video, video? You mean a porno."

"Maybe I lucky, not hardcore. Or CD-ROM—I

slowly take off clothes, rub myself up and down—
take care of myself, you know. Or they click on me
with a mouse—click on hips, dress fall off, click on
breast, bra come off. And they fuck me with robo-
dildo. They tell me all about this already, and pay is
good—five thousand baht for one day working."

Yeah, Stephen thought. *All of a hundred and eight
bucks. If I had this on tape right now, I'd be golden. I can
just see myself uploading a ten-minute Quicktime clip to
the VP of Production tonight . . . she'd have an orgasm.
Not that she ever has orgasms—the Ice Queen from
Hell.* He already figured out how he was going to sell
it. No cold-blooded exposé, no litany of chilling facts
about the sex biz—rather, the story of one woman—
more child than woman, to elicit the maximum
pathos from the situation. One victim struggling to
make a life for herself in the face of an unfeeling and
corrupt establishment. That was how his show dif-
fered from *Hard Copy* and the others—his show was
heavy on finding the human face within every world-
shaking scandal.

*Why am I thinking about nothing but ways to
exploit this child-woman?* he thought. *What am I
afraid of?* He knew they had nothing in common. He
knew that, within the rigid confines of Thailand's
social hierarchy, this was not a woman he could invite
to his grandmother's house, or be seen having brunch
with at the Regent. Only within the context of his
Americanness could they meet as equals. Perhaps
that was why he didn't even hint to her that he could
speak her language fluently, that he was a man torn
between the two cultures. Was that unfair? Why did
he feel he needed to have an edge?

It was because she had an edge, too. Even if she didn't realize it. She had the nightmare. She had been inside his head. Had she, too, had these premonitions? "Do you know who I am?" he asked her. "Have you seen me somewhere before? When you smiled at me, I thought . . . I thought . . ."

She smiled again. "My name is Dao," she said. "Sure, I dream you all the time. You look like Keanu Reeves. Big Hollywood boy, take me away, I no slave to Ai Tong no more, contract—rip."

Dream. Yeah. One word, too many meanings. He studied her face, gazed into her eyes, tried to gauge her level of deceptiveness. She stared right back at him. She didn't do that demure, looking-at-the-floor thing that properly brought-up Thai women always did. She was a child of the slums all right. Her eyes had a steadfast innocence. Being downtrodden hadn't taken away her pride. There was no way for him to tell if she had shared his precognitive nightmare; he didn't want to slip into Thai, didn't want to lose his linguistic dominance.

"I'm not a porno maker," he said. "I'm a journalist. I just want to tell one woman's story . . . one sex worker's point of view."

"You make video about me?" she said. "I give you blowjob, yes?" She giggled. She might as well have been selling him candy or flowers . . . and not her soul.

"No blowjob," he said.

She frowned. "You don't like me?"

"Of course I do. I do. A lot. That's why I think you'd be a great subject for this documentary segment. And there'd be money in it. More than five thousand baht, I daresay. I think . . . I think you could be a poster girl for the whole enigma of Asia. See, in America, they see love and money as almost opposites . . . as mutually exclusive . . . and I want to show how, in this culture, love and money are like brother and sister. You're perfect . . . and the fact that you work at Blockbuster and spout quotes from old movies . . . it's something they can relate to. My audience, I mean. Give 'em something they can grasp firmly before you lead them into uncharted territory." He was really getting into it now. This could be really searing. It could be an Emmy. And she really seemed to be catching his enthusiasm, smiling broadly, encouraging him. "How much of that did you understand, I wonder?" he said.

"I virgin. You want blowjob okay, but no fuck, not till after my big night."

Had they been communicating at all, or were they two people into two private worlds, each conversing with the empty air? He dreamed of corpses, she of Keanu Reeves; he spoke of journalistic breakthroughs, she of blowjobs.

Suddenly Stephen was tired, dead tired. Jet lag sneaks up on you sometimes, and then it pounces. "I've gotta go," he said, and scrawled out his pager number on the back of a card. He couldn't give her his home number, of course; Linda would go berserk. She'll never call, he thought. This whole night was a wasted exercise.

Time to get some real sleep, he thought. *I won't even dream. And if I do . . . I've packed my Valium.*

four

THE PROSTITUTE

WHEN DAO MADE HER WAY BACK TO THE CLEO, THAT other man was there. That nervous-looking man from the U.S. Embassy. Maybe the man thought he was incognito here in Patpong, but the truth was, everyone knew who he was. He wasn't a very good lurker. The way he walked about the street, all puffed up and self-important, made his scrawny little frame seem oddly ludicrous. His nose was his weirdest feature, narrow and pointed. Some of the girls on the strip referred to him as the Woodpecker.

She had hoped to lose him; that was why she'd taken a break after unintentionally luring him to the Cleo. She hadn't wanted him to notice her; she fervently hoped he wouldn't be able to afford to bid on her when the big night came. After seeing him preoccupied with Keo, she had slipped out. Then she stumbled into the American, the TV guy.

What he said to her was confusing. She'd given him the usual spiel about how he looked like a fabulous film star—she picked Keanu because the man had a slightly Asian look to him—much like Keanu

Reeves, a mongrel, didn't you know. He had talked about videos and used a lot of, well, metaphoric language, she imagined. She liked him, but he was one of the ones who liked to be close. Liked to imagine it was all real.

Once in a while a guy like that came to Patpong and ended up investing in a wife, so it didn't hurt to be a little extra charming. White men always seemed to like submissive women. It was probably because, in America, she'd heard, women ran everything. Even President Clinton, she had heard from her best friend, Lek, lived in mortal terror of his wife's wrath. Well, that journalist talked too much. It was a strain pretending to be interested when one could hardly understand a word he said. On the other hand, he *did* look like an American movie star. And even though she didn't know what he was talking about, there was a note of real concern, of real feeling. She wished it could be someone like him who would bid the highest on her precious jewel— precious to all but herself.

Well, all right. She really did like him, a little.

But she was in the wrong profession to like anyone more than a little.

Behind a stall that specialized in pirated software there was a back door into the Cleo. A steep stairwell led to the display room, where sex workers sat in lingerie with numbers around their necks; a one-way mirror displayed them to the patrons of the second-story coffee bar. Leading out of the display room were many narrow corridors that led to trysting rooms, to secret lairs, and to the room where Mr. Tong sat, entertaining his most honored guests; they called that room simply the Tomb, because it was a recreation of an ancient Egyptian burial chamber from the Valley of the Kings. Mr. Tong had a bit of an Egypt fixation.

Dao went to the virgins' dormitory; it was a dismal, ill-lit chamber at the very end of a hallway. Four single wooden beds—no mattresses—lined one wall. No air-conditioning; a ceiling fan wheezed. A gecko chased a dragonfly around the ceiling. When the girls slept, they would roll out some tatami-style mats; while awake, the hard beds sufficed for sofas, lounge chairs, and work surfaces. There was a television. The sound was way down; the picture was an old episode of *Star Trek: The Next Generation*. She had seen it before.

When she sat down, she heard a little giggle. She peered under her bed. "Why aren't you at home?"

It was her twelve-year-old brother Duan. He was shirtless and filthy. "You know why I'm here," he said. "They've got cable."

"You're too busy for television."

"Shit, elder sister," said Duan, "they've got *electricity*."

"Still, you should be watching your little brother."

"Oh, he's back there somewhere." The boy jerked his thumb at the bed. "He's fast asleep, don't worry. *Star Trek* always puts him to sleep. Well . . . he doesn't mind the Borg."

"He's here? How did you get in?"

"That's a dumb question, honored elder sister," he said. "I'm invisible. All street kids are." He laughed. "But seriously, we can't stay there much longer. We're losing the cardboard off the walls. Come rainy season, our house will be washed into the *klong*."

"You know I could get in trouble if you're found

here, younger brother," Dao said. "The penalty for nonpaying overnight guests is ten lashes."

"Don't be silly, elder sister! They're not going to risk damaging your skin. You're a major investment."

"Maybe so. Did anyone see you?"

"Only elder sister Daeng," he said. "But I gave her some pills, and she promised not to talk. Besides, she likes me."

Daeng was the oldest inhabitant of the virgins' dormitory. A bizarre genital deformity, unnoticed at the time of her indenture because no one had bothered to examine her with her clothes off, had made her something of a liability; but she was an expert at legitimate massage, so she was trotted out sometimes for those occasional customers who actually wanted one. Still, at thirty, she looked decidedly shopworn. Where was she now? They kept her pretty busy. She was the one who cleaned the semen stains between customers. Unlike the two boys, she was not an actual sibling; all the employees here called each other elder or younger sister; it was supposed to make for a kind of camaraderie.

Daeng poked her head in the doorway at that very moment.

"Didn't I tell you to stay under the bed, you little rodent?" she scolded. Duan hurled himself beneath the boards. "Oh, little sister," she added to Dao, "the Big One himself wants you. Apparently you've piqued someone's interest."

Dao had a sinking feeling. Piquing someone's interest could mean only one thing: that someone was planning to bid on her virginity.

"Go for it!" said her little brother from under the bed.

"Shut up, little brother," she said. "I only have one chance to earn out Mr. Tong's investment."

"And buy me that television," Duan added.

"First one of those government apartments in the projects," said Dao, "even a one-room would do, and a clay charcoal stove to cook on . . . then, *electricity* . . . then, maybe, just maybe, television."

Dao looked herself over in the broken mirror that hung beside the door, just beneath the portraits of Their Majesties, to whom she whispered a brief word of respect before she began combing her hair. She decided not to use much lipstick. They usually preferred the unspoiled, little girl look. At least when it came to setting a price tag on virginity. There'd be plenty of time to dress sexy later.

I hate the way I look! she thought. That strange pallor of the skin . . . those strangely shaped eyes, neither Thai nor *farang* . . . it was a look that had made her an outcast in the eyes of some, yet it was the look that had caused Mr. Tong to see her as an investment, not just any whore.

The look of not belonging, she thought. Here I am, crushed between two worlds. My mother, a woman from the streets; my father a Frenchman passing through town, pausing to impregnate a bar girl with the same degree of forethought he might have devoted to making a pit stop on the highway.

She smoothed down her skimpy uniform, cautioned her brother to remain invisible and to make sure that the little one didn't fret; then she made her way back along the convoluted passageways to the back entrance to the Tomb.

This was Mr. Tong's little conceit: Lining the

walls of his inner sanctum was a collection of Egyptian sarcophagi, some real, some made of papier-mâché and Styrofoam. Most of these mummiform sarcophagi were firmly glued to the wall, but some had hinged lids; the back entrance into Tong's lair led, through a stiflingly narrow passage, to a little alcove with a velvet-padded seat, and the door itself was one of those sarcophagus lids. Thus it was that Mr. Tong could startle his guests by having one of the lids suddenly pop open to reveal—whatever it was that the client most desired—a naked woman, a rouged transvestite, a leather dominatrix.

A whiff of opium hung in the air. She knew that Mr. Tong indulged in opium. She held her breath, not daring to cough. Mr. Tong's opium was no ordinary opium. Some of the girls said it had . . . *powers*. It could influence a woman's thoughts. Bend her to a man's will. Or even change the future and the past. Girls always chatter about things they know nothing about, Dao thought. Magic is magic.

A little light just above the sarcophagus's face would turn green when the master wanted her to make her entrance. Nervously, she waited in the alcove, trying to breathe as little as possible. In the meantime she was able to eavesdrop on the conversation.

"We know who you are," Mr. Tong was saying—in English, so she had to struggle to make sense of it. "We know you don't have money. But you do have certain . . . uses. For example, our organization might want to avail itself of certain facilities within the United States . . . diplomatic corps. Do you understand my drift?"

"I'm not . . . a powerful man."

"Surely, surely, Mr. Temple, you understand that there is power everywhere, if only you know where to find it."

"But what kind of favors are you looking for? If it's a simple thing . . . slipping something in the diplomatic pouch to avoid U.S. customs, for instance—"

She heard Mr. Tong laugh. A quiet, seductive, menacing laugh. "We already have people for that," he said softly, "but if one of our . . . customary sources were to drop out . . ."

"I see," said Mr. Temple.

The sarcophagus had a peephole. It was not located in an obvious place—the mummy's eyes—but tucked into the crossing of the two arms that held the crook and flail, symbol of Pharaoh's power, in a knot of wood. The temptation was too much for her; she crouched down to look, trying to make as little noise as possible. She saw the man who owned her, an elderly man with a wispy, white beard, his lips tugging on the spout of a bong; trails of smoke encircled him. The smoke . . . this was the strangest thing. The smoke seemed almost alive. It encircled Tong like a serpent. It wiggled, it curled, it mimicked an obscene caress. There was something sexual in the smoke. That didn't surprise her. She remembered, in her childhood, her mother trying to keep her boyfriend by rolling a special incense-icon in her vagina, baptizing it with lubricious fluids before burning it to send its fragrance up to whatever spirit would grant her the favor she needed.

The American was seated across the table from him, his whiskey untouched. He sat in the shadow;

she could not see his face. She saw only that his hands were trembling.

"We'll let you know what it is we need," said Mr. Tong. "But in the meantime, there are always . . . the more subsidiary services. For example, you have access to the commissary at your embassy, and I have a hard time getting some of the more obscure diet colas . . . Diet Cherry Pepsi, for example. I don't suppose they'll ever import that into Thailand. A few six-packs would be worth their weight in gold."

"You would give me access to . . . *that girl* for a six-pack of diet soda?"

"Heavens, no, Mr. Temple. I was merely thinking that it would be a nice little gift . . . for the next time we meet to negotiate."

"You're . . ."

"Insane?" said Mr. Tong. "Not really. Just very, very eccentric. I am eccentric in the manner that only the very powerful can afford."

"I see. So this meeting has been an exercise in power, basically. You're showing me who's boss."

"Very good. And in our studies of you, we've discovered a great deal about your inner workings. We know, for example, that you are the kind of person who is daily tormented by feelings of utter helplessness . . . and who lives for those elusive, fleeting moments in which you feel absolute power over a human being."

"I'd best be going."

"Not until I'm done with you, Mr. Temple!"

Dao looked up. The green light had come on. It was just as well. The air in the sarcophagus was close and stale, and she was starting to panic from the feeling of confinement.

Carefully, she pushed the button.

The sarcophagus lid swung open, and she looked down on Mr. Tong's inner sanctum.

And into the eyes of Temple.

Temple's eyes did not blink; they gazed intently on her, unwavering, hard. They were eyes of surpassing emptiness. They seemed to suck all the warmth out of the room. There was only one emotion in those eyes. She had seen it in many of the customers, but never so naked, never so single-minded. That emotion was hunger.

"Step forward a little, girl," said Mr. Tong in his strangely accented Thai—a bit of Chinese, a bit of Burmese, a bit of something unrecognizable. "I paid good money for you. I want to be able to show off quality." He turned to Temple and said, in English, "This is what you have been looking for, is it not?"

"Perhaps," said Temple in a strained and husky voice.

"But you are not sure. Perhaps you wish to see more."

"Yes."

Tong turned to Dao. "Disrobe," he said.

The opium smoke tendriled about her. It seemed that the smoke became oozy, sweaty hands that clawed at her stays and buttons.

She began to unzip her uniform. It was a simple operation; there was not much to take off. The blouse loosened and began to slide off her shoulders, revealing the upper curve of her slender breasts. She cast down her eyes . . . she was afraid of the hunger she saw in Temple's face. The floor of the sanctum was an intricate marble mosaic that depicted some ancient

Egyptian river scene, fishermen among the reeds, a great lord dallying with two naked Nubians, a naked boy diving after a frog, ibises frolicking. Her blouse slid to the floor. She began to unclasp her bra. But before she could do so, she felt a metallic tap on her bare skin.

It was Tong, striking her shoulder with the mouthpiece of the bong. "Enough," he said. "We do not *give* anything away in this institution. One look is enough." To Dao, he said, "Quick. Zip yourself back up, girl."

She did so. As she had been taught, in one graceful languorous motion, to further inflame the appetite.

"The gate of heaven is not so easily unlatched, Mr. Temple," said Tong. "But we will take you there in stages . . . and for every stage there will be . . . a price. Not necessarily one measured in mere money, of course. A gentleman like you will understand that, I assume."

"I suppose so," Temple said.

"However," said Mr. Tong, "one wouldn't want a valued business relationship to begin without at least some small gratuity. I shall arrange for you to be serviced by one of my more . . . expendable entertainers." He rang a little bell; Dao knew that it would summon one of the older sisters, too broken down for shopfront work, but skilled enough to succor those too drunk or impecunious to care. Sometimes these sisters were tainted with disease. But Cleo's always insisted on condoms; it was a safe house, respectable, patronized by the best.

"Oh," said Temple, surprised. "And how much—"

"Oh, no," said Tong. "Let us not sully this interview with such vulgarities. Just don't inflict any irreversible damage; every one of our little starlets is an investment, painstakingly nurtured."

"I understand." Another sarcophagus lid swung open; a woman stood in the shadows. Dao couldn't see her face clearly, but Tong was already telling her to go with the guest and give him whatever he wanted.

"Now go, my little star," said the old man, dismissing Dao with a quick wave.

She backed up, entered the sarcophagus, and allowed the lid to be slammed shut before she quickly fled down the corridor back to the relative comfort of the virgins' dormitory.

five

THE INTERVIEW

FOR SOME REASON, THE DIPLOMAT HAD NOT WANTED Stephen to come into the office. He had, instead, selected a bar on Sukhumvit Road, in the Nana district, a slightly newer, hipper version of the traditional red light area of Patpong.

"If you're going to interview me about . . . such matters," the man had said to Stephen, "I'd rather it be off the record, and that means not in an embassy setting. That wouldn't do at all. Ambassador Niewinski wouldn't be terribly happy. And you know how ambassadors are. Used to getting their own way. Surrounded by yes-men. Mad with power. Yes. Yes. That's it. Mad, mad, mad."

Stephen put down the phone, perplexed. He had envisaged his documentary segment as a slowly unfolding sort of thing, starting with images of beautiful, touristy, slightly decadent Bangkok, gradually penetrating the surface, and finally, in some searing revelatory moment just before the second commercial break, an epiphany. Instead he was already being thrust into the heart of darkness.

"Grandmother," he said, as they sat down to an alfresco breakfast next to her precious lotus pond, "I need to borrow the driver for lunch; I'm interviewing someone."

"No problem," she said as she spiced up her shrimp and rice gruel with another dollop of chopped chilies. "I have an interview, too, but I won't be needing the car."

"Oh?" said Stephen. "Where will you be going?"

"Narok," she said.

It was barely nine in the morning, but it was already getting hot. Bangkok in the hot dry season is a furnace. But in a few weeks it would be Songkraan, April the 13th, the Thai New Year, when water would flow in the streets . . . a water-splashing Mardi Gras–like madness, which, by sympathetic magic, would summon the life-giving monsoon and cleanse away all the sins and ill luck of the past year. Stephen had been planning to work his Songkraan footage into the end of the segment, creating a sort of joyous quasi-affirmative resolution to the horrors he would have unmasked just before the commercial. Structure was what a good segment was all about. With good structure, you can make an audience believe anything. Good television was the most powerful weapon in the civilized world.

"Wait a minute," Stephen said, as what his grandmother had just said finally impinged on his reverie. "There's no such place as Narok. Narok is the hellish region of Yamalok, the abode of the dead."

"You still remember your mythology, then," Linda said, chuckling a little. "Put some more fried garlic in your soup," she added. "You know what those American doctors are saying about garlic now . . . as if we hadn't known it in Asia for a thousand years."

"So you're not going out of the house, then," Stephen said. "You're going on one of those 'inward journey' things."

"Yes."

"Grandmother, what does '*ka, ka, ka*' mean?

"It sounds like a bird call. A crow, perhaps. Where did you hear it?"

"It's in a dream I've been having, a recurring dream . . . and last night when I slipping out of the house, I heard you say it. You were in a trance, I think."

"If you empty your mind, all the connections will become clear."

"No, no, I don't want any New Age philosophy over breakfast," said Stephen. "I just want to understand how this *ka, ka, ka* can leapfrog out of my nightmare onto your lips."

"Everything in the universe is linked," she said.

"Oh, please," he said. "You're in your Yoda mode this morning, I see."

"Then use the force, Stephen," Linda said, laughing. And then, she added, seemingly out of the blue, "I think you're falling in love."

"C'mon, Grandma," he said, "you know I'd never do a thing like that."

"I'm your grandmother, and I know things long before you do."

"I don't have time for that. Not now . . . not until I'm a little further ahead in my career."

He closed his eyes. A vision of the girl, unbidden, sprang into his consciousness. "I have met someone, but it's not love. She intrigues me. I'm going to center the segment around her. She's like all of Bangkok—a meld of innocence and worldliness—I think she'll appeal very strongly to the American audience."

"And to you," Linda said.

"Wishful thinking, Grandmother," he said. "I'm not getting hitched anytime soon. Besides, she's a hooker."

"But not a well-used, worn-out hooker . . . or she'd never have intrigued you. I know you better than that."

"Grandmother, you've told me plenty of times not to fraternize with people of a lower social class. No, no, it's not prejudice, you keep saying, it's just the hierarchical nature of Thai society, it's just too difficult, causes too much confusion."

"I'm afraid you're far too American to be bothered by that kind of thing," she said with a rueful smile. "And at this stage, Stephen, I think your family would be happy with almost any kind of bride."

Dolphin's Paradise was a bar with a bestiality theme, though there was something quaintly clinical about the way the girls, nude except for their knee-length boots, swam around the big glass tank in the center of the room being nuzzled by lethargic porpoises. Oh, the music was bouncy enough, and the girls thrusted and heaved earnestly as they swam, but it all seemed a bit Disney-fied. In fact, there were even a few families there. There was an excited-looking German one, for instance, the two very blond kids posing in front of the water tanks while an imposing hausfrau-type snapped pictures and a father guzzled beer. At another table, two chador-clad women—Middle Easterners—sat intently hunched over a laptop. Few of the customers seemed to notice the zoophilic floor show.

Stephen had been kept waiting for an hour; he had almost decided to leave when the subject of his interview showed up. A little man with glasses, shuffling, hunched over. Harmless-looking.

Dirk Temple walked over to the table and sat down before saying a word. As Stephen was about to talk, though, he stuck out his hand. "Temple," he said. "I've been asked to . . . help you out, and steer you through any awkward situations. Don't know why they sent you to me, really. You're part Thai, I hear. And my secretary says that your grandmother talks to spirits. You should feel right at home."

"You've researched me," said Stephen.

"We research all journalists," said Temple, and he charged into what was clearly a rehearsed script, "and the ambassador's asked me to have a talk with you. It's a standard talk we give—about not rocking any boats. You see, Thailand's an important link in the economic chain of being. When the baht went south, when all of Asia went spiraling out of control, well, that chain got rattled, you know what I mean? A strong Thai economy helps make for a strong U.S. economy, and the ambassador knows that a docu-segment with the wrong spin can send the tourist industry into a nosedive, which would impact on *our* interests. . . . Are you getting my drift?"

Stephen pulled out the mini-DV in his tote bag. This was great stuff. Awesome television, for this shuffling, beady-eyed man to be mouthing laissez-faire platitudes while virgins were being auctioned off down the street. He pointed the camera at the man and adjusted the angle of the screen.

"Would you mind saying all that again for my camera?"

"You're joking, of course," said Temple.

"No, seriously. You've always wanted to be a star, haven't you?"

"No!" Temple said in a vehement whisper. "Those actors, those self-aggrandizing, egocentric whores who strut and strumpet their way across empty celluloid vistas—horrible, horrible! The world should be cleansed of their hypocrisy!"

Stephen hardly dared breathe. Obviously Temple hadn't known—couldn't have known—that the camera had been on at the time. He had undergone an abrupt transformation, from spineless geek to something quite different . . . and frightening. Excellent footage . . . which didn't belong in the documentary.

"You feel strongly about that," Stephen said.

It was over. The man sort of morphed back into his ineffectual former self.

"There's more to me," said Temple, "that people can imagine."

"I guess so."

"One day, I'm going to burst out of my cocoon," said Temple, "and then I'll devour the world." His hands were shaking. "But meanwhile . . . ," then he went right back to his prepared lecture. "You're an American citizen, but it's a delicate situation. Free speech is a wonderful thing, and if you get into trouble, we'll pull you out, of course, but you have to be careful. And . . . there's a secret pager number you'll need." Temple wrote it down on a piece of paper and held it in front of Stephen's nose for a full ten seconds, then yanked it away, tore it into little pieces, put them in the ashtray, and set fire to them with his Dunhill lighter.

"This is the fun part," he said, giggling. "My job is so, so, so, so boring, you know; I rubber-stamp cultural exchange proposals. Occasionally, when I can actually indulge in a bit of pyro, or pass out the old secret decoder ring, why, it makes my day."

Dirk Temple watched the little bonfire in the ashtray. He imagined it a hundred times bigger, blazing, perhaps leaping from brothel to brothel in the confined alleyways of Patpong.

He looked at the silly little reporter with his sculpted Eurasian features, his too-pretty eyes, his perfect hair jelled solid. *If he only knew me! If he only saw what I am inside! If he only understood the extent of my power! Last night, for instance, last night—*

Tong had tormented him with that perfect little vixen. Baited and switched him. Given him some used-up, loose-lipped whore to do as he pleased with.

He hadn't totally kept his word to Ai Tong. Toward the end he hadn't been able to avoid a couple of bruises. But the bitch would mend quickly enough. And he'd tipped her enough to buy a few painkillers.

Dirk Temple sat across the table from some green, starry-eyed journalist, but his mind was far away. Reliving. Thinking about power. The fear that flecked that woman's eyes . . . probably actually thought he was going to kill her. When he'd had his hands around the woman's throat . . . the energy, the naked energy that pulsed under his fingers! He should have squeezed harder. He should have sucked the life force into his hands . . . absorbed her . . . devoured her, yes, devoured her.

But then again, it wouldn't have been *perfect*. No. She wasn't beautiful. Her skin was mottled. Not smooth and creamy, not like the other one. It would have been like wasting a fine steak knife on a tough slab of stewing beef instead of a tender filet mignon.

No. The big moment was yet to come. His shining, secret self was still trapped in the confines of the chrysalis. But the moment was getting closer.

Suddenly he realized that the journalist was staring at him. Why? He hated being stared at. Perhaps the man had somehow caught a glimpse of the transcendental self, cloaked though it was in the chrysalid darkness. *Be careful, Dirk*, he told himself. *No one shall know. Not until I'm ready.*

Deliberately, he intensified his nervous tic, allowed his gaze to wander erratically across the table. *I'm just another geeky bureaucrat, dotting the i's and crossing the t's while moral turpitude reigns around me. Yes, he despises me! He thinks he knows my kind! And he himself is so superior. He is the media. The bringer of light. The savior of the reluctant world.*

"You were telling me about the secret pager," the man was reminding him.

"Ah yes! The pager! The pager! I trust you've memorized the number?"

"Yes, yes, but what does it do?"

"It's a hotline to our . . . special division."

"Oh, I see. The marines will come and rescue me if I get in too deep."

"We'll take care of you," said Temple, "as long as our names aren't attached. You know how it is. Some of our friends aren't quite as . . . enlightened as we are, but if a shady character has what you want, you do business with him; you don't become the greatest nation on earth by counting your scruples."

"No," said Lelliott, "I suppose you don't."

"And I'll deny everything . . . I hope you understand. There is no secret pager number, no special division . . . and the press is as free and unfettered as the wind."

Temple smiled. He wondered whether Lelliott fully understood the double meaning inherent in that sentence, "We'll take care of you." *I have him in my power,* he thought, *and he doesn't even realize it.*

Lelliott said, "Well, I appreciate your help. But I probably won't be needing it. This isn't going to be a political story. I'm not going to rock any boats. I'm just going to tell the story of one woman, one life. Television's better that way."

"Wonderful." They shook hands. Temple had the distinct impression that Lelliott felt he was soiling his delicate, squeaky-clean skin. *Good. Let him think he's better than me,* he thought. "Oh, by the way," he added, with schooled indifference, "what are you into?"

"I beg your pardon?"

"Into—girls, boys, transvestites, transsexuals, sado-masochism, golden showers, monkeys, dolphins . . ." Temple pointed out the dolphin in the tank, now humping furiously at the swimming nymph's leg. "Dolphins have become very fashionable of late. As, for some reason, have Russians. The Slavic *poontangski* is widely available in Thailand, you know, since the collapse of the Soviet Union and all that.

And the Russian gangsters have moved in, too. If there's something you particularly want, well . . . I'm authorized to dip into our expense account a bit. Anything for the press, you know."

"I'm not here to partake," said the man. A little too quickly, thought Temple. Good. He had a weakness. "Just to document." Then, recovering his composure, he said, "And you?"

"Me? Oh, my, oh, my," said Dirk Temple. "I don't even *like* sex that much. I yearn for . . . other things. And so, alas, I'm starving in the midst of plenty here in the Big Mango."

And with that, he got up and walked out of Dolphin's Paradise.

six

THE SHAMANESS

IN ANOTHER TIME AND PLACE, THE CROWS WERE WHEEL-
ing through a bloodred sky. And yet the sky was blue
and blazing and cloudless. Linda was in many places
at once . . . her *vinyaan* was soaring above the city and
through the landscape of dream, even though she was
actually sitting, cross-legged, in a teak pavilion over-
looking a lotus pond . . . in the merciless, breezeless
heat of Bangkok's hot season.

Just past the huge shopping mall nexus, where
four street corners with five shopping malls con-
verged, and the shrine of the Four-faced Brahma was
crammed with devotees, and the modern Taj Mahals
that were the Hyatt and the Regent pierced the
bright sky, stood the Dusit family's temple, one of the
toniest temples in Bangkok, though little known to
the tourists. Many establishment families had their
family pavilions here, where the ashes of their dead
were kept. Once the only spires in a very pastoral corner, the temple was now overshadowed on every side
by gaudy skyscrapers, and Linda had often thought it
might be time to endow a pavilion somewhere more

remote, upcountry, even. Would it not be better, when the day came, for her ashes to rest in some nice wooded setting, with birds and fawns and flowers? But that was not a very Buddhist attitude. It was clinging to the material. And there was no more powerful a street corner than this one; it was not just a nexus of shopping malls—more lines of spiritual force ran through this square kilometer of territory than anywhere else in Thailand.

She let her *vinyaan* drift along the wind. What she did was a dangerous thing; that was why, seated in the lotus position next to living lotuses, she held a *saisin* cord in her folded hands, to anchor her soul to the material world; it was a sort of spiritual kite string. The cord looped around her hands several times, binding them in an attitude of prayer; it then stretched toward the railings above the pond, twining through the teakwood; it ran all the way to a niche inside the house, where a statue of the Four-faced Brahma sat, surrounded by jade elephants.

From its vantage point above the chaos of the city, she could see those lines of mystic power . . . glowing, crisscrossing, circling about the Brahma shrine like divine yarn. Oh, the ecstasy of flight . . . oh, the joy and the terror of giving in to the wind, to the waves of sunlight.

She circled over the temple with the sun directly behind her, allowed herself to penetrate the gilt-tiled roofing of her family pavilion, a gaudy *sala*, its murals depicting scenes from the epic poem "Phra Abhaimani," the story of the flute-playing prince abducted by a lovelorn ogress. The main chamber was designed to impress visitors; there was a dais with cushions for monks to squat while chanting, and a gilded chair for the abbot to sermonize from, and the floor was covered with an intricate Persian carpet.

For a while Linda allowed her soul to siphon in and out of the carpet's patterns, enjoying the clash of textures, the rushing pink, the stolid maroon, the delicate filigree of gold thread. It was a sensuous pleasure she could not experience in the flesh; but here, where the abstract and the corporeal blurred into each other, she could truly feel the patterns within patterns: within the rug, the warp and the woof and the interlinking filaments; within the threads, the twisting symmetry of the strands of fiber; within the fiber, the long wiry molecules of once-living organisms; within those molecules, the fandango of subatomic particles. It was good to be one with all things . . . to let go of the ego completely. But one could not do so for too long, or the chains that linked the *vinyaan* to the flesh might snap.

For a split second she was back by the lotus pond. *Almost lost myself for a moment*, she thought. She sent her *vinyaan* back, but did not allow herself to be drawn into the carpet's hypnotic patterns.

Incense in the air . . . close and still and charged with sunlight.

She allowed her soul to flatten, to flit along the fresco. She was two-dimensional now, like the paintings themselves. Suddenly she could hear the rustle of the waves, the whisper of the wind over the sea, the anguished wailing of the forsaken giantess.

There was Phra Abhaimani and his magic flute now. The song was like fractured wind chimes; the exiled prince sat in the mouth of a cave. Linda hovered over the entrance, whispered a mantra of unlocking, and pulled herself through the thin layer of pigment, through the thick stucco to a room in the back.

It was a storeroom. Here, things were a lot less organized. This was where all the paupers' coffins Linda had ordered over the last few months were stacked. The latest one, too wide to stack properly, lay by itself in the middle of the room. And she was soon staring right into that crimson crow's eye, being carried aloft by the whirlwind, racing over that blasted terrain she had visited before. Now, having meditated over its images for more than a day, Linda was experiencing it all with far greater clarity. She stood at the entrance to Narok . . . and looked down into the flames, flames fanned by the wings of a gigantic crow whose shadow blotted out the sun and moon and stars.

The wind was screaming now. Narok was not hot. There was fire blazing somewhere in the bowels of the rocky earth beneath her feet, but it was a fire without warmth. The wind whipped at her . . . she gazed into the abyss. An ocean of black seethed beneath her. But when she stared hard enough, she could make out the shapes of crows. The wind sprang from the flapping of a million black wings . . . the howling in the air the sum of a million cries of *ka, ka, ka.*

"Who is this coffin for?" she screamed. "Why did you make me buy it?"

She knew that to get the answers, she would have to descend further. She would have to enter the abyss itself. She would have to risk not coming back—let go of the *saisin* she held in her hands. No safety net. Nothing to pull her back to consciousness, save her own determination to live, save whatever she encountered at the bottom of the bottomless pit. And that was bound to be hostile . . . wasn't it? Wasn't it?

She teetered at the very edge. She felt the cord that connected her to the material world. It was fraying . . . weakening. *If I leap*, she thought, *I will be gone . . . the thread will snap . . . and I will drift forever in a world between worlds. Is this what my karma has led me to?*

Ka, ka, ka, ka, ka!

Linda hesitated. Beneath her, the black maelstrom churned.

Then the perspective shifted. It was as if the whirling chasm had become a scrying bowl. She knelt at the edge. The wind was more powerful now, and the shrieks of the maddened birds more dissonant. But in the chaos she could see images . . . pieces of the real world. The bottomless pit was also a window into the world . . . a sort of two-way mirror between realities.

She saw a graveyard. She saw a woman. She saw a crow.

The woman was standing next to a headstone topped by a cross; and that was in itself a strange thing, a Christian symbol invading one of her visions. She could not see the woman clearly, but it was a young woman with long hair, wearing a simple uniform, perhaps the uniform of a restaurant or chain store.

The crow sat on the headstone with its wings spread, shielding the woman's face from the sunlight as she stooped down to lay a jasmine wreath on the ground.

Sunlight streamed down. The woman's hands were drenched with sweat.

Who could this woman be?

The perspective shifted again. She saw tall stucco walls topped with glass shards, typical in a crowded city studded with very private estates. She could hear the putt-putt of a canal bus; this had to be near the Chao Phraya, the river that divides the twin cities of Bangkok and Thonburi.

The woman paused . . . she seemed to have heard something. She looked behind her.

Linda saw a white Mercedes pull up to the gate of the cemetery.

My car! she thought. *Is it me? Or is it Stephen?*

The car windows were mirrors; she could not see inside.

The woman was getting up now. Linda caught a glimpse of her face. It was a half-breed's face, neither Thai nor *farang;* pale-skinned, deep, dark, haunting eyes. The woman's lips moved . . . a greeting, perhaps.

Who are you? Linda cried.

The woman turned. Perhaps she heard something . . . a rustle of leaves in the mango trees that lined the wall. Her lips moved, she was about to say something directly to Linda . . . then, all at once, another fleeting image . . . an old man in a dark room, surrounded by Egyptian sarcophagi and flashing neon lights . . . a glittering knife, slashing through the darkness . . . and blood, and . . .

. . . the scream . . .

. . . crows, leaping from the abyss, their amber beaks dashing straight toward her eyes, crows swooping on her face, crows ripping the flesh from her bones, slurping the gelatinous ooze from her eye sockets, the images blurring, growing dark, and—

And suddenly, Linda was back inside her body. Obviously, the *saisin* had tugged her back. What she was about to see had to be too traumatic, or too intimately related to her own life, and therefore too dangerous. She took a deep breath, unwound the *saisin* from her hands, and called for the maid to bring her an iced tea.

seven

THE GRAVEYARD

DAYTIME, SHE HAD SAID, I WORK IN THE BLOCKBUSTER in Soi Six.

Leaving the Dolphin's Paradise in Soi Nana, Stephen realized that the Blockbuster was only a few minutes' walk away, though with the traffic, it could easily be half an hour by car. He told his grand-mother's driver to bring the Mercedes around while he walked. To get across the street the driver would have to go all the way to the corner of the four shop-ping malls, then circumnavigate a great circle of one-way streets, all packed with traffic. Stephen was happy to walk, though not happy to brave the early afternoon sun; the pollution hung brown and thick in the air; it streamed from the exhausts of motorcycles, *tuk-tuks*, and microbuses; and Sukhumvit Road, jammed with vehicles, was a pandemonium of car horns, street hawkers, and clashing music. Multilin-gual rap, abrasive techno, Chinese opera, and the bland pap that passed for pop music poured from every conceivable source.

A precarious *sapaan loi* made it possible for

pedestrians to cross the street without risking death. A steep stair led to the concrete walkway, which was lined with beggars, all kneeling, with their McDonald's drink cups in their prayerful hands, each one more miserable-looking than the last, many with young infants bawling in their laps. If they weren't as aggressive as the street people back in L.A., it was because charity is a cornerstone of Buddhism, and many regarded the disbursement of a few coins to the poor as simply the toll for crossing the street . . . and assuaging the guilt of being nouveau riche.

Stephen dropped a ten-baht coin in every cup. Each beggar made obeisance. It made him a little uncomfortable that a mere twenty-five cents could trigger such obsequiousness, and he walked on quickly.

The Blockbuster stood in a shiny new shopping plaza, with a brand new Brahma shrine by the sidewalk, all in gilt and marble. There were posters advertising some Gary Busey movie in the window. The look of the place was jarringly American next to the Brahma shrine and the row of little boys hawking lottery tickets and *phuangmalai*—jasmine garlands used to make offerings to deities and the Buddha. Stephen stopped for a moment, decided to pull out his mini-DV and get a few seconds of footage of this cognitive dissonance to add to his B-roll. The little boys smiled at him, and he gave each of them a shiny ten.

Inside, despite the Thai language signs alternating with the English, he might as well have been in America. Even the customers had a decidedly American look here in the touristy section of town. He glanced at the women behind the counter. Petite, pert little things. Two of them, one a little more willowy, the other a little more squat.

He spoke to them in English, once again not wanting to betray his edge: "Is there a young lady named Dao who works here?"

"Oh, Dao," said the taller of the two. "You one of her friends?" The two girls giggled.

Stephen wondered how much the girls knew about Dao's nighttime activities. "I don't know her very well," he said, "but she told me she could be found here."

"Dao never come in Tuesday afternoons," said the squat one. "She gets afternoon off, go to the cemetery."

"Yes," said her companion. "Visit parents. They all dead, very sad."

"You no need Dao," said the other. "We get off at seven. We show you all the good clubs . . . practice our English."

"Well . . ." Stephen said. The two of them laughed in chorus. Another customer approached, and was asking a complex question, and he took advantage of the moment to disappear into the horror movie aisle.

He was surprised to see one of the jasmine garland vendors standing by the Roger Corman display. A tiny boy, maybe four-foot-nine, his shirtless shoulders completely covered with strands of jasmine. He wore outlandish plaid shorts, with holes in them, held together with a belt with a shiny buckle that sported the misspelled legend *Ralph Raulen*. He had big eyes, messy hair, and several scars on his chest and arms, like thin white worms. He had an even tinier kid in tow. He was earnestly looking through the video boxes; he had put aside a couple of gore-drenched Dario Argento movies. He didn't look like the kind of kid who rented videos— or, for that matter, who would be allowed in a place like this. Street kids stayed in the street.

The boy flashed him a dazzling white grin. "You looking for Dao?" he said.

"You know where she is?"

"Yes. In graveyard. You want to see her?"

"Yes," said Stephen.

"You have car?"

Stephen began to wonder if this was some kind of con. "Yes, yes," he said, "I have car."

"Okay. You come, I show you where."

"Wait . . . who are you?"

"I Duan. I Dao brother. This littlest brother— Din. Dao, Duan, Din—Star, Moon, Earth—clever names."

"And you know who I am, then."

"Yes. You movie man. You look like Keanu Reeves, my sister say. You pay her for big movie, you take her away to America, take me and little brother, too. She tell me."

"I didn't exactly—" What was the use? Why shatter anyone's dreams? What did this kid have except these streets?

Suddenly, Stephen realized that he was about to do the unthinkable . . . to cross a boundary one never crossed in this culture. He was about to let a member of the lower classes ride as a guest in his grandmother's Mercedes. He was sure that the driver would be absolutely appalled . . . that he would undoubtedly report the entire incident to Linda, who would think that Stephen had finally lost it. If these kids thought for a moment that he was Thai, they wouldn't even have suggested the idea. They themselves would not have felt the wrongness of it. It was good, sometimes, to be an alien in one's own land; the rules did not apply to the *farangs*, who, as even the lowliest street urchin knew, were incapable of ever achieving fully civilized status.

Just as Stephen knew he would, his grandmother's driver was disdainful when the two street kids piled into the shotgun position. He immediately began scolding them: "Don't let *any* dirt rub off on the upholstery," he said. "This leather is worth more than your lives."

Stephen said to the boys, "Now tell the driver where this cemetery is." He got his camera ready. There had to be something worth documenting.

The driver seemed to sense that Stephen didn't want to speak Thai; his eccentricities were well-known to Linda's staff. Young Duan began to rattle off a series of complex instructions; the driver proceeded to ignore all of them, as they were clearly based on bus routes, which did not have to observe the arcane one-way system that regular vehicles had to follow.

"Well," Duan said, "at least buy a *phuangmalai*. I spent all morning stringing these. They smell good, too."

The driver ignored him. The boy chattered for a while. Meanwhile, Stephen called his grandmother on the cellular to tell her he'd be late getting back. He was careful to speak only English to her.

"Where are you going?" she asked him. She sounded alarmed—unusually so.

"I'm following a lead for a story," he said. "Don't worry, Grandmother. I'm not wandering into any dark alleys. No one's gonna ambush me."

"I know, my dear," she said. "But I've had one of my premonitions. I know you're a skeptic, but for my sake, avoid cemeteries today."

"I'll try, Grandma," said Stephen, and clicked off.

Eventually, the boy, sensing the chauffeur's disapproval, lapsed into silence.

Despite the boy's instructions, the driver pulled into an alley alongside one of the luxury hotels along the Chao Phraya River—not the Oriental, made famous by Somerset Maugham and Michael Jackson, but one almost as splendid, a few blocks away—so that the ragamuffins would not be publicly seen leaving Linda Dusit's Mercedes. They understood the scenario well. They didn't protest when they were dumped at the curb; the driver then pulled round to the front of the hotel, dropped Stephen off, and suggested that he page him when he was ready to be picked up.

As Stephen left the car, the driver added, under his breath, "I don't know what's happening, *Khun* Stephen, but those boys are filthy; watch out for disease, that's all I can tell you."

"I will," he said, tipping the man a hundred baht so he wouldn't go spilling the beans to Linda, such beans as there were. It occurred to Stephen that the driver probably thought there was something faintly prurient about bringing two dirty little boys into the car, but was too well-mannered to comment, though doubtless it would become the basis for another wild tale in the drivers' lounge at the Country Club about the unfathomable eccentricities of the upper classes.

His camera in his tote, slung over his shoulder,

Stephen slipped furtively through the lobby—this hotel lobby was popular with the well-heeled, who liked to be seen sipping Blue Mountain in their Versace suits, and Stephen didn't feel like having to converse with some dull distant relative—and managed to make it, unseen, past the pool area and down to the riverbank itself, where the boys were waiting. Duan was doing brisk business; a boatload of tourists was disembarking, and he'd divested himself of all the garlands except one or two.

"You come now," said Duan, and tugged at Stephen's arm. On the far shore stood the Temple of Dawn, a landmark seen in every movie set in Bangkok, its porcelain pagodas glittering in the sunlight. "Come quick," the boy said. "Too hot here. You be cooler in mango orchard."

Another alley. Tall walls on either side, all topped with shards of glass. They were entering the former Christian Quarter of Bangkok, granted to the Catholic Church by an ancient king; the Jesuits had been given permission to spread their gospel, but had succeeded only in building some magnificent churches, schools, and hospitals; it had never been easy to make inroads on Buddhism, a philosophy that easily absorbs other religions and transforms them into itself.

The deadly glass glistened in the sunlight.

"Where *is* this cemetery?" said Stephen.

Duan said, "Is old *farang* cemetery, built by Jesuit, long time ago. My sister father was *farang*, you know, yes? *Farangset.*"

"French?" said Stephen. "And your mother?"

"Oh, she die." He did not volunteer a reason, and Stephen was afraid to ask.

"Where do you live now?"

"Nowhere," said the boy. "Terrible. No TV. But I watch in Central Department Store. I never miss *Star Trek.*"

Stephen's heart went out to all of them, living on the fringes, always on the outside looking in. He wanted to help. He wanted to be involved . . . and yet there was something within him that held him back. Perhaps it was the old journalistic objectivity thing: for the observer to influence the observed was a Heisenbergian heresy. But this kind of TV segment was hardly supposed to be unbiased reportage. *Who am I fooling?* he thought. *The reality is . . . I'm scared.*

The woman had something about her that scared him shitless.

The alley twisted and turned. He could smell the river. Down another side alley, and they were at the edge of a *klong,* one of the ancient canals that had once been the city's transportation system. Wooden steps led into the muddy water, where children swam. Large brown rainwater jars, each as tall as Duan himself, lined the waterfront. Next to the wooden dock, incongruously, was a stone church, its walls encrusted from the pollution, with carved mahogany portals. Stephen was already taping. He couldn't resist this sudden touch of New Orleans Gothic bang in the middle of Sin City East. *No one can ever believe this city,* he thought. *It's cultural schizophrenia on every corner.*

Stephen wondered if the church was actually in use; one of the stained-glass windows was broken. Another incongruity: just out of the church's shadow, a spirit-house such as every house and commercial building in Bangkok possessed—put up to house the displaced spirit of the land whenever a dwelling place was built; the spirit-house was well kept up, with plastic garlands heaped around it, fresh incense, and a table of offerings including the roasted head of a pig. More footage. At this rate the B-roll would be better than the storyline.

The church grounds were unkempt, full of weeds; next to the spirit-house, and just as well-tended, was a lottery tree. It was hung with dozens of garlands and ribbons and messages of hope or thanks, and he could see one or two suppliants, on their knees, running their fingers along the gnarled bark to see if the outlines of any winning lottery numbers might have been scratched into the wood by the spirit within the tree.

Behind the church was the graveyard—one of the Christian burial places that could be found in this quarter of the city. Much of the cemetery was over-grown; the headstones were grimy, cracked; masonry weathers quickly in the tropics. Rising from the weeds was a somber angel with an outstretched sword. One grave was topped with a scale model of Michelangelo's *Pietà*. A stone path led through the tangled vegetation. The names, when he could read them, were mostly French.

Vegetation always runs rampant in the tropics unless it is constantly beaten back, pruned, cropped, mowed . . . but toward the far wall, there was a cleared space where someone had carefully cut the grass and pared back the foliage and weeded and planted; there was a rosebush . . . and against the wall, a line of mango trees . . . the sick-sweet scent was almost overpowering.

And there, in the middle of the clearing there was a simple headstone with a cross. Perched on the cross was a crow, peering down at the woman who was laying down an offering . . . a garland of jasmine, three lit joss sticks that poured their bitter incense fragrance into the air. Oh, and the sunlight streamed down. Not a cloud. She knelt, planted the incense in the ground; it was a strangely syncretistic thing, the Buddhist ceremony in the Christian graveyard . . . and Stephen had caught the whole thing on tape.

He held his breath. She had not yet noticed him, nor her two brothers, half-hidden by the waist-high weeds. She stood up and lifted her arms to the heavens in a timeless gesture of imploring. She was weeping. He knew that because the digital zoom went in tight enough for a closeup, losing nary a pixel in the process.

He went on filming. He was already editing the piece in his mind. The ravishing, ethnically ambiguous woman in the suffocating sunlight, the little clearing and the encroaching wilderness—there was your big visual metaphor—and then that universal gesture upward—to whom? The Christian God, or the more abstract principle of karma?

This was your perfect opening shot, setting up all the moral ambiguities of the situation, and introducing our heroine to her millions of new fans.

He thought of Duan and his naive belief that Stephen would somehow, godlike, pluck the three orphans out of their stupefying lives. And then he thought: *Here I am, arrogantly composing the shots, orchestrating these people's tragedy into a show entertaining enough to sell deodorant soap.*

Finally she became aware of him. She turned to him. She smiled.

"I know you come," she said.

He walked toward her across the flagstones veined with moss, and they met on either side of the gravestone. She folded her palms together and inclined her head toward him in a graceful *wai*. He nodded.

"I know you come for me," she said. "I know you will save me." And she began to weep.

Meanwhile, that same afternoon, under the same scorching sun that streamed into a back room through holes in the canvas blinds, Dirk Temple was hunched over a prone woman, who was passed out from a combination of downers and alcohol. He was slicing away her uniform with a steak knife. The woman was out of it; she hardly seemed to be breathing. She was an ugly woman, and not that young anymore; but Dirk did not mind. It would be a waste to practice on a truly beautiful woman until he had perfected himself, completed his transformation.

She stirred, moaned. Didn't she understand what she was supposed to do? Dirk fumbled about in the darkened room, found the first available heavy object—a pewter ashtray with images of *kinari*, the half woman, half bird of Thai mythology—and slammed it down on the woman's head a couple of times. She lost consciousness again. Dirk resumed the slitting of the skimpy cloth. He had her breasts exposed now—and he was hacking away at the material, down to the nether parts—the shaved, curiously dainty vulva. *Such a pretty organ for such a tainted whore!* he thought.

He had all her clothes off. He folded the shredded uniform and put it in a neat pile at the foot of the bed. It squeaked. He began arranging the woman on the bed in a more artistic posture. First he tried to emulate classic paintings like *Maia*, draping her arms coyly over her pubes and arranging her hair; she was plump enough, certainly. But somehow she wasn't alluring that way. So he finally laid her out with her arms spread . . . a sort of supine crucifixion needing only a few nails to complete the picture.

Now that was exciting. It made him think of his own childhood. The father and the mother. He hadn't thought of them in a while . . . because they had been taken away when he was six years old. The father was a big man. He had a stale smell. Dirk never drank beer because of that memory.

When Dirk Temple was four years old, they would fight all the time. They were violent fights. Dishes thrown, black eyes, leather belts, punchings. He remembered how he tried to stop it. How in church the preacher had explained it all: Jesus, nailed to the tree, sucking into himself the pain and horror of the world . . . paying with his agony for our transgressions.

Dirk always slept in his parents' bed when he was little. He could hear everything that was going on downstairs. One night he decided to be like Jesus . . . to take their pain unto himself. Yes. He took off his pajamas and lay on the bed with his arms outstretched. He called for the pain to come into himself. And waited. There weren't any iron nails around, so he tried digging his own fingernails into the palms of his hands. It hurt some, but maybe not enough. His heart was pounding. He could hear them still hollering . . . well, mostly the father, and the mother was whimpering and shrieking. Then it began to subside at last. Maybe the magic was working.

They came into the bedroom now. He closed his eyes. *I have to be dead,* he thought. *Jesus died for our sins.* It was dark. He squeezed his eyes tighter, till the tears came. The father was speaking softly. *I'm sorry, baby, I don't know what happens, some demon comes over me, I'd never hurt you for the world, I love you, I love you.*

And Dirk was thinking, *I did it, I am like Jesus.*

A sticky wetness on his palms. Was it blood? He dared not look. He had to maintain the pose of the crucified one. He had to take away their pain. Sometimes the mother would be so bruised she would limp around the house, and never look up at anyone, because she didn't want to show how much makeup she had plastered over her black eye.

They moved toward the bed. It was dark. It was as if they didn't know he was there. She was flung on top of him. She could scarcely breathe, he knew; she had had the wind knocked out of her so many times that night; she just lay there, barely moving, her head crushing his arm, but he dared not extricate himself; he didn't want to lose the power. And then he heard the father speaking, *Oh I love you baby baby,* and then the sound of cloth tearing and the father was throwing himself on top of her and moving, up and down, like a choo-choo engine maybe, stinking up the air with his beer breath, up and down and up and down and squeezing little Dirk, too, but at the same time he felt powerful because he was replacing their pain with joy . . . and then finally he heard his father rasp out, *You bitch you cunt you fucking slut whore pig woman I can beat you like a dog and you still crawl back for more you fucking whore oh I love you I love* . . . words whispered in such primal passion that Dirk knew he had become the savior of the world and that the phlegmy ooze that spurted over his closed eyes must be his own sacred blood, the redeeming force of the universe . . . and . . .

The older Dirk looked down at the unconscious whore. How could he have thought her ugly? How could he have criticized the sagging of her breasts, the mottled complexion, the tired circles about her eyes? This woman, too, was beautiful. Her blood was the same blood that had spewed over him in the dark nights of his childhood. And was she not about to take his pain upon herself, to draw away the thousand torments he had endured, from being teased at school, being whipped at the institution, being derided by his social peers, being looked down on in his job as a mindless, rubber-stamping flunky?

Woman, he thought, you know not what you do.

With surpassing tenderness, he kissed her finger-tips, her lips, the soles of her feet.

Then he dug the steak knife into an open palm. He barely broke the skin with the first thrust. This was harder than he thought it would be. The flesh resisted. Of course it did. It wouldn't be redeeming agony if it wasn't *real* agony. He pushed the knife in harder. A few drops of blood oozed from the cut. It was so different from his imagining . . . the real flesh, so much less pliant. He rocked the knife back and forth. Maybe it wasn't sharp enough.

Suddenly the woman's eyes opened. She was

shrieking. He leaped on top her, slapped her repeatedly to try to knock her back into oblivion. She bucked against him. It was infinitely exciting. He jabbed the steak knife down harder, sawing against bone now. She pulled her hand free of the knife. Blood spattered the bed. He sat down hard on her stomach, winding her, flailing with the knife, cutting here, cutting there, not knowing what he was cutting . . . letting the blood spritz over his face, his clothes . . . with a superhuman effort, she rolled away from him, got him off balance . . . ran screaming into the bathroom . . . slammed the door shut.

. . . and Dao said to Stephen, "Big day coming soon. You help me, I know you help me. I pray at the Brahma shrine. You know the Brahma shrine answer any prayer if you make the right promise. You ask, you must make promise. I say, let the man who look like Keanu Reeves, the handsome Hollywood movie man, let him save me from my big night. I know he like me. I love him good, very good, all night, many night, maybe even forever. Many men bid on big night say good-bye virgin. One man put big money. I afraid of him, be afraid, be very afraid." Always the quotes from Hollywood blockbusters.

"What man?" said Stephen.

"Look, look. Mr. Tong give me picture."

They wandered over to a stone bench in the shade of the mango grove, and she pulled a little photo album from her purse. They sat down. Duan picked a mango and was feeding it to his brother. Dao was showing Stephen the album. There were several photos, in dim lighting, as though captured by a hidden camera . . . snapshots of men sitting at a coffee table, with a faux Egyptian mural in the background. The room was smoky; in the foreground, the shadow of a bong suggested opium. The pictures were of old men mostly, men who seemed uncomfortable—even if they didn't know they were being photographed. But the final photo shocked him because it was the man he had just lunched with in Soi Nana.

"Dirk Temple?" he said.

"He bidding a lot of money . . . one hundred thousand baht, I think. And I afraid. The girls say he like to hurt them." She looked right up at him, searching his face, perhaps, for some sign of compassion. And found it.

"Oh, God," said Stephen. He knew he couldn't let that happen. He watched one brother feeding the other, thought about the vacuity of their lives and how they had still managed to learn tenderness and gentility. "I'm going to do it," he said. "I'm going to find a way of saving you."

She stared at him. For the first time, he saw confusion, even suspicion. Even the boys looked up from where they sat, several yards away. What was wrong? It dawned on him. In his eagerness to be these people's savior, he had dropped the deception, the ace in the hole that was to have allowed him to remain the dispassionate observer, the camera-eye, the journalist from the distant west.

He had forgotten to speak English.

"That girl will never work again," said Ai Tong. "I've had her soundly beaten, of course, but she is useless to us now."

"I'm sorry," said Dirk Temple. Five minutes after

the prostitute ran off screaming, two burly flunkies had shown up to escort him to Cleo's, to the secret room. He hadn't expected that. He hadn't even known that this low-class institution across the alley was part of Tong's business . . . although he should have realized that the old man had a finger in every pie. And now Tong was staring him down, blowing opium in his face, making him feel like his father used to when little Dirk hadn't taken out the garbage.

Why wasn't this going right? Wasn't he the all-powerful one anymore? No. That opium-smoking prunelike old man had effortlessly assumed the role of master. Dirk hadn't felt that way since . . . since . . . his father used to stuff him in the garbage Dumpster to wait for his spanking. He shrank back in his chair . . . just as he used to when his father spoke to him. This wasn't good. Not good at all.

"Mr. Temple," said Tong, "there are plenty of women where she came from, and my business will not suffer unduly as a consequence. But she did have a year left on her contract, and we do have, ah, obligations, financial instruments, paperwork, paperwork, paperwork. I'm sure you know what I mean . . . of course you do . . . you're a diplomat. You have your own sea of paperwork to deal with."

These miserable human beings, he thought. *They always end up talking about money, when there are bigger things at stake . . . such as perfection . . . metamorphosis . . . transcendence.*

"How much?" he said.

Ai Tong laughed. It was the standard cackle of an old Hollywood serial villain, cavernous and self-indulgent. "I told you," he said at last, "money is never mentioned in Mr. Tong's inner sanctum."

"I see," said Dirk. "But there *are* . . . other services you want me to perform, are there not?"

"Perhaps."

"And by never putting a monetary value on that woman's injuries, real or perceived, you will continue to hold me in your debt, with the interest escalating, from now until the end of time."

"Oh, hardly, hardly, hardly, Mr. Temple," said Tong. "We are not heartless here at my little operation. Merely . . . practical." All business now, he pulled a file from a hidden compartment in the coffee table. "These are the names of certain visas we would like issued."

"Visas aren't my department. Cultural exchange, bringing over pop groups or artist workshops—that's my line of work."

"Nevertheless," said Tong, "we're in a bit of a bind. It's the Los Angeles operation. We need a few quick replacements. And our helper at the embassy has become . . . incapacitated."

Temple immediately wondered who their man at the visa office was. He could easily find out if anyone had recently left or fallen sick.

"No, no, no," said Ai Tong. "Counterproductive. Nobody knows who our operatives are. Especially not other operatives!"

So I'm an operative now, thought Dirk.

"Don't worry," said Ai Tong. "It's only rubber stamping, isn't it? And that's all you ever do there anyway, isn't it? Now, at least, you'll have the frisson of danger when you sit down to do your very mundane tasks."

"Let me consider it," said Dirk.

"Perhaps . . . another go at the woman who ran from you? I can arrange for her to be a little more compliant."

"I see."

"There are relatives of hers whom we could, ah, get to."

"I see."

"But . . . if you want to inflict violence on anyone I own, you must do so within strict limits . . . do you know what I mean? I am not running a rehearsal studio for serial killers here. Burns, scratches, and stab wounds must be, within reason, reversible."

Control me! All they ever want is to control me! thought Dirk. Temporize for now. Say what you want to say. Be their flunky by day. By night, rule over the quick and the dead. By night, return in glory, be the judge and jury, be the executioner. "Yes," he said softly, "I'll do what you say. I'll be your secret weapon." Be subservient for now. Be nice. He does not need to know you are really his master. Play him as he thinks he's playing you.

If only they knew, he thought. If only they knew. I'm burning the candle at both ends, and when the flames meet, there's gonna be a Big Bang . . . the kind that sets all of creation in motion.

He wondered how it would feel to flay the old man alive.

Finally, it was Duan, the boy, who broke the silence. And it was as if the surprise had never occurred—as if they had always been speaking Thai the whole time— as though no shift in perspective had ever occurred.

He said, slipping immediately into the kinship language that creates a comfort zone for Thai speakers, "So, older brother, can you drop us home? I have to pick up a new consignment of *phuangmalai*, and respected older sister has to change her clothes before she goes to her night job."

Dao continued to just stare at Stephen.

"Yes . . . yes . . . of course," Stephen said, slipping ever further away from responsible journalism. It was, he admitted to himself, a relief not to have to listen to the kid's strained, broken English, to have a real conversation.

Duan went on, "You'll want to film our home. I know they always have to show the house the heroine grew up in. They always have a picture of the outside of a place, and then they jump into the inside."

"Establishing shot," said Stephen in English. The boy mulled over the strange words, tried them out a few times, then uttered a surprisingly accurate rendition.

"Respected older brother, maybe I shouldn't ask this yet . . . but . . . when I work all night long, sometimes I only sell twenty or thirty—or even ten—and my profit is only five baht a garland. I've been saving my money a long time, and—"

Dao finally took charge. "No, little brother," she said. "You are not to ask *Khun Phii* for a television set. You are not to ask for anything at all. Or he will get tired of your constant demands and he won't like any of us. Let alone try to find enough money to save us from . . . the big night."

"I wasn't going to ask for that," said Duan. "It's just . . . I've been saving up to ride the roller coaster at Sea-con Square. And I can never get enough money somehow." He turned to Stephen. "C'mon, elder brother," he said, "it's not much. Me and my brother, we don't have an uncle or anyone to take us places. I'll get you some extra big garlands to hang on the statue of Four-faced Brahma at the Erawan. I'll rub your feet, too. I can even . . . you know . . . I know how to do what elder sister does. I haven't told her before, but it's because I don't want to bother her sometimes when I don't have enough food for my brother and me. I know how to do that mouth thing. But I'm not good at it. I gag. But I won't with you. You'll see."

"Be quiet!" said Dao. She raised her hand to slap Duan, but he shied away. "What will he think of us if you say things like that? This isn't some *farang* sex tourist. Apologize to the *Khun Phii* at once!"

Appallingly, Duan began to cry. Stephen did not know how to console him. He wasn't good with kids. Should he hold him, comfort him? After the grotesque proposition the boy had made to him, the thought of hugging him made him queasy. And yet that was what he needed—to be held by someone he could trust, who would keep him safe from the horrors of his world.

"And stop crying!" Dao said. "Nobody's died. It's bad luck to cry when someone is offering us a ladder out of Narok itself."

"I'm not sad," Duan wailed. "I'm happy. I'm too happy. I don't understand it." And brother and sister comforted each other, while the little one, full of mangoes, burped happily.

"Come on," Stephen said at last, "I'll take all of you back."

• • •

When the American man suddenly became a Thai, Dao was convinced she had witnessed a miracle. As she replayed their brief encounters in her mind, she realized that the Four-faced Brahma must have granted her wish. Everything was going to be all right.

She didn't dare speak as the man paged his car and as they stood in the alley by the churchyard's back gate, waiting for the white Mercedes to pull up. As the driver got out to let Stephen in, she flinched from his disdainful glance. It did not surprise her. Perhaps she herself would have been that way, had she been working on the estate of a high and mighty *khunying* and a tradesman had tried to come in through the front door. She could endure such disdain. It was natural. She knew that it was far above her station to ride in such a car, to share the backseat with such a personage. But there was something different about this man.

Was it love?

Dao did not know.

As the Mercedes moved out of the alley, worked its way down Silom, already thronged with tourists as the night market stalls were being thrown up along the sidewalk, she marveled at the smoothness of the ride, the luxurious texture of the upholstery. Did people really live like this, and not even appreciate it? she wondered. They drove past the entrance to Patpong. The neon was already beginning to blink on, though sunset was still a ways off. She shuddered when she saw three or four of her coworkers, arm in arm, getting off the microbus and marching down toward the back entrance to Cleo's.

Perhaps she would never have to go back there after this man bought her contract. She would make him so happy. She knew that she could. She would love him more than other women could. Their meeting had been foreordained by karma. Perhaps they had been lovers many times already in past lives. Perhaps that was why it had only taken two brief encounters to reawaken the buried memories of passion. He had not even asked her for one kiss; did that not prove that she was more to him than a whore?

But was this love?

She knew that there are many kinds of love, and that love can be a woman's highest duty. She knew of the myths of women whose duty and love led them beyond the grave itself . . . women like Savitri, who had snatched her husband's *vinyaan* back to the real world out of the realm of Yama, out of Narok itself.

Am I capable of such love? she wondered as they left behind the world of high-rise condos and the driver began to take them down Rama IV, toward the shanties of Klongtoey. Would this man be so horrified to see her dwelling that he would reject her? It was too late to worry about that now. Duan, her much-too-forward little brother, the boy who never seemed to know his place in the hierarchy, had pushed the two of them over the edge. Perhaps they would both become outcasts, beyond society's comprehension. But she had heard that in America, no one knew his place. That servants could become masters, that executives could find themselves destitute . . . that the wheel of karma spun so fast that one could be reincarnated many times even within a single lifetime.

There it was: An overpass reared up. There stood

the last of the spectacular skyscrapers, jeweled obelisks in the setting sun. Before them an expanse of garbage. Houses built of cardboard and corrugated iron. Houses slapped together from the discards of the affluent. No streets in this slum, just narrow walkways. The whole shantytown a powder keg—one accident with a match could set the whole thing on fire, had already, more than once.

"I should walk from here," she said. "Your car can't go any further and . . . shouldn't be seen in this neighborhood anyway."

As the Mercedes pulled over to the curb, she opened the door and stepped out. She didn't feel right having the driver open it for her. "Come on, younger brothers," she said to Duan and Din. They followed quickly.

"When will we see each other?" asked the man.

"Um . . ." She realized that she still did not know his name. It was too late to ask. Both of them would lose face. For now, she would think of him as *Khun Phii*—respected older sibling. It was good that they were now speaking Thai; the requisite respect language meant she would never have to address him by name, not until she'd had a chance to find out what it was.

"Do you want to call me?" asked Stephen. He pulled out his last business card. She wondered whether she could read, and was relieved to see her scanning the Thai and English without appearing to struggle.

"*Khun* Sa-tee-*ffen*," she said, sounding out the Thai transliteration of his name. "Yes, we'll meet soon. But I couldn't possibly call. You will come to Cleo, to arrange the . . . ransom."

"Yes," he said. It was the first time she had heard

him explicitly agree that this was, indeed, the plan. She smiled, at last. She wanted to throw herself into his arms and kiss him, but she couldn't view him as a *farang* anymore, so she didn't want to indulge in such a vulgar display of physical affection. Instead she inclined her head and brought her palms together in a graceful *wai*, then shepherded her brothers down the steep, sloping hill of garbage.

Stephen watched the three siblings descend into the wasteland. The galvanized walls of the shacks glowed bloody in the polluted sunset. The air was dusty and moist. The skyscrapers cast zebra-stripe shadows over the slum. The smell of putrid garbage mingled with spices from cooking fires and Bangkok's ever-present whiff of gasoline. He was taping, but his heart wasn't in it. Even though it was heart-rendingly good television.

He wanted to sort out his feelings about this woman. It wasn't love, he was sure of that. How could it be? They had known each other for twenty-four hours, and for most of that time he had deceived her. He wasn't exactly proud of that, but it had been in the interests of the story, hadn't it? And the story was getting better and better every minute.

The girl was a miracle by herself; the two little street urchins just added to the pathos. How could you look at this thing and not see *Pulitzer* written all over it? And yet . . .

"Take me home," he told the driver. Then he picked up the cellular and dialed Los Angeles. What time was it there? Three A.M.? He didn't care. The voicemail was open 24/7, and he knew that this couldn't wait.

When his producer's voice answered, he began talking up a storm, not even caring if he was addressing a human or a machine. "Listen, Marcie—I've stumbled on the real story. I've got the human interest to end all human interest. I've got the gorgeous, vulnerable, girl-on-the-verge-of-womanhood, tear-jerking, liberal-guilt-compounding, award-winning story you want. Oh, and there's corruption, too, corruption wherever you look. Even among the good guys . . . the cops . . . some U.S. Embassy personnel . . . there's dirt to dig, everywhere you go. I had lunch today with some embassy flunky who made veiled threats. And then I find he's got a finger in . . . okay, okay, I'm not gonna spoil the tomato surprise. But you need to wire me at least another five grand. It's not much, but we're going to buy this girl out of bondage—right on camera—and we're gonna lead her and her little kid brothers out of Egypt, and America's gonna hold its collective breath while it falls in love with this poster girl, and our ratings are just gonna hit the roof. Promise. Promise."

He hung up the phone.

The slums were well behind him. In front of him was a wide avenue crammed with cars; overhead was the unfinished L-train, that monument to high-tech futurism and fiscal feudalism.

There were big issues here. There was momentum. There was a career to be made, maybe more than one career.

And the woman? Was this going to be one of those *Pygmalion* deals, an innocent girl's heart and mind awakened to the glories of a brave new world, only to learn that the brave new world had no place for an uneducated ex-hooker who once lived in a cardboard box on top of a refuse dump?

No. I'll take care of her, I'll make sure she gets set up somewhere . . . starts a little business . . . I don't know . . . selling cloth or flowers or noodles . . . but not on the street . . . somewhere nice, maybe one of those shiny new shopping malls. It's in our budget, I'm sure. And they'll be glad to do it. A small price to pay for a slew of Emmys.

It was good to think of ways he was going to improve her life. It assuaged his sneaking suspicion that he was abetting in a display of shameless exploitation. And it prevented him from thinking about something else—the girl herself.

The feelings she aroused in him—they were pity. Compassion. Perhaps a little bit of lust—who wouldn't feel it? This was an exquisite woman . . . the orchid in the jungle's heart. Compassion, lust, and, yeah, okay, a hefty dose of liberal guilt. But not love.

Surely not love.

part two

The Love That Never Speaks

Earth, sky, and sea
Shall one day cease to be:
But not this love.
  —Sunthorn Phu,
    18th-century Thai poet

eight

THE SANCTUARY

STEPHEN FOUND HER A ROOM. IT WASN'T EASY—SO many factors to juggle—the network wanted a photogenic room, one that could easily be filmed in, one that had enough of an ethnic look to it without being so alien as to unstabilize viewers in Peoria. Stephen required a place of utmost safety, one whose location would not be discovered by the pimp-mafia nexus or any other curious media. He wanted a comfortable place. The older brother, with his independent spirit, could be a loose cannon, running off somewhere and blowing the whole cover. He wasn't worried about Dao; he believed that she would stay put for the duration of whatever it would take.

The network wasn't shoving a lot of money at this segment. The price of a young girl's future, and the entertainment of a couple of small children, were huge in terms of the local currency, but small change in show biz. They weren't seeing this as Emmy or Pulitzer material yet, but they were willing to dare at least a little money—more than they'd ever risked on Stephen's previous assignments, even the no-brainer save-the-whales show he'd done last year.

But Stephen was thinking about the little sanctuary he'd prepared for Dao as he scribbled on his bid sheet. He was in a private booth at the Cleo. He was being entertained by his own go-go-cum-lap-dancer, and the music was turned way up. He had thought the auction was going to be the sort of thing you see in Roman spectacles—"What am I bid for this enticing piece of flesh?" "Two thousand sesterces!" "Show me her teeth!" and other clichés of the slave market, but the reality was a lot less spectacular—and a lot less telegenic.

Of course it would be this way. The last thing any of Ai Tong's top clientele would have wanted was to be seen by another member of that elite. No scandal, of course—this was not the sort of thing that Thai tabloids were interested in—but knowledge was power, and details of the sexual habits of some political figure were a valuable commodity.

When Stephen found out that none of the bidders would see each other or even be in the same room, and that the bidding would be a matter of sealed envelopes discreetly carried from room to room by silent waiters, he was afraid that the scene simply wouldn't work on television. You can't convey much excitement from people sitting in rooms writing on little bits of paper.

It was lucky he had the inside track on this auction.

He had been spreading a little of the network's bribery fund around. As he sat there, sipping his Bacardi and Coke, the waiter came in again. He was a cadaverous, stony-faced man in a yellow tuxedo, carrying a tray with drinks and a rose in a vase; that was not, of course, a vase at all, but a clever shell that concealed a microsized digital video. How small they made them these days! And capable of registering an image under minuscule- lux conditions, too. He'd trained the waiter to hold the tray at just the right height to record tight face shots of the prospective purchasers. A few of these faces were going to become world-famous come the sweeps. But there wouldn't be any names; and with the faintness of the light, there would probably also be deniability.

A private TV monitor on the table showed Dao herself, gyrating in slow motion to what sounded like an insipid Thai version of Britney Spears. She was wearing a silver lamé bikini under a short, open leather jacket, and she was rubbing herself against a revolving shaft of light. A black bar at the bottom of the screen had a running tickertape display of stock prices . . . with one of them, labeled simply X, going steadily up as the evening progressed.

The figure was now eighty thousand baht, but Stephen had not yet put in his bid. He knew, after all, that Temple was planning to top out at a hundred grand—that indeed, an arrangement to that effect had already been made with the boss, making this entire auction a rigged sham. He was counting on the element of surprise.

It cost a nonreturnable ten thousand baht just to get seated at this auction, and Dao was only one of seventeen virgins on the block. But she was clearly one of the star attractions. It was already midnight, and she had only just gone on offer.

Dao continued dancing. It was all very vulgar, but

somehow the tackiness had not touched her; though she shook and shimmied like a second-rate Vegas girl, he could see that there was something in her that remained untouchable.

It was a pity there was no way for him to see the footage until later tonight, when he would dub them off and courier them to Los Angeles. He wondered whether they would be forced to pixelate key bidders' faces to avoid lawsuits . . . or whether the studio considered the third world too remote to bother about such matters. He sipped his drink. He had ordered only one. He had nursed it all evening.

"You ought to order something else," said the waiter. "They begin to think something wrong with you."

The lap dancer undulated.

"Is the girl a spy?" said Stephen.

"No, no," the waiter said. "Only her feelings a little bit hurt, because you no groping her. She think you no like her."

"I do, I do," said Stephen, though truth be told she was not that attractive. She was tall for a Thai girl; in fact, her pronounced Adam's apple made him suspect she wasn't a girl at all.

The girl's endowments, now revealed for the first time as she twirled her leather bra in his face, were overly large, too, and overly solid.

"She doesn't have a dick, does she?" he asked the waiter.

"Why you care? It only a lap dance. You no fuck this one. Save your cum-juice for later, huh. I know you buying virgin meat tonight. You don't want me film inside the bedroom? I no charge extra."

"No, you won't," said Stephen. "The pirated porno would be on sale at Pantip Plaza by noon tomorrow."

The waiter laughed—a strained laugh—and commented, "You sure know a lot about Thailand, boss."

The private dancer was down to a G-string. The suspense should have been unbearable, but when she finally slithered out of her last stitch of clothing to reveal a little stub of a penis, Stephen barely noticed. The bidding on the monitor had reached 96,000 baht, and he knew that the moment of truth would soon be upon them all.

He turned to the waiter, but he was gone. Perhaps he was even now recording Temple's face for posterity. What a shock it would be! He wondered whether the embassy knew of, even condoned, Temple's off-hour behavior. The lap dancer had her—his—hands on Stephen's shoulders and was wriggling about in a passable imitation of sexiness. Stephen ducked and slid out of his chair. There was a bell he could ring to summon the waiter again. And it had to be quick. The hundred thousand had been offered, and the screen was flashing the "going, going" signal.

The waiter surfaced at the last minute—ten seconds or so before the light would stop flashing. Stephen handed him the bid sheet. "Hurry up," he said. "Don't just stand there with your eyes bugging out."

"Yes sir, yes sir," he said, and retreated quickly from the chamber.

Stephen had bid 300,000 baht. Okay, it was only about ten grand, but still, it was about five years' salary for the average Thai chauffeur, for example. When in doubt, he thought, preempt.

Dao was waiting with the other girls in a room with gray walls and a couple of TV sets. The dancing had been prerecorded; the girls were being pampered today—no jumping about, nothing to ruin the new red uniforms they were wearing, red being a color that Mr. Tong favored, since it is the color that Chinese brides wear.

One TV set was the in-house video feed, showing the bids and the dancing girls. On the other, a dubbed episode of *The X-Files* was running, but no one was paying any attention to it. The girls were chattering about nothing, but she could tell they were nervous . . . avoiding the subject they most wanted to talk about.

She sat apart from the others. She knew they were all worried about who they'd get tonight. Would he be some handsome *farang* too ignorant not to overtip, who wanted to talk about his wife and kids back home before doing anything? Or a wealthy Chinese businessman, deflowering virgins in the folkloric belief that it prevented aging? She had heard a rumor that men from the Arab countries, whose belief system devalued women, were often cruel. What did it matter? Dao knew that she would be saved that night. She didn't want to talk about it; the other girls would only make fun of her for overreaching her station in life.

At length, she saw herself on the screen, and saw the bid rising steadily. It was hard to believe that anything could be worth that much, least of all herself.

When the bidding hit 100,000 baht, the other girls gasped, and a supervisor beeped in on the intercom: "Dao, go to the Golden Room and make yourself ready."

He's done it! she thought.

"Got yourself juicy *farang*, did you?" said one of the girls. "I hear they have huge dicks."

"Yes," said another, "big and prickly, like a cactus."

She didn't even bother to respond, but slipped away quickly, down the side corridor, to the Golden Room, the special chamber for deflowering virgins. She was happy. She wanted to be good for her new-found friend. It was a beautiful thing, to be yielding up her richest treasure to a man she actually loved.

The lacquer panel door slid open. The room was golden indeed, the walls inlaid with delicate gilt designs that represented angels and demons, the bed a four-poster with a gold-plated frame and golden drapes.

In a few minutes Stephen would be there . . . and all would be well. Although she had never experienced a man inside her, she'd received extensive training in the techniques. She knew she was going to be good.

As she stood beside the curtained bed, a hand reached out and grabbed her arm. Hard.

"I can't wait anymore," said a voice. "This auction is a joke."

She turned. The curtain was whisked aside. It was Temple, the strange man from the embassy, the one she had heard rumors about. He looked harmless enough . . . ineffectual, even. But he would not let go.

"I did not know you pay for me already," she said.

"I didn't," said Temple. "But it's a foregone conclusion. So why not taste, you know? While no one's looking."

"Taste?" said Dao.

He whipped out a paring knife from his pants pocket.

"Sometimes it takes a little adrenaline to get the lubricious fluids flowing," he said—she could not understand Americans when they used those long, alien-sounding words—"and the only way to taste it is in the blood . . . the blood tastes sweeter . . . like velvet . . . like honey."

"You crazy man! No touch me!"

"Au contraire," said Temple. He leapt off the bed and put an arm around her, his nails still digging into her wrist. He was going to kiss her. His breath was sour . . . it reeked of alcohol and strange American spices. "You come at the culmination of my personal odyssey, you nameless little whore. Oh, if only you knew how lucky you are. My whole life has been a bitter journey to reach this meeting point, this unwilling conjoining of our souls." He crushed her hard against his body, which pulsed against her with an inhuman energy. "But you are destined to fuel my transformation. Oh, you will see. You are the chalice of my sacred communion. You are she who will shatter the cosmic egg"—he squeezed her so she could barely breathe—"the soul-smasher, the heart-render, the co-redemptrix."

He paused for a moment, panting heavily, not letting go of her, and now she could feel his lips and tongue against her neck, and the jagged sharpness of his teeth, and he went on, nuzzling against her neck so that each incomprehensible word came drenched in sputum, "As a child I meant nothing to anyone . . . I was discarded, fending for myself, even though I gave of my flesh and blood so that the parents might survive their nights of violence . . . oh, oh, the interminable darkness of that childhood . . . and even as I grew up, the child within was never let out to play. You know what they think of me at the embassy? You think they know about the greatness inside me, the greatness you will awaken?"

She whimpered. He had bit down on her shoulder. She could feel the hot blood against her stone-cold skin. She wanted to scream, but suddenly his mouth was on hers, his tongue pushing against her closed lips. With a superhuman effort she extricated herself from his arms.

"Do not be afraid," he whispered. His tone was harsh and rasping, even though the words appeared passionate, amorous. "Through you I am about to touch the edge of an absolute beauty. Yes, yes, truth and beauty are in the taste of you. You don't know how I sought you out, how many I rejected so I could find the perfect vehicle for my metamorphosis. . . . Don't be afraid, child, this is love, the true, eternal love that consumes the soul with supernal and ineffable flame."

He lunged at her throat with the paring knife. She stepped aside, and he crashed into an ornamental gong suspended between a pair of elephant tusks.

"I love you," he rasped.

"What are you trying to do?" she managed to blurt out.

The doors opened. Dirk watched in astonishment as people began piling into the room. There were two of Ai Tong's bodyguards—a matched pair of henchmen, in quasimilitary uniforms—with guns. Behind them was Tong himself, preceded by a whiff of opium smoke. He wore an ancient mandarin's outfit, complete with tasseled hat. He looked like a decrepit incarnation of Christopher Lee's Fu Manchu.

"How dare you!" Dirk shouted. "This is all paid for. I need my privacy. How can I enjoy my purchase if people keep barging in?"

"I am sorry, Mr. Temple," Tong said mildly, "but you were simply outbid. A surprise offer at the last minute."

"You assured me there would be no surprises."

"That is not always entirely up to me," said Tong. "We all have our price; I run a business establishment, not a charity."

"A hundred thousand baht is charity?"

"You have been outbid, in cash, and within the time limit allotted. Had you been watching the monitors in the private lounge we assigned you, you might have been able to forestall this outcome—assuming you have the wherewithal to raise three hundred thousand at short notice." Disdain dripped from the man's voice. "But the rules are, alas, the rules."

"You told me," said Dirk. "You told me there are no rules except the rules you choose to make. Maybe you're not really a god after all."

"I'm hardly claiming divinity for myself," said Tong. "I am just a humble businessman, and every scruple has its price."

This was worse than being exiled to the Dumpster by the father. This was worse than sitting in the office day in, day out, watching the others with their supercilious faces, looking down on him, treating him like a lower being, never noticing the glorious creature that was hiding under the mask of the geek. *I am being tested*, he thought. *Sorely tested. Job himself wasn't tested like this.*

A murderous rage welled up inside him. I could kill him with my bare hands, he thought. And those henchmen with bullets, why, they could rain bullets on me, and the bullets would pass right through me, because I am as insubstantial as the wind. I am pure energy, not matter. I am thought, not substance. I am spirit. Ah! Let them live. They are testing me.

Compassion, he thought. Compassion and pity must be in my every glance. I must not show them my true self. Or they will be consumed alive . . . in the burning fiery furnace of my resplendent being.

My outer body is a shell, a carapace, and it's getting brittle. Like porcelain. If I'm not careful, it will crack, and the light inside me will leak out and devour the world. No, no, no, no, I'm not ready.

He had thought that tonight would be the night of transformation, but he still had a little more time.

A god had to take the long view.

At long last Stephen was ushered into the Golden Room. It was a luxurious-looking chamber, but the luxury was all skin-deep: gold paint, not gold; plaster statues, not marble; the Louis XV chairs upholstered in vinyl. It didn't matter. She was there. She was clothed in red, and veiled, like a Chinese bride, in keeping with the chinoiserie-themed room.

Even without seeing her face, he knew her.

A whole retinue had followed him into the chamber; there were two handmaidens, two security guards, a valet, and Ai Tong himself, beaming as an assistant counted and wrapped the 300,000 baht on a lacquer tray.

Stephen had not seen the notorious Tong until only minutes before. Of course, a man like Tong did not visit with the customers . . . not unless they happened to arrive with brown paper bags stuffed with thousand-baht bills. He wasn't even certain it *was* Tong—a man who never let himself be photographed. His studious command of the English language gave him away. It was well known that Tong spoke a disturbingly refined English—looked like the Yellow Peril, sounded like Sir John Gielgud.

"Well, Mister—ah—Smith, was it? The commonplace names are the hardest to remember. You've certainly come up with the money. I'll have them write you a receipt, if you like."

"No need." Why didn't they all just go away?

The handmaidens moved into position on either side of Dao. One tugged at her robe, the other prepared to whisk away the veil; everything she wore was designed to be removed with a single flick of a servant's wrist. She was like a presliced ham, ready to eat straight out of the package.

"I'm not going to screw her here," Stephen said at last, trying to sound like a finicky customer. "The atmosphere is too oppressive. I'll take her to my hotel."

"You may certainly take her where you wish," said Tong. "For now, you are her master. But if you take her off the premises, there will of course be the bar fee."

"Bar fee?" Stephen knew that in most of the girlie bars in this district, a man could pull most any woman off bar girl duty and take her for the evening with the payment of a fee to the management. "But I've already paid three hundred thousand baht."

"Then you won't mind paying another two thousand," said Tong. "Oh, and . . . since you're leaving, you might want to settle your drinks tab."

The little assistant, with his tray, sidled up to him with a handwritten piece of paper. He was being charged about fifty dollars for the single rum and Coke, plus a cover charge in the same amount. They didn't miss a trick around here. Stephen took out his wallet. He was running low. Luckily, he had the studio's American Express card, to be used only in emergencies. He watched as the assistant pulled out his abacus and his portable credit card machine—a very sophisticated one, with a wireless modem—and completed the transaction by handing him a bar release chit, stamped with the date and time. All very proper, all very soulless.

The attendants removed the veil. The assistant brought in some street clothes and left them on one of the faux Louis XV chairs. And then . . . and then they were alone. He took out his video, set it up on top of a fake T'ang dynasty horse statuette that rested on a lacquer armoire.

She looked disheveled . . . her hair in disarray, as if someone had gotten to her first. "Are you all right?" he asked her.

She began to weep. "You almost lose me," she said. "Someone else here earlier. I think maybe he want hurt me."

"They almost gave you away?" he said.

"Yes, yes. Terrible man. He want to play rough, too rough. No look like Keanu Reeves . . . more like . . . Freddy Krueger."

He couldn't help smiling a little; she smiled back

at him, and dabbed at her tears with a sleeve of her
red silk wedding dress. Was she happy? You can never
tell with the Thais. Smiling is a reflex, ingrained from
childhood. You smile when you're happy—you smile
when you're in the direst anguish.

She said, "You want fuck me now?" Why was she
speaking English when they were alone together?
Perhaps she suspected that the walls had ears. He
shushed her with a finger on her lips, felt the per-
fumed moisture of them, whispered, "No, no . . . no,
you don't understand . . ."

"I work very hard," she said. "I make you very
happy, I know."

"Let's go now," Stephen said. "I don't want you
here for one more minute. This place degrades you. I
want you to be somewhere real, somewhere human."

They kissed. Not a sexual kiss, Stephen told himself. No, I'm not taking advantage of this. I'm comforting her. And she's only doing what she's been told
to do . . . what she's been trained to believe . . . that
her value only lies in one thing. That will change, he
thought. It *must* change.

But the kiss became disturbingly less chaste.

Abruptly, he broke away.

"Oh," she said, crestfallen. "You no like me."

"Yes," he said. He took her hand. Squeezed it gently, as you might the hand of a frightened child.
"Come with me now."

The Mercedes drove them to a hotel. They entered
the lobby and then went out through the back. Duan
and Din were waiting in a side alley with a taxi. The
sanctuary was only about twenty minutes away; they

took the toll highway, totally deserted, speeding on the elevated road past Bangkok's art-deco-contempo-Oriental skyline, a vista so far removed from the cardboard houses of the shantytown that it might as well have belonged on a different planet.

At last they were in the hideaway. It had just two rooms, one with video games and a pullout bed, the other with a bedroom and private bath. Dao gaped. It might as well have been the Ritz-Carlton. Stephen got footage of her admiring everything.

He really didn't know what his plans were going to be for her. He was playing it all by ear. Presumably his 300,000 had bought at least a temporary respite in her life. Then what? Media stardom? Would she do a book, as told to Andrew Morton, perhaps, like Princess Diana and Monica Lewinsky? Or would she get tossed back into the slums, to fend for herself after her fifteen minutes of fame? These were questions that didn't have easy answers. But for now she was safe. He watched her; she disappeared into the bedroom and emerged in a simple silk robe—he had picked out a wardrobe for her on the network's dime, hoping that it would please her. She had cleaned off the makeup and let down her hair.

The younger brother was already asleep on the couch. Duan was deep into a game of *Final Fantasy VIII*, lost to the world, his tray of jasmine garlands wilting away on the counter.

Holding his breath, Stephen set up the tripod and turned on the video camera. He caught her perfectly, in the doorway to the bedroom, backlit by the rose-shaded nightstand lamps, her hair caught in a slight breeze from the wheezing window air conditioner. She was the fragile child-woman, the white man's wet dream. God, she was beautiful.

"Tell me how you feel," he said to her in Thai.

"I'm afraid," she said, in English. She had a natural aptitude for this. She played to the camera, and even her broken English seemed to have been crafted by the screenwriter's art. "I no deserve this. This no can be true. Something bad will happen. My karma no good. I born bad, grow up bad, I finish bad, I think; and then you come to me, like angel, lift me up, show me the face of heaven. I think I dreaming. I think tomorrow wake up, and I still in my house made of cardboard and steel, on big pile of garbage, next to rotting canal. But for now I so happy, if I die in the morning, I die happy."

Brilliant television, Stephen thought. The more this goes on, the more it makes me wallow in my moral ambiguity. I want her. Why don't I admit it to myself? I want her so much and yet something's preventing me from possessing her . . . even though I know I can turn the camera off and throw her on the bed and screw her until morning, and she wouldn't even care that I was treating her as a mere sex object, she'd *thank* me for it . . . a scenario straight out of Sex Fantasy 101. But why can't I do it?

Because there's more to this than just sex?

It was impossible. They had barely spoken to one another. And it had all been generalities. Their worlds were so far apart, they wouldn't be able to have more than a ten minute conversation about anything significant. How could a relationship be built on such flimsy foundations? Not to mention the fact that she could never be accepted by the Thai side of the family . . . that she wouldn't even be allowed in the tradesmen's entrance of most of their houses.

Stephen suddenly felt very out of place.

"I should leave," he said abruptly, causing her to switch back to Thai.

"Leave, *Khun Phii?*" she said. "But I've spent weeks preparing for tonight . . . learning the art of love. You have to stay . . . I promise you, it will be more than just the techniques I've learned. You deserve more than just technique . . . you saved me."

"I want you to spend one night—one night at least, without being the slave of some man's whim," Stephen said in Thai. "After that, I don't know, we'll see . . . I'm too confused right now. Sleep tight tonight. Feel safe. Feel protected. Watch the boys play their games and think how they don't have to spend all day out on the streets hawking those flower garlands. Tomorrow, we'll think about real plans, long-term plans. I'll be back in time for lunch."

Quickly, too quickly, he let himself out, the video-camera forgotten, still running. He slammed the door . . . because he could see that the elevator was in the hall with the door still open. He did not want to turn back, did not want to risk seeing her in tears. He was doing the right thing. He had to be. He knew he was. Teaching her to love herself again, to respect herself. In the next few days, he'd videotape her eating, smiling, talking softly about herself, reliving the horror of the past and reveling in her new hope.

And he'd have time to figure out how he really felt about her.

• • •

Dao sat at the edge of the bed for a while, trying to puzzle it out. Now and then, from the next room, her brother's video game chimed, beeped, or erupted into pert music.

Why was *Khun Phii* so uninterested in having sex? She knew that his feelings for her were real, not just a sham cooked up for his Hollywood show. Tomorrow I will work on him, she thought. Tomorrow I'll lure him into bed, or to a spot on the couch that he can't easily wriggle out of, and I'll start exercising all the things I learned.

Dao decided not to go to bed right away, but to have a soothing cup of Chinese tea, which she found on the counter of the pantry . . . there was *everything* . . . even a small refrigerator with some carryout green pork curry and noodles. What a considerate man Stephen was. He had even thought about how hungry she must have been, sitting in that room full of chattering whores, waiting all evening long for the winning bid.

She sat on the couch and watched her two brothers, one sleeping, the other completely absorbed in his video game.

"Aren't you afraid?" she asked Duan.

"No," her brother said. "He's a good man. He'll take care of us, he'll nurture us and love us. Don't ask too many questions. Just accept your karma."

She sipped her tea. I won't go to sleep at all, she thought. I'll just sit here, in the cool of the air-conditioning, and wait for him. Then I'll show him how much I love him.

In a few minutes, she had drifted into slumber.

• • •

She dreamed of flying over fields of green young rice . . . feeling the wind and the sunlight against her wings. It was glorious. She buzzed the Temple of Dawn, skimmed the rippling river flecked with gold, soared skyward over the city . . . and north, toward the mountains . . . toward the cool of the forest . . . to the country of the elephants. Wheeled above the canopy of the jungle. Kissed the edges of the clouds. In the foothills, dragon steps led to gilded stupas shrouded in mist. Higher still, shimmering in the haze, the blue of distant mountain ranges . . . stairways to the gods themselves. *Is this freedom?* came her own dream-voice, echoing from mountaintop to mountaintop.

Suddenly, in mid-flight, she looked down at her own shadow . . . huge and black against the reeling landscape. *I'm a crow,* came the dream-thoughts. *Why am I out in the sunlight? I belong in the darkness.*

And all at once she was plummeting toward a burning abyss where a million crows swarmed, and all of them screeched *ka, ka, ka, ka, ka* . . .

There was a knock on the door. Duan looked up at the clock on the television set. Six o'clock in the morning. Too early for *Khun Phii* to come back. Or was it? He saw his sister on the couch, his toddler brother in her arms, saw them sleeping . . . went to the door.

Then he thought, My sister should really do this. I shouldn't even be here. I should take my little brother and get out of the way.

Last night, he thought, they didn't do anything. Maybe it's our fault. We're always underfoot. Elder sister's put up with a lot from us, but they can't get in her way now . . . not now . . . not with the most important moments in her life.

The knocking went on, more insistently now. Tenderly, not wanting to wake little Din, he pried him from her arms. His brother put his little arms around Duan's neck. He kissed him gently. Then he went behind the counter and sat cross-legged on the carpet with the child on his lap. Dao stirred. Softly, he called out to her, "Elder sister, elder sister . . . someone's here for you."

The knocking became violent. Suddenly the door came open. Ripped off its hinges. It wasn't Stephen at all. It was someone else. A white man with blazing eyes. He could hear the door crashing onto the concrete of the landing. The man stormed into the room. He was soaked in sweat.

"I'm glad I had to break down the door," he said. "It hones my strength. I'll need all my inner power to survive my metamorphosis."

He marched over to Dao and pulled her from the sofa. Without even waiting for her to wake up, he forced her into a suffocating embrace. He tore at her clothes and threw the scraps of cloth around the room.

Abruptly, she came awake. "No!" she cried. "I no belong to you!"

"Hasn't your friend read the small print in the agreement? The deal was for one virginity. Your one commodity's been sold now, you bitch. Now your price is the same as any used whore's price. But I paid a premium so I could come and pick you up myself." The *farang* spoke rapidly, feverishly, as though possessed. Duan could not understand much of what he said. But he knew the man was dangerous.

"No one know where this place is! How you come?" said Dao. "You wait, please wait. *Khun* Sa-tee-fan coming back, make everything right."

"There is nothing that happens in the city that I cannot find out. You must know that by now. I am omnipotent. I am the eyes of the almighty. Look, look!"

He flung her against the wall. He waved his hands in her face. Pressed against the floor, peering through the narrow slit between the counter's legs and the floor, Duan saw that the man's hands were bleeding from deep gashes in his palms . . . like the statue of Jesus in the Christian temple where their father was buried.

The video game continued to fill the air with trite, tinkly music. The man kicked in the television set. The smell of burning plastic filled the room. I'm gonna choke, Duan thought. But he held his breath.

Dao screamed. Duan tried to scrunch himself farther into the space behind the counter. The terror seized him. He couldn't move. He couldn't speak.

The man lifted Dao in his arms. He may have been skinny, but he had the strength of a demon. Dao was whimpering, "I haven't told him yet . . . how much I love him."

"Be quiet!" The man slapped Dao resoundingly, dropped her on the floor. He drew a small paring knife from his shirt pocket.

He's going to kill her, thought Duan, *and I can't even move. I can't even stop him.*

And then something appalling happened. His little brother woke up. *No!* Duan mouthed. *Don't cry, don't move, don't go in there.*

The boy wriggled out of his arms and ran bawling out into the living room. He kneeled next to his sister's prostrate body, shrieking out her name over and over . . . and Duan could do nothing to prevent what happened next.

nine

THE DETECTIVE

LINDA INTERCEPTED HER SON BEFORE HE LEFT THE NEXT morning. She didn't want to pry too much, but as he put on his shoes in the hallway, she pressed something into his hand.

"Take this . . . please take it. Wear it around your neck," she said.

Linda had gone to great lengths the previous night to find it in her armory of fetishes and amulets. It was a jade crow. He was looking at it—he seemed annoyed that she was pushing one of her occult objects on him—but she could see in his eyes that sense of recognition when an ancient object triggers a buried memory from some former life. "Good," she said, "you know what it's for."

"No, Grandma, I have no idea," he said. He was very distracted. It had to be that girl. If only the boy knew how well she could read him. "But it's beautiful. Is it jade?"

"Black jade." It was a curious artifact; its smooth polish and angular, almost surreal outlines had caused one expert to tell her that it was very old indeed, a neolithic carving from the Hongshan culture—five thousand years old, perhaps—certainly, when she had used it as a meditating object in the past, she had felt its resonance.

"Thanks, Grandma. It's for protection, isn't it?"

"We've all been dreaming about crows; I think that the spirit within this amulet will lead you wherever it is you're destined to go."

When Stephen arrived, the police were already there. They were dusting the counter for fingerprints. They were snapping pictures, and one of them was poring over the door, ripped from its hinges, propped against the balustrade of the stairwell.

There was no sign of Dao or her two brothers. A police officer stopped him at the door. He was tall for a Thai, and prematurely bald. "Are you Khun Stephen?" he asked deferentially—he must have already done all the research on who had paid for the apartment, and checked into his family background in order to figure out what kind of kid gloves to use. You always had to obey the rules of the social hierarchy. Sometimes Stephen didn't mind shamelessly exploiting the fact that his Thai family members had real clout.

Stephen said, "The woman—"

"Yes. I'm afraid she is."

"Gone? Kidnapped? Or—"

"Yes," said the man. He smiled, as all Thais do when bringing tragic news, for it is the height of bad taste to impinge upon another's private emotions. He proffered a business card.

"Police Detective Samreung?" said Stephen.

"I've admired your work," said Samreung in clear,

though accented, English. "I was in Cincinnati last year, you see; observer, you know; American forensic techniques. I liked it very much there, and we did occasionally see your name on some of the stories on the show."

"You can surely speak Thai, if you wish," Stephen said.

"Oh, no," said the detective. "It's important for me to keep up my English. Lot of Americans in heroin trade these days. You cannot interrogate without, you know, the language. Interrogation is particularly difficult, you know, because they're often in such pain—you have to have the language skills of a dentist to understand what some of them are saying—even in your own language."

"Oh," said Stephen. "So you're a torturer."

Samreung smiled. "Semantics," he said. "I'm a good guy."

Stephen sat down on the couch. There was a smear of blood on the upholstery. He was nauseated. What had happened, who had done it, and what about the kids? Samreung offered a cup of tea. "It's good tea," he said, "imported; you've stocked the place well. As if you intended to keep the woman here for some time. May I sit with you?"

She was dead. That had to be what the man was telling him, but Stephen couldn't face that. He had videotaped her standing in that doorway, back-lit, her eyes shining. "Who did it?" he said.

The detective said, "Khun Lelliott—you're an important man. I understand you paid three hundred thousand baht for this woman. You're not a monster. Do you know how many years it would take me to make three hundred thousand baht? And I'm at the top of my division. People like you . . . you don't have to face the inner darkness of your souls . . . you can buy the darkness off. I envy you."

"Where's the videotape?" Suddenly Stephen noticed that the mini-DV was still sitting where he'd left it, on the tripod. The tape had to still be in it . . . that moment was still there, digitally preserved . . . the beautiful young woman snatched from perdition, standing precariously at the doorway to a new existence. If someone had broken in here and slain her, it was even more important to preserve that lost beauty, to broadcast it to the world, to let the world know there had once breathed a woman as beautiful as Dao, as proud, as full of hope. Stephen got up and went over to the camera. He popped open the tape door. It was empty. "Give me the tape!" he said. "People have to see the tape. People have to know."

"I'm afraid not," said the police detective. "Oh, we're not confiscating it or anything. In fact, we were hoping you would turn it over to us. The evidence, you know."

"You think the killer—"

"Please, Khun Lelliott. We're all grown-ups here. We won't pretend. Nothing will happen to you. You have many friends. No one is going to upset the boat."

"Rock the boat." When Stephen was nervous, he always corrected people. Bad habit. This was going in a direction he didn't much care for. A direction he didn't want to believe. "You're saying that *I* did it. That's what you're saying."

"I'm saying that I was not born a member of the elite. I'm saying that the upper classes are different. That's what I'm saying."

"You're saying that I did it—though I don't even know what *it* is at this stage—and that you're just going to walk away from it—to let me go. It doesn't make sense."

"I am only obeying my superiors," said Detective Samreung. He sipped the tea slowly and gazed at Stephen. He did the inscrutability thing well; Stephen could not tell where compassion ended and the hatred began. "Thailand will not, ah—rock the boat. Thailand will—how do they say it on *Star Trek?*—Thailand will comply." He laughed ruefully. "You are half Thai—and that half is of the upper classes. You are half American—and that American wields the power of television. But if it was just you and me, things would be different."

Stephen was too stunned to respond. This man had a vision of him as some kind of arrogant pervert who had paid for his pleasure and expected others to clean up after him. This man thought him a monster, and yet he was sitting down with him, explaining pragmatically why he was not going to prosecute some hideous murder . . . or multiple murder, perhaps! Where were the children? Stephen's stomach soured as he thought of the two boys. Had he created a safe haven for them, or had he lured them into some serial killer's trap?

Samreung was on a roll. Officers were methodically taking photographs and making notes around them. The two of them sat there—the innocent man whom everyone was assuming was a brutal killer and yet were treating with the deference due to his place in society—and the angry policeman, who was saying, "If I had any real power, Khun Lelliott, I would take you and release you in the jungle, and I'd hunt you down like an animal. You and your friends have raped my people and my culture. We're the laughing-stock of the world because of you and all your media exposure . . . that stupid definition of Bangkok in Longman's dictionary—'city of temples and whores'—who put that there? People like you. You're worse than the tourists who come here trying to buy cheap love. You've taken the illusion and turned it into *fact*. And they've told me to leave you alone."

"I didn't do it," said Stephen.

"Of course not," said the policeman softly. "The record will reflect a random murder, no motive, just one little girl and one little boy who happened to collide with a *farang's* sadistic fantasies."

"Wait!" said Stephen. "You said one girl and one boy?"

"Don't you even remember? How many drugs does it take to forget something so gruesome?"

"I didn't do it, Detective. And . . . there's someone missing in all this. Another boy. You have to believe me. Perhaps he's in danger. Perhaps the killer thinks he saw something. Perhaps he's tracking him down. Perhaps the boy has the tape . . . the evidence!"

"And perhaps pigs will fly. And perhaps the department will release the funds and manpower necessary for the investigation of the disappearance of a nameless, worthless street kid," Samreung said bitterly.

"I want to help you," said Stephen.

"Please . . . please, go back to your house. In fact, go back to America."

"No," said Stephen. "Not until you believe me."

"In a week will come Songkraan. We will all be washed clean in the blessed waters. Our evil karma will be swept toward the great ocean that is the past. I beg you, Khun Lelliott, you who stand between two worlds, pick the *farang*'s world and go home."

ten

THE DOORWAY

THERE WAS A DOORWAY.

Behind the doorway raged the flames of hell.

And in the doorway stood a woman.

She wore the remnants of a robe, ripped, bloody, and dark bruises showed through the tears in the fabric. Blood streamed from her breasts, and in her arms, curled up against her chest, its lips against the wound where a nipple had been sliced away, a child suckled. The child had no eyes. Blood streamed from the sockets. The woman had no eyes. The empty gouge holes wept a viscous and congealing blood.

Yet she was beautiful.

Linda screamed. Abruptly, she snapped out of her trance. And yet she did not find herself beside the lotus pond. *I must still be inside my vision*, she thought. Yes. She was in the room at the family pavilion . . . the room with all the stored coffins.

There was the coffin with the burning crow's eye.

The woman floated above the coffin. A blood-tinged mist enveloped her features. The child in her arms screamed soundlessly. His tiny hands and feet had been pierced . . . blood spewed from the stigmata . . . the woman hovered, her feet barely skimming the crow's head.

Mustn't show fear, Linda thought. *The dead are not here to frighten us. They have needs, just like the living. Sometimes they only need a little reassurance . . . just to know they are loved.* Linda forced herself to look at the apparition. Yes, she was beautiful. Or had been once. She *knew* this woman. She had seen her in other visions. But this time . . . this time she was dead. You can always tell the dead. They have a kind of emptiness. No living soul, even one on the verge of passing beyond, has quite that sense of the hopeless void, the hungry dark.

"What do you want?" Linda whispered. "Don't you know that this is a blessed place, protected by the *saisin* from vengeful spirits? Who have you come for? What is your name?"

The eyeless sockets twinkled, then began to burn with a cold and distant light . . . like stars. "Is that your name?" Linda said. "Star? *Dao*? And the child?"

The dead woman opened her lips. Earth began pouring from her mouth . . . earth, with the odor of fresh-turned soil . . . muddy earth, earth crawling with worms and spiders. "Is that your little Jesus' name?" said Linda. "Earth? *Din*?"

The dead woman clutched the child closer to her breast. She was an obscene Madonna, an affront to the faith of the Christians . . . but if a Christian ghost, how was it that she was in a Buddhist temple? The spirit world was a strange place, with constantly shifting boundaries. The world beyond the grave is an abstract world, incomprehensible except in terms of the illusions cherished by the living . . . spirits usually stayed within the confines of their own belief systems. "Are you Christian?" said Linda. "If so, maybe you have wandered into the wrong temple . . . but I do have a friend, a Jesuit. On Tuesdays, we often play bridge. Perhaps all you need is a good exorcist to send you on your way."

Behind the dead woman the doorway shimmered again.

"You must go through that door," Linda said.

The dead woman howled. Her lips were like the opening of a womb. A feathered shape was forming inside her mouth . . . she could see it struggling, could see the woman choking as the creature fluttered inside the moist cave of her cheeks. Suddenly there was a beak, tearing flesh now, rending the woman's cheeks from within . . . like a chick breaking loose from an egg. The cheek ripped and she could see the bloody tongue and uvula inside . . . and the crow emerged . . . the same crow sculpted on the coffin. The crow ripped the woman's head asunder . . . the skull shattered with a sound like breaking glass . . . brain tissue dribbled in gray globules down the shards of flesh and bone. The child screamed aloud now, and the whole room seemed to blur, to slide back and forth, and the coffins tumbled, and the big coffin pitched and yawed like a ship in a tempest, and in the center of it all was the woman . . . and now there were many crows, crows inside her, eating their way out, slicing through the paper-thin flesh with razor beaks, shrieking as they tore through her lungs, her intestines, her abdominal wall, devouring the child as it squirmed in arms that were animated by birds beneath the skin, and Linda thought, curiously, of that old English nursery rhyme:

> *Four and twenty blackbirds*
> *Baked in a pie . . .*

The incongruity of it, the horror and the lilting innocence of the children's song . . . that was what finally broke the spell. Linda found herself back at her house. She was shaking. The *saisin* fell from her hands . . . or rather, was yanked from it. When she looked up, her grandson was there. He was distraught. He was trembling. He was so upset he had not even removed his shoes before stepping onto the pavilion.

"Grandmother," he said, "I'm lost . . . I'm afraid."

Her grandson, the tremendously successful one, the one who never needed anyone or anything, was weeping like a child.

"You've seen something," he said. "I know you have. I don't believe in what you do, but there's got to be something to it. Grandma . . . she's dead, and I killed her . . . I *killed* her."

"Yes, yes," she said. The torrent of emotion had taken her by surprise. He had always been so balanced, so reasonable. But it would not do to go straight into a big wallowing scene, her grandmotherly instincts kicking in automatically. "But first, you have to eat something . . . just look at you."

"Grandmother, how can you think of food?"

"You need it," she said, "and besides, it will give you time to gather your thoughts. We're going to have to figure out how to deal with her."

"Her?"

"The woman—the dead woman. It's about her, isn't it?"

"Yes." He had to be really overwrought. Normally, when she said one of those psychic *Twilight Zone*-like things, he'd never have let it go without challenging her, or at least picking a few nits. Now he didn't even bother to ask her how she knew.

"Stephen, we may have to enlist the Catholics on this one. When the apparition comes, there's a certain Christian imagery to it all. I find it perplexing."

"Grandma," Stephen said, "I *killed* this woman . . . I manipulated the network, and her, and *everyone*, just to get this fucking story. I *killed* her . . . as surely as if I'd pulled the trigger myself."

"She wasn't shot," said Linda. "Now, you see, if you had actually *been* there when she was killed, you would have known that."

There were times when Stephen believed his grandmother was the only person in the world who understood him. Now, as she fussed over him, making him eat the elaborate *khao chae* meal she'd had the servants preparing all morning, letting him tell the story in little bits and pieces, he felt like a little boy again. Whenever he'd been dejected as a child, it had always been his grandmother who ended up getting to the bottom of it all.

Khao chae is served only in the hottest months of the year. The rice comes over a bed of jasmine-scented ice, and each of the side dishes requires elaborate preparation. As she waited for the story to come

out in dribs and drabs, Linda gave her lecture on the
complexities of *khao chae*. It was one of many stock
speeches she had—he had heard it often enough—
but this time he didn't find it annoying. In a way, it
was strangely comforting.

The events of the last twenty-four hours didn't
seem to make a connected story. They were fragments of many different stories . . . disjointed images.
But she listened quietly, and discussed the food when
he was stuck for something to say, until she pieced
together enough to get a general chronology. The odd
thing was, she seemed to know a lot about it already.
In fact, she seemed to know things he didn't know.

"I see only two dead people," she kept saying,
"but you talk about a girl and her two brothers."

"I want to see . . . what you see," Stephen said.

"I don't think you do," she said.

"Isn't there a way of showing me? You know, a
kind of telepathic e-mail or something?"

She reached her hands across the table. He held
them. They were cool and soft as lambskin. "I could
try," she said, and told him to close his eyes.

He saw:

—her face jerk back, the knife slashing down,
gleaming, and—

"No," he said.

—the grapefruit spoon gouging the eyes from
their sockets and—

"No!" A terrible chill seized him . . . though it
was high summer and the sunlight was streaming
down.

—the dead Madonna clutching the bleeding
Christ-child to her bosom and—

"It's trickery," he said. "It's all illusion. I've got to have proof. I've got to find the kid."

"It *is* illusion," said Linda. "The universe is illusion."

"She's dead, and you're giving me semantics."

"She loved you," said Linda. "And you love her."

"That can't be true," he said. "There was so little time. We came from such different worlds. You can't have love without at least something in common."

"Oh, Stephen," said Linda, squeezing his hands— he dared not close his eyes again because he knew he would see that vision again, that grotesque Madonna, those bleeding, sightless eyes. "How can you ignore all that I've taught you since you were a child? Are you so completely seduced by the *farang* culture that you don't remember the truth . . . that all the souls in the universe are caught in a cycle of Maya, of illusion . . . that your love for this woman could have been honed over a thousand lives . . . that you could have lived your entire life in preparation for that single moment when you knew you had found her once again. Do not fight your karma, Stephen, my beloved grandson. Now close your eyes."

—a doorway—

"What do you see?" she whispered.

—behind the door, the burning flames of Narok—

—in the doorway, the woman—

—and suddenly he was feeling the knife slice into his flesh, feeling the bite of the jagged steel, feeling his own blood well up, feeling the soft crying child against his bleeding bosom—

"Do you see a doorway?" said Linda.

"Yes. Yes."

—the doorway beckoned to him—it was the portal of an Egyptian temple, its lintel covered with hieroglyphs and sigils—a crow, carved in basalt, its wings outstretched, its eyes flaming rubies, stood watch over the entrance, and from its stone lips there came the plaintive cry of *ka, ka, ka, ka, ka . . .*

"What does the doorway tell you?"

"I don't know. Can I open my eyes now?"

"No, Stephen. You must speak to the spirits. You must ask them why they have come."

—*It wasn't love—couldn't have been—we never even told each other we loved each other—*

"Does the spirit ask you to enter the doorway with her?"

—*Can't you see it, Khun Phii? In life, we dared not face this truth—we are each other's neua khu—we are mated flesh, destined to seek each other out from incarnation to incarnation—but in this life I've been cut off before I could even tell you who I am—*

Stephen wept. He barely felt the comforting pressure of his grandmother's soft hands.

—*Come through the doorway—*

—she smiled at him. And he knew that if he stepped into that vision, if he lost himself in the dreamworld, if he reached out to her and held her, that he could stanch the bleeding, that he could restore her sight and beauty—if he would only take her hand and walk through the doorway into the kingdom of Yama, Lord of the Dead.

"No," Stephen whispered, "not yet . . . prove it to me . . . show me something real . . . show me the tape . . . show me Duan."

—Is a tape real? Is it more than just a dance of bits and bytes, a flurry of electrons? Is it more real than love?—

"I don't know!" Stephen cried. And abruptly he pulled his hands away from his grandmother's grasp, severing the connection.

. . . into the slums in the white Mercedes, stopping when the paved road became dirt too narrow for the car to pass, going on on foot . . . and all the while keeping up the act of the impartial media man for his producers, who were on the cellular every five minutes, because, my God, this was even better television than ever before.

"Yes," he was saying, talking fast because talking meant he didn't have to think about what really troubled him, "now we have an even deeper tragedy . . . and corruption . . . and we have the journalist, the observer, suddenly at the center of the controversy as well . . . the observer altering the thing observed . . . you see, it's all very postmodern. The audience is gonna eat this up, you know it, you just know it. And I'm gonna need more money, and you might need to FedEx over some more audiovisual equipment . . . and the lost tape? The tape, the tape, probably too raw anyway . . . if I can't recover it, we might have to go to the old 'studio recreation' scenario."

Night was falling. On one side of the canal was a ten-foot wall thrown up almost overnight a few years back, because the city officials didn't want the members of an international economic conference to see the slums from their penthouse hotel suites. The side that faced the affluent world was beautifully decorated with children's murals, lovingly contributed by earnest, environmental-minded art departments in a dozen elementary schools. This side he had never seen. This side was covered with graffiti.

There were no beggars here—there was no one to beg from. Stephen walked alone down the streets that were mere planks suspended above the mud. Children scurried out of the way. Where was Dao's house? He had been there once, surely he could find it again. But the houses shifted every day, didn't they? Didn't they spring up and get torn down in a matter of hours? He saw a toothless old man at a sewing machine . . . wondered which power line they had tapped into to steal electricity. Somewhere, a portable radio blared out snatches of gangsta rap. From farther away, the tinkling heterophony of xylophones and gongs, perhaps a radio play in folk opera style. The planks he walked on settled uncomfortably into the soft mud. Behind the smell of decaying fish and fruit, and the fumes of pollution, Stephen could detect the scent of jasmine. He knew there were no jasmine groves here . . . but the fragrance reminded him of Duan and his tray of jasmine garlands, and he followed it, deeper and deeper into the heart of the shantytown.

It seemed that the walkways became ever narrower, the heat and the closeness of the air ever more oppressive. Soon the roofs of the shanties were virtually touching across the path, and there were fewer planks. A little light came from the distant neon billboards and the condo-skyscrapers on the other side of the great wall. The light fell sparsely through the gaps in the corrugated roofing . . . pools of garish colors . . . here and there one of the buildings had a little light, from stolen electricity or a guttering kerosene lamp.

Then Stephen turned a corner, and the fragrance of jasmine hit him so hard it almost choked him. There was an open doorway, and behind it the jasmine petals were piled in woven baskets, piled almost as high as the ceiling. A dozen little boys were huddled in the room. A window—an irregular hole in the siding—let in moonlight and the lights of the city. A naked lightbulb was suspended on one wall, but its light was meager. The boys' faces were in shadow. Stephen saw what they were doing— threading the jasmine into the *phuangmalai* they sold on the streets. Everybody in the city used the garlands: as offerings to the Buddha or various deities, as greetings, as a gift to the spirit-house, as an aid to prayer or meditation.

Stephen had seen the maids in his grandmother's house gather together mornings, sometimes, to weave garlands; they would laugh and gossip as they threaded, and the kitchen would be suffused with the scent of the jasmine and *phuttachaat* blossoms, and the banana leaves on which the garlands were piled up. Weaving garlands was a happy thing; garlands are sacred, and making sacred things can only add to one's store of karma.

But this was different. The thin fingers worked relentlessly to the accompaniment of a portable radio, which was playing, improbably, one of the Backstreet Boys' latest hits. They worked silently. They were grim. Their bare chests looked skinny, malnourished. They had not noticed Stephen come in. He stood for a while, watching them, waiting.

One of them finally looked up.

"We don't know," he said.

"You don't know what I've come to ask," said Stephen.

"Whatever you're looking for," said the boy, "you've gotta ask Loong." *Loong*, a generic word for an uncle, seemed to have a menacing connotation. Perhaps it was the entrepreneur who owned this jasmine garland business.

"I don't need any *phuangmalai*," Stephen said.

"Wait a while," said the boy, "when Loong comes, he'll give you a wholesale rate."

"Where's Duan?"

No one spoke.

"I'm looking for a boy named Duan. I'm his friend. I'm trying to pull him out of danger."

No response.

"Listen. Two have died already. I just want to find him. I won't hurt him; I'll keep him safe."

Like you kept the other two? he asked himself bitterly.

The boys went on threading the garlands. Hundreds of jasmine blossoms went into each one, and the ends were accented with a dash of color, an orchid bloom, a bit of ribbon. The finished garlands were handed down the line to a boy who laid them neatly in baskets. As the baskets filled up, one or two of the boys would slip away with them slung across their chests, and other boys would move in from the shadows, bringing in empty baskets. Soundlessly they worked, while trite pop tunes bopped and bebopped in the background.

I shouldn't stay, he thought. It was depressing to

see the kind of life a kid like Duan led . . . in a city where, a block away, Armani-clad millionaires dined on caviar and traded stocks on their cellular fax machines. Bangkok's shiny crust hid many dirty secrets.

"Good-bye, boys," he whispered.

None of them looked up as he left the room.

But as he was turning back—he knew that the driver must have circled the slum several times now, even in this deadlocked traffic—he felt a small hand brush against elbow.

"Little brother?" Stephen said. But it wasn't. It was some other lad, one of the ones inside the jasmine room, perhaps, though it was hard to tell in this half-dark.

"No one's seen Duan in a couple of days," said the boy. He put out his hand. Stephen reached into his wallet, pulled out a twenty-baht note, waved it in front of the kid, decided to go for a little more information first. "Um," said the boy, "the word on the street was, he and his sis found some rich *farang*—not the usual fuck and run type—this one was maybe good for a month or two—if you knew how to squeeze him."

Stephen wondered if the boy realized that *he* was that *farang*. Perhaps not. Since he had only spoken Thai inside the room, and it is inconceivable to most Thais that a *farang* would be able to speak Thai with any real fluency, the boy had perhaps not even made the connection.

"I was looking for Duan's house," said Stephen, "but I can't find it."

"Are you a landlord?" It astonished Stephen that

a place like this would even have landlords. Perhaps it was only some thug collecting protection money. Surely illegal, and surely completely ignored by the authorities.

"No," said Stephen. "Look, I've come to help him . . . and, well, just look at me. You know it must have been difficult for me to come here. I wouldn't have come if it wasn't important."

"Well, that's true, sure," said the kid. "I'll take you as far as . . . the corner. But you can't tell anyone. And I don't want no twenty baht." Stephen pulled out a hundred. He could see the boy's eyes grow big. He probably didn't pull a hundred baht in a whole day's work.

The boy took the money—furtively stuffed it in his pants—and led Stephen by the hand down a few more alleys. Suddenly there were bright lights . . . searchlights perhaps. There were policemen. Stephen recognized the house—if you could call it that—but now it had been lit up. The garbage glittered around it.

"Thank you," Stephen said, but the boy was nowhere to be seen.

Stephen made his way toward the house. There were no planks at all now, and he was stepping ankle-deep in waste as he climbed the little hillock of refuse to the dwelling. The lights hurt his eyes. He didn't even recognize Detective Samreung until the man was almost on top of him.

"You ghoul!" Samreung shouted. "Have you no shame?"

"I'm looking for the brother," said Stephen. "Leave me alone."

"There's no brother . . . and if there was, I wouldn't tell you," said Samreung. "Although my superior officers wouldn't give a shit, frankly. He's just a statistic. Maybe you already killed him, anyway. Where's the damn body?"

"Let me in the house," Stephen said. "Maybe there's something there . . . some little piece of evidence. I could help you."

"You are unbelievable," said the police detective. "We're not here to collect evidence." He barked some orders at his subordinates. "We're here to destroy it."

Two of Samreung's henchmen were pulling on a rope. Stephen saw it go in one window of the shanty and out another, forming a kind of noose. On the detective's signal, the two men tugged sharply. It only took one pull. The building was flat. A metal object—perhaps a washbasin—went clanking down the side of the garbage heap.

"There," said the detective. "You didn't get it on tape, did you? For that precious television show of yours."

"No," said Stephen.

The henchmen were dousing the remnants of the house with gasoline. One threw in a match, and all at once the flames were spewing into the night. Just like that. All gone. The hovel this woman once called home.

As Stephen stared at the burning shack, he saw a black-winged creature burst from the bonfire. A crow. A bird of ill omen that circled and soared and swooped and swerved in and out of the fire . . . surely an unnatural creature, for there was in its movements a strange feeling of purpose . . . a message for him alone.

Who are you? he thought. My mind must be turning into mush . . . I'm starting to think that birds and inanimate objects can talk to me . . . my grandmother's starting to rub off on me.

The crow descended. It was wheeling above Stephen's head. The policemen were backing away; they must have sensed something supernatural. The bird spread its wings wide. Against the backdrop of the flaming hovel, the bird was onyx-black, and its eyes seemed to be crystal windows through which Stephen could see the fire engulfing Dao's home . . . or was it the icy flames of Narok itself?

At the detective's signal, more policemen stormed the burning home—hosing it down, spraying it with fire extinguishers. The blaze died down to a pitiful smolder in only moments. After all, the house had been little more than a cardboard box. Here and there small pyres blazed among the heaps of refuse. A veil of mist hung over the embers. The smoke was making his eyes tear up. The mist whirled, swirled, shifted, but did not dissipate. It embraced the hulk of the dead house . . . like the ghost of a lover. There was no wind. Thick moisture clogged the air.

The crow fluttered above him, cawing above the hiss of the dying flames. Where the house had stood in flames, there was a great rectangular nothing . . . a doorway into darkness. Was he the only one to see it? *Ka, ka, ka!* The Thai word for crow, the Egyptian word for soul. It all made a kind of sense to him. It was the same doorway he had seen in the brief vision his grandmother had allowed him to see. A doorway into a hidden kingdom, where light and dark are one.

Like a sleepwalker, he began walking toward the

house. The mist churned about him. It caressed him.

There was something almost biblical about this scene. Jesus being baptized in the river, the dove circling his halo, the voice of God acknowledging his son to be the chosen one . . . except that this was a blasphemous parody of that scene. The Jordan was a slew of garbage . . . the dove was a dark bird of ill-omen . . . and Stephen could hear a voice, not from above, but from within . . . from his own inner darkness . . . a voice telling him that he was being chosen . . . not to redeem the world, no—there was rage in this summoning, not compassion, not love. Or if it was love, it was a bitter love, a love that could never be fulfilled, a love born on unquenchable longing, a love that was music to a deaf man's ears, a jasmine blossom for one who had lost the sense of smell or touch or sight. This was not a love he could ever have chosen . . . yet it had chosen him.

In the mist, the outline of a woman . . . a horrific Madonna who wept blood, who suckled a sightless child from her bleeding breasts. . . .

Stephen howled in the empty air. He sank to his knees in the mud, heedless of ruining his tailored clothes. "Don't summon me anymore!" he cried out. "I don't want to be the chosen one! I don't want to live in perpetual darkness—I want to be left alone!" Unnamable emotions seized him, powerful, incomprehensible. He dig his fists into the offal, screamed, wept.

"You're evil," Detective Samreung shouted abruptly at him. "Even the birds are singling you out."

"You're wrong," Stephen said. "Don't you see

her? She's calling me from beyond the gave . . . she wants me to take vengeance. Oh, God, I loved her, I loved her."

"You're pathetic. Go back to America," said Samreung. "There, crazy killers get on *20/20*."

One of the detective's men tapped Samreung on the shoulder. "Detective," he said, "I think you ought to take this call." He handed him a cellular phone.

After a brief greeting, Samreung appeared to be listening to something, and not much liking what he heard. He turned to Stephen, on his knees in the mud. He was suddenly much less hostile. He touched Stephen's shoulder. "Look," he said, "perhaps I was overhasty."

Stephen listened numbly as the police detective continued. "There's been another murder. Another prostitute. Same M.O."

What was happening? Was Dao's death only the beginning?

The detective wrote out an address. He handed it to Stephen. "Perhaps we may need your . . . input," he said.

He was doing what Thais are prone to do when they realize they have been wrong: avoid confrontation at all costs, do a bit of quick revisionism . . . and suddenly they've never been wrong . . . they were always one of the good guys. It was a cultural thing.

Stephen took the piece of paper. The torrent of emotion, the bizarre, quasireligious vision that had just seized him, had suddenly segued into pure reality, leaving him with nothing but an aching emptiness. He got up. "Another woman?" he asked Samreung.

"No child this time, just a Pekingese dog," Samreung said wryly. "Listen, maybe there's more to you than I thought. Anyway, you're a link in this chain, even though I don't know how. Come and take a look. Maybe it will trigger some memory, some useful bit of info no one's thought of yet."

Samreung turned, barked out some orders, and then, with appalling suddenness, they were all gone.

Stephen stood at the center of the sea of garbage. Dao's house was gone; even the smoke was finally dissolving as a humid, foul-smelling wind sprang up from across the distant *klong*. Only the crow remained, hovering above the clearing mist.

In the car, on his way to the new murder site, Stephen finally thought about the pager number Temple had given him. The magic number that would, apparently, summon the marines and good old American know-how to make everything right.

He contemplated the number. He had ambiguous feelings about Temple; he knew that he had wanted to purchase Dao's virginity. But, he thought, that doesn't necessarily make this phone number bad, does it?

They'll take care of me, thought Stephen. Isn't that what he told me? As long as they still have deniability, the Americans will take care of their own.

He fingered the crow amulet his grandmother had given him. How cool it was to the touch. Jade was a magic stone, according to the Chinese: It becomes the person who wears it, becomes a double of his personality, a spiritual double.

Double. *Ka*. That was what the ancient Egyptians meant by *ka*, Stephen remembered from some

obscure moment in Freshman Anthropology. The
Egyptians believed in two souls: the *ba* and the *ka*.
The *ba* was in the shape of a bird . . . it could fly
around. But the *ka* was a ghostly double of the corporeal form of a person; funny how *ka* meant *crow*
in Thai. And *ba*? That's Thai for *crazy*. And do the
Thais believe a man has two souls? Yeah. The
vinyaan and the *kwan*. One is the soul proper, the
personality, the self—the ghost that comes to haunt
the living. The other, the *kwan*, is the breath of life,
the animus.

Strange how many connections you can see in
the world when you started free-associating . . . to
keep your mind off the things you dread.

The car was threading through Silom now, the
familiar red light district of Patpong left far behind.
They were turning right at the river, driving past the
labyrinth of alleys that had led to the Catholic cemetery Dao loved to go to . . . into Bangkok's Chinatown,
a wilderness of decaying buildings, goldsmiths, and
hole-in-the-wall restaurants. Soon they were crossing
unfamiliar *klongs* on rickety wooden bridges . . . they
were far from places frequented by tourists . . . or by
the affluent.

I'm sliding down a slope, Stephen thought, *and at
the end of the slope there's that doorway, and to go
through that doorway must mean . . .*

Death.

That's what it was all about, wasn't it? The crow,
the raven, the black emissary of the underworld, that
was a death symbol no matter what culture you came
from. Dao was dead, her infant brother dead, too, in
all likelihood Duan was also lost forever. It was Death

that was calling to him from beyond that door . . . and God, he didn't want to die.

If I don't do something, he thought, *I'm going to slide all the way into the abyss.*

The phone number was a slender lifeline. Perhaps just the illusion of a lifeline. But it was all he had right now. On one side the apparitions, the dreams, the pull of a love he was still trying to deny, and his grandmother's darkling visions. On the other—rationality. Apple pie. Cable TV. His apartment in Santa Monica, his hoped-for mansion in the Hollywood Hills. Normalcy.

This is my last chance, he thought, and dialed.

Hello, Mr. Lelliot. It was a female voice, flat, unemotional. "You know who we are. There is no need to leave a message. Do not worry. You will be contacted."

Well, Stephen thought, *I'm in the middle of a low-budget James Bond movie.*

Flashing lights! Motorbikes were pouring into the street. Men in uniform—no uniform Stephen recognized—were riding the bikes. The whole street was blocked in a matter of seconds. Some of the men were Asian, others clearly clean-cut white Americans. Two hopped off their bikes, saluted, and motioned that the Mercedes should follow them.

"Police escort," the chauffeur said. "Shall we follow?"

"We don't appear to have a choice," said Stephen. "What kind of police are they, anyway?"

"I don't know, *Khun* Stephen, but they're packing AK–47s."

"Well," said Stephen, "let's go."

• • •

Linda received a phone call from her friend Father
Santini, the Jesuit. And that was strange, because the
priest had been in her thoughts . . . because of that
strange lost soul she had been encountering, the
woman with her child.

"Are you calling to cancel Tuesday's bridge?" she
asked him, though she already had a feeling he had
something else in mind. In Linda's life, there were no
coincidences.

"I'm sorry to call so late—" Santini began.

"Oh, don't worry. I was just watching *Oprah*,"
said Linda. *Oprah*, dubbed in Thai, was indeed on the
bedroom television, embracing a battered woman,
being her wonderful empathic self. Linda always
thought that if she and Oprah were in a room
together for a few hours, she'd have the talk show
host flying through supernatural realms in no time.
That woman had to be a natural.

Still, she flicked the remote and turned off the
set. "As I was saying," said Father Santini, "I don't
want to disturb you, but I've had a call from the
morgue . . . and I know you have a collection of coffins."

"A pauper?" said Linda. "Yes, I have coffins to
give to charity."

"There's something weird about this woman.
She's a pauper all right . . . a prostitute. They thought
she might be a Catholic because of the . . . way she
died."

*The obscene Madonna, the crows ripping their way
through her flesh, the child with the sightless eyes.*

"They want her dealt with in haste, Linda. I
thought of you. We can't bury her in a Christian

cemetery until we find out more, but the morgue wants to dump her now. Something about . . . orders from higher-ups . . . I don't understand it, but they're adamant. It's some kind of hot potato for the authorities."

Father Santini, in his seventies, was an atypical priest. He was headmaster of one of the many Catholic schools in Bangkok, with their upper-class students—almost all of whom were Buddhist—and he himself was a student of Eastern philosophy. He'd even attended one of Linda's exorcisms—and had a pantheistic, vaguely heretical notion of the nature of God. "You're the only Catholic priest I know," Linda said, "who would call a shaman and ask to borrow a coffin."

"I know," Santini said.

"You want me to . . . keep the body in my family pavilion until you're certain if she should be buried by you, or cremated in a Buddhist ceremony."

"Yes, that's it, Linda. I knew you would understand."

"You'd better have the morgue deliver them both to the temple," Linda said. "I'll meet them there and supervise the transfer."

"Them?" said the priest. "I didn't mention—"

"There's a woman and a child."

"Yes. Very mutilated." He paused; even on the phone, Linda could tell that he was crossing himself. "I know better than to ask how you know these things," he added.

"I don't know myself," said Linda. "It's just an inborn talent, I suppose."

Stephen was still out in the Mercedes. Well, at this hour a taxi would be all right, she thought. The traffic should have died down a bit. "I'll be there in a couple of hours," she said.

"You're a godsend," said Santini.

Linda hung up the phone. She felt the spirit's closeness. Someone breathing in the room with her . . . a gust of decay-scented breath . . . the cry of a dead child in the wheeze of the air conditioner. The fragrance of jasmine.

We're going to meet in the flesh at last, she thought. *I've known we were going to meet ever since I bought your coffin only a few days ago.*

The wheel of karma was turning.

Ka, ka, ka.

Soul and *crow* were about to become one flesh.

eleven

THE AMBASSADOR

THE POLICE ESCORT—IF THAT'S WHAT IT WAS—TOOK
Stephen in the Mercedes along the river for a while,
then crossed over to the Thonburi side. The Temple
of Dawn glittered in the moonlight. At length, they
got off the main road and went down a narrow,
unpaved lane; it meandered past some wooden
shacks, and finally led to a walled and gated estate. No
name, no number. The gate slid open automatically,
and on the grounds there were several American-
style split-level houses—the area resembled a typical
suburban land development of the 1960s. They
might as well have been in Ohio. There were even a
couple of white picket fences. Only the walls—at
least twelve feet high, and topped with razor-sharp
spikes—served to remind the eye that this was not
Middle America.

"Where is this?" he asked his grandmother's
chauffeur, who knew almost everything about the
byways of the city.

"I don't know, *Khun* Stephen," he said. "It's like
another country."

The convoy came to a halt in front of the biggest house in the enclosure. Stephen was ushered into an anteroom—American colonial, a lot of brass eagles and hunter-green leather, even a moose head on the wall—and then into a dining room where a black tie dinner was in progress. One wall of the chamber was completely covered with velvet drape, purple silk, interwoven with fine gold thread.

At the head of the table sat a balding man with a ruddy face and a pug nose. Stephen recognized him at once; he'd seen his photograph in the *Bangkok Post*.

"Sit down, Lelliott!" he said. To a uniformed staffer, he barked, "Bring Mr. Lelliott a chair. Quickly. He's a big man, an important man. TV personality! Yellow journalist extraordinaire! Woah, sorry, Lelliott. Yellow journalist—get it? Better than yellow peril, I suppose."

"Don't be such a racist pig, Kevin," said a slender black woman with a booming voice. To Stephen's amazement, he recognized her, too. She was Eliza Dashforth, the jazz singer. In fact, everyone at that dinner was a celebrity of one kind or another.

At the opposite end of the table, deep in conversation with a drop-dead gorgeous woman whom Stephen recognized as a well-known model, was Ai Tong. The infamous flesh-monger looked up at Stephen and leered.

"You . . . !" said Stephen. "You know something about all this. You must know!"

"Ah, Mr. Lelliott," said Tong. "I had no idea that you moved in such exalted circles."

"I don't."

"I understand you enjoyed the merchandise very

thoroughly indeed, Mr. Lelliott," said Tong. "But termination of a prostitute's contract usually costs a little extra; I'll send you the bill. Or does the network pay?"

"I didn't do it," Stephen said.

"Of course not," said Tong. "I assure you, the matter goes no further. And if you can't, ah, make up the difference right way . . . I am disposed to be sporting about it. Maybe a friendly game of poker. Or do you play chess, Mr. Lelliott? It would be somewhat Bergmanesque of us, would it not, to play chess for a dead whore's soul?"

Stephen started to answer, but Tong had already returned to his previous conversation.

A chair was brought in, and His Excellency Kevin Niewinski, Ambassador Extraordinary and Plenipotentiary of the United States of America to the Kingdom of Thailand, motioned Stephen to sit beside him. Then he clapped his hands, and maids in black uniforms with frilly lace aprons scurried to bring him a plate. "Bit of everything all right?" said Niewinski. Stephen didn't respond in time; they were already carving him a slice of turkey, picking out a lobster tail, slathering a duck drumstick with orange sauce.

"Unorthodox way of getting you to come to dinner," said the ambassador, "but I'm glad we finally get to host you."

Have to think on my feet, Stephen thought. "So . . . where am I?" he asked. "This isn't the official ambassador's residence."

"Well, this ambassador," said Niewinski, "gets a little tired of the old pomp and ceremony now and then. This ambassador likes . . . a little something on the side sometimes. You should appreciate that, being Thai, or half Thai, or whatever the fuck you are. Every self-respecting Thai male has a second wife, a *mia noi*, stashed away in some secret apartment. Same with me. Well . . . I don't have a second wife here, but it's almost as good—I have no wife here at all! Mrs. Niewinski doesn't even know about my little Americana theme park here."

"And yet . . . *this* Middle America has entertainments you can't find in the real U.S. of A.," said a wiry little man—whom Stephen recognized as a famous Czech film director who was not allowed to work in the U.S. because of a sex scandal involving a nun and a Boy Scout.

"Vaclav is very appreciative of what we do here," said the ambassador. "Would you care to see a little?"

He nodded to the head waiter. A bell rang, and the velvet curtain was whisked aside to reveal a stage. Pink and green spotlights danced. A woman writhed with a boa constrictor. A languid waltz played over the speaker system. It was a little tame until the serpent began to burrow its head into the woman's vagina. The crowd *ooh*ed and *aah*ed, and applauded . . . though there was a certain bored tone to their reactions.

"You don't like?" said Niewinski. "Well, well . . . what's next on the schedule?" A gong sounded, and the dancer bowed and exited. She was replaced by three couples in leather: one mixed, one lesbian, and one all-male. "You're surprised at the all-white revue," said the ambassador. "I can explain. They're all a bunch of Russkies. Economy's so bad in Moscow, the hookers actually get a better deal here."

"So I hear," said Stephen. This was a far cry from

being rescued by the marines. Although there was nothing going on that any tourist couldn't see in a bar in Patpong, there was something sickening about it happening here . . . and doubtless at the U.S. tax-payer's expense.

The three pairs of sexual gymnasts were switching off now, turning into two threesomes. And now it was one woman in the center, simultaneously fellating and being fucked and sodomized while the other two women did cartwheels in the background.

"His Excellency's a fun-loving guy," said Eliza, while Vaclav merely stared at the orgy, slavering. Everyone else was too busy eating, or having some intellectual discussion, to watch the show.

"Enough of this nonsense!" said the ambassador. "Let's have a bit of culture."

The gong sounded again. The curtain fell and rose immediately on a female string quartet. They were playing Bartok—Stephen recognized it from an interminable music appreciation class he'd taken in college—grimly sawing their way through the music's astringent dissonances. They were all naked. "Perhaps this suits your fancy better," Niewinski said. "A bit of cognitive dissonance. The acerbic and the sensual all rolled into one."

"I like how their tits flap with every downbow," said Vaclav.

"Mr. Ambassador," said Stephen, trying to keep his voice low, as though he sensed that the other guests were craning their necks to hear, "I was hoping for some help in my investigative reporting. One of your aides gave me this pager number and . . . I need to get back. Someone is killing women—mutilating, raping, I don't even know all the details—and I'm being thwarted . . . and the authorities keep burning the evidence."

I sound like an idiot, Stephen thought. God, if only I could get this on video. No one would believe this. The corruption reaches into more levels than I'd ever dreamed.

Stephen saw the ambassador wrinkle his brow. The waiter took away his plate and substituted some kind of flambé dessert. "My young friend," Niewinski said, "you're overreacting."

"But Mr. Ambassador—the murder of an innocent woman— a child—"

"Hell, Lelliott! I was in 'Nam. Life is cheap around here. And you're one of those pinko liberal types . . . your heart's bleeding all over the damn carpet—Kurdistan by the way, about 1903, nice, isn't it?—surely you don't blanch at a bit of kinky sex from time to time . . . it's just good television."

"I'm in danger."

"Yes, yes. Of course. We'll keep an eye out for you. I'll send someone to look after you. How about that Temple fellow? You had lunch with him, didn't you? He's the one who told you how to get help."

"I see."

"But you have to promise to lay off. I'm serious now. Do your exotic story—all the sex in high places you want, all the human interest, everything—but lay off this particular . . . thing. Rocking boats is a dangerous exercise, and a rocked boat does have a tendency to sink without a trace."

All the levity was gone now. The ambassador was gazing intently into Stephen's eyes. Stephen wasn't good at staring contests. Niewinski said, "All right. I'll make it all a little more clear, lad. You have a lot of very fine footage already, right? You boys are clever, and I'm sure you can edit it into some remarkable little piece. But Thailand and the United States have a bit of an understanding, you know.

"It's like . . . well, you're a bleeding heart, let's take an example you can relate to—it's like the environment. You think wolves are pests, you shoot 'em all, the next thing you know, there's too many rabbits or something, and the crops are all devastated. The great balance . . . the great cycle of being. You understand my drift, pal? I'm a career diplomat. I'll be here when all the politicians have been voted out . . . here or in some other shithole country. It's not about grand ideals. It's not about bringing the great adventure of western culture to the poor demented third worlders. It's not about agendas, my friend . . . it's about the status quo. Dog will always eat dog. When we control the rate at which dog eats dog . . . we control everything."

He took a huge swig of red wine, settled back, and seemed to be enjoying the astringent strains of the Bartok.

"So you're telling me that I can do what I want . . . but I can't do what I want."

"This is a fine country," said the ambassador, "and they'd appreciate it if the tourist trade were not thrown into a tailspin. As would happen if it were generally known that an ax-murderer was on a rampage in the red light district."

"I see," said Stephen.

"Chang will show you out. Oh, by the way . . .

nice amulet. Hong Shan period, isn't it? Or is it fake? If you can get it authenticated, you could make a cool hundred grand from it. You should get a nice gold chain to hang it on, not that cheap-looking red cord."

One of the uniformed waiters took Stephen by the arm. He had not touched his food, but his plate was suddenly gone. The interview was clearly over; the guests had gone on to a discussion of ancient murals in Buddhist monasteries, and did not seem to notice as Stephen was escorted to the antechamber. Only Tong appeared to see him leave. He looked up from his conversation and stared at Stephen . . . a moment of unmitigated animosity.

Chang, the waiter, said, "The motorcycles will escort you to Silom Road . . . please find your way back from there."

He bowed, and they were soon on their way.

twelve

THE HOTEL ROOM

AS SOON AS THE MOTORCYCLE COPS TURNED AROUND, in the Silom area, and left Stephen to brave the traffic unaided, he told the driver to go to the murder site.

He had to go there.

The pager thing . . . that had all been just a delaying tactic, that much was clear. Whatever was waiting for him was still waiting for him. What had he learned from the encounter with all those decadent celebrities? There was more rage than ever before. Rage was good. With this much rage, he did not have to think about other things.

The wheel of karma was turning.

He saw their destination now—a third-class highrise hotel, a few blocks past the luxury hotels on the Erawan corner, moving toward the middle-class area of Pratunam . . . the Shiva Hotel. There were several police cars in the lot.

"Wait for me," he told the driver. "Keep the motor running in case I have to get out of there quick."

The lobby was swarming with cops and plainclothesmen. He didn't see Detective Samreung anywhere. He was probably with the body. Or bodies. Guests and curious onlookers were milling about, adding to the confusion. Only one elevator was working, and that had an officer standing in front of it, assiduously questioning anyone who wanted to go upstairs.

"I'm with Samreung," he told the officer.

The officer looked him over. He mumbled something into a walkie-talkie, and jerked his thumb toward a corridor. "Take the stairs," he said.

Linda had the coffin taken out and placed in the main *sala* of the pavilion. She lit a dozen white candles. She waited. Tomorrow was the first day of Songkraan . . . the festival of renewal, of cleansing. It was good to spend these hours on the grounds of a temple, close to the other world.

Dirk Temple intercepted the walkie-talkie message— the police detective had been busy swabbing blood samples—and told the officer what he wanted to hear. Then he informed Samreung that Lelliott was on his way up.

"What will I tell him when he gets here?" Samreung asked.

"He won't," said Dirk.

Samreung nodded soberly.

"The ambassador thanks you for your cooperation," Temple said.

"The police department thanks the embassy for its cooperation," said Samreung.

"We always come as quickly as we can when American citizens are involved," said Dirk Temple. "I appreciate you calling us in."

"Still, the speed with which you responded . . . it seemed you got here even before we did."

"There are those," Dirk said, "who attribute almost godlike powers to me." Inwardly, he laughed. It was always astonishing how gullible people were. How else had they deemed him a mild-mannered, ineffectual geek all these years? He surveyed the carnage in the hotel suite. *It is good*, he thought, *it is very good*. Everything was in perfect order; it ached, knowing that the tableau must be taken down, that the immaculate image must be shattered.

There had been no child this time, but the dogs provided the perfect foil for this woman. Placing one halfway up her cunt was a great idea. It looked like she was giving birth . . . or maybe that the creature was gnawing its way out. And the Pekingese pooch nailed to the bathroom door was a nice touch. It hadn't been quite dead when the police came; pity that detective had shot it. These people had no concept of poetry, of art. They were condemned to perpetual mundanity. It wasn't even worth showing them what they were missing. Fucking yellow philistines. Sometimes he didn't know why he condescended to share the earth with them. Next time he had to find a more appreciative audience. He'd make it all perfect.

Killing was like a Chopin Étude; you could spend your whole life practicing it, and still not have it perfect. *Brilliant simile*, he told himself, *and I don't even give a shit about music.*

He felt particularly bad about the young American tourist who had had to be . . . terminated to make the picture complete. It was good to give the police the illusion that the woman had been entertaining a

customer other than . . . well, I am no ordinary customer. *I am he who comes by night and grants the boon
of eternity.* Still, he felt a twinge of discomfiture about
how he'd lured the kid in from the tourist mall down
the way, when all he'd been doing had been picking
out some fake Polo shirts for his friends back in the
States . . .

　　—*Hey, kid, you want a woman?*

　　—*No, man, I don't go with no hookers.*

　　—*But she's already paid for, and I found out my
wife's flying in a day early, gotta go to the airport.*

　　—*Well—*

　　—*Young guy like you, what, nineteen, twenty?*

　　—*Eighteen. I'm on tour with my church choir. We're
doing a concert for blind orphans tomorrow. You should
come.*

　　—*Gotta be horny. Look, here's the key, my hotel
room's—well, just over there—check it out. They'll never
miss you. She's hot! You can do her and be on your way.
You know the best pussy's in Bangkok—live it up a little!
The choir can hang out without you for a couple of hours.*

　　—*I don't even know you.*

　　—*Gimme a break! I'm an American.*

It was too easy to lure people to their deaths.

　　—*Dude don't kill me—*

　　—*Write this note. Then I'll let you go. I'll untie your
hand. Here's a piece of paper. Now write:* Don't come
looking for me. I've found what I've been looking for
all my life. I love you, Mom and Dad—

　　—*My father's dead.*

　　—*All right, then. Just her. Now sign it.*

　　—*You'll really let me go?*

　　—*Yes.*

—I swear I'll never tell anyone.

He had been sobbing like a little baby. Pathetic. Dirk hadn't even hurt him that badly. His own father hurt him more than that, at least once a day, before it ended. Dirk missed his father.

—I'm going to let you go now.

—Thanks.

—I'm going to let you go.

They never get the joke, he thought. You give them the chance to laugh along with you, and they never fucking get the joke. *Let you go*—yeah, right. Go where? Back to your filthy half world with its lies and secrets? Go where? There is only one place where all mortals go. It's just a question of when.

"The embassy will take care of its own," he said to the police detective. "We'll have the kid shipped off to the family . . . and we'll all keep a lid on it; I hope you understand."

"So I've been told."

Dirk Temple sauntered out of the crime scene, down the hall, toward the elevator. He had the letter in his pocket; he'd make sure the choir director or whoever got ahold of it; the boy would just be another nameless kid wandering around trying to find himself in the mysterious East.

And tonight, he'd eat in. He thought of a song he'd heard on the radio once, from the gothic-punk band Senseless Vultures—hideous music, but the words had struck a chord:

Not human hearts in aspic.

Linda did not watch as the pitiful remains of the woman and the child, which arrived in a small plastic

trash bag, were placed in the coffin. As soon as Father
Santini arrived at the pavilion, there had been a subtle
change in the spiritual atmosphere. The woman's
vinyaan, which was lingering in this plane from rage
and love, had been assaulting her thoughts—the image
of the bleeding Madonna and child had seemed to lurk
everywhere—but now there was nothing. The fury
seemed to have suddenly abated.

Spirits are like that, Linda thought. When they
want something, they bother you until you become
obsessed. When they get what they want, they fade.
No positive reinforcement. Spirits are like junkies,
raging, raging, raging, until their fix puts them under
for a while.

When you're ready, Linda thought, *you'll talk to
me again.*

Her conversation with Santini was mostly pleas-
antries, discussions of next week's bridge schedule.
He had clearly been profoundly perturbed by what
he'd seen.

"It's all right, Joe," she said at last. "I understand.
You spend all day stilling the tempests in the souls of
others; with yourself it's something else."

"Yes," Santini said. "See you next Tuesday, then?
Irma can't make it—she's in Finland for the week,
looking at inventory for her import-export business."

"Yes, of course," Linda said.

Father Santini was eyeing the murals. The can-
dlelight danced over angels and demons, over the
haloed face of the serene Buddha, his palms forward
in a gesture of benediction. The coffin had been
closed; the ridges and furrows of the wood carving,
shadowed in the pale flames, made it resemble some

scale model of a moonscape. And the eye of the crow glittered, crimson, angry.

"What will you do with . . . with her?" said the priest at last.

"The bodies of the rich and important remain in their coffins for a hundred or more days before the final cremation service, with monks chanting daily, and mourners coming to pay their respects," said Linda. "But in the case of a poor, lost, unclaimed streetwalker . . ."

"Perhaps, if you would permit a few rituals on my end as well—a novena, perhaps, in her name—covering the bases, as it were . . ."

"Yes, of course," said Linda. "You know that Buddhism acknowledges the validity of all religions—all worldviews are possible within this great cycle of illusion."

"All right, then."

Linda accompanied the priest to the sliding door, to the little alcove where he'd left his shoes. As he stepped outside, a bucket of water was emptied over his head.

"Happy Songkraan!" Some temple boys—every temple has a few orphans it looks after—were laughing, refilling their bucket from a nearby rainwater jar.

The priest managed to smile. "Doesn't the festival start tomorrow?"

"Not for you!" said one of the kids. "You a *farang—farang* day start at midnight, not at seven in the morning."

"I'm soaked," said the priest.

"It's a blessing," said Linda.

"Yes, I know," Santini said, shaking himself like a wet poodle.

As Father Santini made his way toward his car, Linda realized that it was drizzling a little. How unseasonal, she thought. April is the month of the harshest heat, when the sky is constantly pregnant but never gives birth to the life-giving waters—that is one of the meanings of Songkraan . . . as in earth, so in heaven—the casting of waters will bring the torrential sustenance of the monsoon.

Linda stood a little farther in the courtyard. The moon was disappearing behind a cloud. The temple children were already getting ready for tomorrow, the first day of the week's celebration, dashing behind jasmine bushes and stucco statues to shoot each other with water guns, dousing each other will little plastic pails of water, laughing and shouting, their cries melding with the heady music of a Bangkok night: the traffic, the crickets, the clashing boomboxes, the chanting of monks. . . . The rain felt good. She stepped farther from the doorway . . . droplets pelted her bare arms, her face. Her dress got caught in a cross fire.

"Sorry, respected granny," said one of the kids, bowing in apology.

"Oh, no," said Linda. "It is a blessing."

In the center of the courtyard, overgrown with vines, stood a miniature pagoda. The outer stucco was in disrepair; layers of brick showed through, and underneath, in the intermittent moonlight, there was a silvery glint. A boy stood in the shadow of the pagoda, apart from the others. He was a garland seller, perhaps; plenty of them walked around in this neighborhood, clambering onto windshields and tapping at car windows to sell their *phuangmalai.* Something about him gave her pause. He bore a strange resemblance to the woman she had seen in her visions, the woman whose mutilated corpse, she was sure, now rested in a box inside her family shrine.

The boy was hiding from the rain, perhaps. The rain was coming down harder now. The temple boys didn't seem to mind it; but this boy was shying away from it. He seemed very frightened.

She left the doorway behind and walked toward him. She saw him clearly now. The terror in his eyes was unmistakable. He looked toward the pavilion with a kind of longing . . . as if he knew that it contained something that belonged to him.

"Don't be afraid, boy," she said. "I won't hurt you." Then she said what she never dreamed she would ever say to a member of his class, not here, where one's place in the cosmic hierarchy defined every aspect of one's existence: "Come in, child, come in out of the rain."

Behind the door there was a stairwell. Stephen slammed the door behind him; it latched itself. The crime scene was on the eighteenth floor. He looked up. The staircase seemed to spiral to infinity. He heard a pattering sound. Could it be rain?

He made his way slowly up the stairs . . . tightly clutching the cold, chrome banister with one hand until his fingers touched something something gooey. He looked at his hand. Was it blood?

Light from fluorescent bulbs, high overhead, flickered. From somewhere far away . . . the beating of wings. Grimly, he ascended. With every step, he seemed to be pulling harder . . . his joints seemed stiffer . . . the flapping of wings grew louder. Where was it coming from?

Breathing . . .

He climbed faster. He did not want to look behind, did not dare look. An echoing, metal clattering, like a set of keys being dragged along the concrete walls . . . gray, gray, gray . . . Stephen climbed. Climbed. His fingers were slipping and sliding now . . . There was definitely blood here, blood congealing as it sluiced down the slick metal, blood clotting as it clogged his pores—

Footsteps!

Faster now, faster.

They're just my own footsteps, it's just my own breathing, faster, faster.

Now stop. Take deep breaths. Listen.

Khun Phii . . . Khun Phii . . .

No! Turn around. Go back.

He whirled around. Beneath him the fires of Narok were raging. The flames were licking the balustrade, reflecting off the chrome, dazzling, searing his eyes . . . rivers of fire flowing uphill, up toward him, and beyond it all a doorway . . . and Dao in the doorway, softly whispering his name.

Illusion! Illusion! He began running, now two steps at a time. Eight more floors to go. Gasping for breath. Barely grabbing on the banister, and now scraping his hands against the rough concrete, running headlong, heedless, fleeing the rising flame and—

Stephen tripped! Skinned his wrists on the stair. Reached out, felt a hand, grasped the hand, pulled himself up and—

—a severed hand—

Dainty painted fingers, the wrist stump still dripping a dark red rheum, the cracked radius and ulna poking out, and—

He flung the hand away . . . it sizzled in the flames that were even now encroaching more and more, and—

Dreams, dreams. None of this is real. It's like I'm trapped inside one of my grandmother's vision things. Gotta stay calm. Gotta move slowly. Slowly.

Stephen pulled himself together. Forced himself to look down again. The spiraling stairs swirled, swirled, like water flowing down a faucet. He swayed. Some kind of vertigo.

Khun Phii—

A shadow flapped across his face—a crow!

Ka ka ka ka ka

Stephen hurled himself up the steps now. He tripped. He clawed his way higher, heedless of the abrasions on his hands.

More footsteps now. Laughter. Mocking laughter, soulless laughter of demons, and—

The thirteenth floor. The door was swinging open. Creatures in the doorway—demons—demons with guns!

Laughter—

Calm yourself! It's just kids' laughter. Not the high-pitched screeching of demon voices. Just prepubescent children . . . children with water pistols.

"Happy Songkraan," they cried, giggling, and trained their water pistols on him.

Songkraan begins tomorrow, he thought. *Typical kids, getting an early start, can't wait. I'm going crazy. Get a grip. Get a fucking grip.*

He stared down toward the abyss. Nothing there at all. Just the shadows, the staccato flicker of old fluorescent light tubes. No flames of hell, no doorway down to darkness.

Stephen put his hands up in mock terror. "You got me, kids. Do your worst."

They surrounded him. Little kids, just like Duan, street kids in tattered clothing. It struck him as strange that they were in the stairwell with him . . . but hey, it was Songkraan, wasn't it? On Songkraan, the social barriers waver a little.

Stephen laughed.

They all laughed. Then they began to spray him.

It took him a split second to realize they were spraying with him acid.

He smelled his own face burning before the agony hit him. The acid hit the concrete, which began to hiss. He fell forward against the banister. His head smashed up hard against metal. The steel dug into the flesh. The kids crowded around him now. The metal was starting to dissolve. The balustrade was going to give way. He writhed, he twisted. As he raised his hand to ward off the acid, his hand began to melt. He screamed and screamed and the acid was squirting into his mouth now, dissolving his tongue, penetrating his cheekbones, slicing up his vocal cords so he could no longer scream, and still he screamed, silently, as the metal wore through and he began to fall—

The amulet! he thought. He had forgotten that his grandmother had made him wear it. Why isn't it protecting me? Suddenly he realized that it had never been there to protect him . . . she had never said anything about protecting him . . . it was about leading the way toward his destiny . . . whatever that was—

—and he fell and fell and—

She was waiting in the doorway.

She was not blind anymore. She was beautiful. The wind that whipped her hair was tinged with flame. Her lips were parted in a half smile, and her eyes were wide with wonder. She opened her arms to him. He was floating . . . floating . . . borne toward her in the talons of a great dark bird . . . whose beating wings were the source of the wind. Stars streamed from her fingertips.

I love you, Dao! he cried out in his mind, understanding at last that it was true . . . that it was the last truth he would know . . . before he passed through the doorway.

Linda clutched at her heart. She was falling, falling . . . but the boy ran toward her, held her, as the unseasonal shower pelted them.

"Don't die," Duan whispered, "please, old granny, don't die."

"Who are you?" Linda gasped. "And where is my grandson?"

"I've been searching high and low for him," Duan said. "They burned my house. He said he'd protect us . . . but something terrible happened while he was gone."

Duan could not get the story all out. Trudging through the streets, his sandals finally giving way, walking barefoot on the burning pavement, hungry, burning up from the heat, turned away from the crisply air-conditioned shopping malls because he looked too much like a vagrant . . . and the horrible memory of the man who had killed his brother and his sister . . . he couldn't tell it all fast enough. Instead, for the second time in his life, he started to bawl like a baby.

"I have to see *Khun Phii*," he said. "I have something for him."

The kind old lady didn't answer. She seemed to be suffering as much as he was. That was strange. The rich never felt any pain—they had servants to take the pain. She must be different . . . like *Khun Phii* was.

Finally she said, "I have a terrible emptiness inside me. I think, perhaps, that your *khun phii* will not be coming back . . . at least, not as Stephen Lelliott, my beloved grandson."

Duan reached into his shirt, which was tied around his waist like a belt, and pulled out the thing he'd been guarding since he had fled that apartment. "I think *Khun Phii* will want this video," he said.

Dirk Temple, walking through the lobby, heard the thud of a body on concrete, somewhere toward the back of the hotel . . . where the stairs were. He smiled.

I am ready to transform all the way, he thought as he stepped out of the hotel, into the rainswept night. *Tonight I will go to sleep a mortal; tomorrow I will wake up a god.*

And in the sanctum of Linda Dusit's family pavilion, on the sarcophagus that held two paupers wrapped in a garbage bag, the ruby eye of a carved crow wept real blood.

thirteen

THE CROW

A DARK PLACE. SUNLESS AND HORIZONLESS. A GRAY place, empty and cold. A void, without spithout time, without feeling, without form. A chaos pregnant with creation. A word waiting for the breath to animate it. A world as yet unmade.

An ocean of unborn souls. The waters are still and deep, for they reach down to the very heart of darkness.

A sourceless cold light that plays over the unmoving sea. Something is stirring in the abyss. The currents of eternity have begun to shift. There is a wind: a bitter, icy wind has sprung up, and the ocean is beginning to churn. In the wind there is a bird . . . a dark bird with crimson eyes.

He is Corvus, the messenger of death. He is the bringer of tidings to Valhalla. He is the Raven who pulled the first men out of a clam shell in the northwestern Pacific, the Deathbird who prophesied from the lips of the decapitated Bran of Ireland. He is the bird whose coming is the omen of death. He is the eater of carrion. He plucked out the eyes of Cinderella's sisters. Once white as snow, it is said, until the god Apollo turned him black, so that all would know his messengers came laden with doom. In its earthly incarnation, the Crow mates for life; in this place, beyond the confines of earth, he mates for all eternity. He is the disconsolate one, the one who mourns. His burden is the world's sorrow, the world's despair.

It was long past midnight. The old woman and the boy stood under the eaves of the pavilion. They watched the children playing in the rain, and when they finally left, exhausted, to go to sleep, they watched as the rain slowed to a drizzle.

Linda could not go back to the house. She knew that her grandson had passed through the doorway. She had to wait here; she knew that in some form or another he would soon be arriving here, in the family's house of the dead. What did this boy know, what had he seen? What she had glimpsed in visions . . . he had seen with his own eyes. *How scarred he must be*, she thought. She had never seriously thought about the children of the streets before; subtly, imperceptibly, her view of the world was changing. She had hob-nobbed with spirits and dark forces in other planes of existence . . . but she had never so much as noticed these other planes that coexisted, intersected with her own life in a thousand ways.

And now the rain had stopped.

"Is *Khun Phii* coming soon?" Duan asked her.

"Yes," she said. "He's coming now."

A purple twilight had begun to steal over the gilt-fringed eaves of the temple. The white Mercedes was pulling into the courtyard. "How long till dawn?" she wondered to herself.

"One hour, maybe a little more," said the boy. "I know because an hour before dawn is when I gather all my garlands and get on the bus to go to the corner of Rajprasong to get the predawn rush, the faithful ones who offer their *phuangmalai* to the Four-faced Brahma every morning. I'm usually up all night . . . when the sky turns this color, I know it's time to get the flowers ready."

"Good."

"Why do you need to know? A rich lady like you never has to see the dawn."

"But I do, my child. Tonight I have to do a potent magic . . . perhaps the most far-reaching spell of my many years as a *khon song*."

Wide-eyed, the boy said, "You speak to spirits? Can you speak to my sister?"

"I already have," she said.

Yom was parking the car. And another car was following the Mercedes into the courtyard. It was— somehow it did not surprise Linda—a police car. The man who stepped out wore no uniform; she surmised it must be someone of some authority . . . or a police detective, perhaps.

Somberly, he opened the trunk. He took out what looked like a porcelain vase . . . blue and white . . . like an ancient Ming artifact, or one of the cheap imitations sold in souvenir shops all over Bangkok. The vase had a glass stopper, like a perfume bottle. He carried it carefully, reverently.

Linda knew what it contained. But how? What could have reduced her strong, tall grandson to the contents of a blue and white vase? *I have let go my grief,* she told herself. *Attachment to the material is*

bad . . . Stephen is not dead, only transformed. What-
ever's in that vase . . . it's just a shell. The vinyaan *has*
passed beyond.

"*Khun* Linda," said the policeman, "I am police
detective Samreung . . . and I'm afraid I have distress-
ing news about your grandson."

"I know," she said.

"Of course you do." He bowed his head. "You are
well-known in some circles as a *khon song.* You will
already have seen what happened."

"I felt a terrible pain, as if my heartstrings had
snapped," Linda said. She smiled. That was the appropriate thing to do—to show composure at all times,
especially when one's heart was breaking. She could
tell that the young detective was moved by her stoic
poise. "Thank you, Detective," she said, and raised her
palms in a *wai* of thanks.

He *wai*ed back. "I am profoundly sorry," he said.
"Especially since . . . I must bear some of the blame.
At one stage I thought him the killer. I said many
cruel things to him. I am sorry, *Khunpuying.* For me to
intrude upon your grief is . . . unforgivable."

"The fault is mine," Linda said graciously.

"Mistress," said the driver, "it was bad, very bad. I
went into the lobby of the hotel to look for *Khun*
Stephen. The police had all the elevators cordoned
off, and they were strictly controlling who came and
went. Something prompted me to look in the stairwell. I saw . . . it was terrible, terrible. I saw the police
detective when I emerged . . . and he helped me
to . . . collect the remains."

"This was all we could salvage . . . these shards of
flesh," said the detective. "They literally tried to con-

sume him with some chemical. And I could have inadvertently . . . *caused* his death by encouraging him to come. You see, there have been instructions from above."

"The department wants the whole thing hushed up?" Linda allowed her anger to show. Not good. One should be civil in these circumstances. When all is lost, all you have to sustain you is your good manners.

Samreung bowed again. "It could have been anyone! Perhaps the killer didn't want him snooping. It could even be the police department. Certain officials have a vested interest in the sex industry, and your grandson was, to put it mildly, rocking the boat. Oh, *Khunpuying*, I am so infuriated sometimes, so frustrated! Even bringing you these remains . . . I have been ordered to tell no one, least of all the press. Yet there's a madman out there, killing women and children!"

"Can I trust you?" Linda asked him.

The police detective seemed pained. He was a good man, Linda decided, in an untenable position.

"There's supposed to be an amulet. He was wearing an amulet," she said.

"Mistress . . . I couldn't find an amulet," said Yom.

"Detective Samreung, the amulet could be the key. Do you believe in the power of ancient objects to retain some memory, some aura of what they have witnessed? There was an amulet . . . a crow . . . a jade crow."

"He was wearing it in the car, mistress," said the driver, "and the acid wouldn't have dissolved the jade."

"So someone must have taken it."

That was a blow. Jade was a living stone, absorbing unto itself the events and personalities it was close to. The carving knew what had happened to Stephen, knew the identity of the killer or killers . . . but now, falling into the possession of those killers, its clarity might become tainted.

"If you find the amulet," she told the policeman, "you may also find the truth. Though what you do with the truth . . . may lead you where your bosses do not want you to be led."

"If I find it . . . shall I contact you?"

She did not answer him, but turned away. This was something he would have to agonize over himself, and perhaps he might have to come to terms with his own loyalties . . . whether to the institution he worked for or to the justice he was sworn to uphold. After a decent interval, the policeman *wai*ed, she *wai*ed back, and she turned toward the pavilion as his car drove away down the gravel path.

"Come," she said to the boy. "Help me. Every shaman could use an assistant, sometimes."

They went into the pavilion, where the candles were still burning for the lost souls.

Animals! Mere animals! Dirk thought. *They exist to be slaughtered . . . just as I exist to be sacrificed to.*

Dumb animals. They could not even speak. Of course, they had all been gagged, and were gazing at him with numb, terrified expressions. But if they had any spark of the divine in them, they could have fought off the pesky little encumbrances of bondage. After all, Jesus himself could call legions of angels to rescue him at any time. And he and Jesus were very much alike.

Another hotel room . . . another rampage. So easy here, where the prostitutes were cheap street-walkers who would suck a guy for ten bucks. Just go downstairs, pick one out, bring 'em up . . . and before they could react to the sight of their sisters all bound and gagged, whack 'em quickly and truss 'em up.

This was the tableau of transformations. He was arranging the women in a circle around the king-sized bed, like the petals of a flower. It would be a rose when he was finished with them, a gorgeous red rose. And he, in the center, would rear up like the flower's sexual organs, the stamens and pistils, scattering the pollen of godhood into the air. It was a pity he'd had to tie them up so tight that they couldn't move on their own; it would have been nice, to allow them to sway back and forth a little . . . But on the other hand, he thought, this isn't a painting . . . it's a grand metaphor of life and death, creation and renascence.

Look at them! Creatures of all sizes and shapes. Even one or two *katoeys*—those transvestites Bangkok's always crawling with. Equal opportunity to guard the gateway of eternity.

He had cut away all their clothes now. Their legs were bent back and their ankles shacked to their wrists, so that each petal had a triangular design; not wanting to mar their beauty, he had fashioned the gags from clear plastic sheeting, and wound clear packing tape round and round their heads, leaving only their eyes free.

He hummed as he worked. This was a joyous act. As he pulled out the grapefruit spoon to scoop out the eyes of the first woman, you could just feel the adrenaline pumping into the air-conditioning. The eyes were pretty. The girls (well, they were almost all girls) began writhing as soon as he started to gouge out the eyes. Since they were quite hobbled by the way he had trussed them up, they succeeded only in sort of jiggling up and down; they couldn't even scream properly. But the squeaking of the bedsprings, in time with their wriggling, did add a kind of rhythmic counterpoint to the proceedings. An unexpected bonus—a soundtrack.

The eyes were good. He remembered once, when he'd been briefly posted to the embassy in Riyadh, that the guest of honor in an Arab banquet always had to eat the raw sheep's eye. A delicacy to end all delicacies . . . only the guest of honor was ever so privileged. Well, as a god, Dirk was going to be guest of honor at his own banquet, he could have as many sheep's eyes as he wanted. And these creatures were, in fact, sheep—for had not God commanded Abraham to substitute a ram for his beloved firstborn son?—all mortals are as sheep.

Temple knew that the old God was dead—one only had to look at this filthy, degraded world to realize that there was no longer any life left in old Yahweh. I mean, he thought, look what happened to the Chosen People in the Holocaust—a sure sign that it was time for a fresh master of the universe. The whole Abraham and Isaac thing had started the downhill slide. The minute you get soft on human sacrifice, the minute you let human emotions cloud your divine vision, it's all over. Well, not that *exact* minute, but then, a thousand years is but a moment in the mind of God. After all, Methuselah lived nine hundred years; today, Dirk thought, they live about as long as ants and bugs.

Lovingly, he pried more eyes loose. It was amazing how adept he had become at that; it was now no worse than shucking an oyster. The platter in the center of the flower petals was filling up nicely. The sacrificial lambs were all shivering; he turned the air-conditioning up even more; the cold was a good thing; it symbolized the coldness of his heart.

"Do not despair that you are prevented from crying out, from making your pain known," he said, pausing to straighten out one petal that had managed to inch out of position by wiggling its knees and inching slowly out of the circle. "Silent pain is the most telling. No one reports that Jesus screamed on the cross, nor that Tyr wept when the wolf Fenris bit off his hand. You must bear it all silently; that is the whole point. Being human and weak, you need help; believe me, I'd loosen the gags if I knew you had the superhuman endurance of a god . . . but you do not."

Switching to the paring knife now, he began to slice the nipples off, one by one; nipples were unnecessary, and they made an attractive garnish for the eyeballs. Oh, it was good to be the God. It was good to be able to rearrange the elements of creation.

There was a lot of blood. He hadn't realized that there would be quite this much . . . right away. After all, he'd only just started. This was going to be very messy. It could not be helped. He thought of eating one of the eyes right now. But there couldn't be any snacking between meals. Even a god has to have order in his life.

Carefully, Dirk took off his clothes, folded them neatly, and put them out of reach of any blood splatters.

He looked through his selection of utensils. He

couldn't make up his mind at first, the razor blade or the samurai sword: one was more dramatic, the other easier to fine-tune.

He turned on the hotel television. The pictures would settle his mind; the noise would filter out all the noisome rattling in his head, so he could focus on the grand vision. A music video was playing . . . rather pleasant, really . . . some bouncy Oriental girl bobbing up and down and flashing her skimpy tits to a vacuous synthbeat.

Good.

I'll use the sword. Drama over detail. He seized it, made a few passes in the air. It was sharp. He'd been honing it all morning. He almost sliced off one girl's ear. Gotta calm down, or I'll ruin the tableau, and then I'd have to start all over again from scratch, he told himself.

He climbed back into the middle of the bed. He made sure all the petals were correctly positioned. If this was going to be a bloodbath, he was damn well going to set the shower heads lined up perfectly.

Here goes nothing, he thought.

With a single twirl of the blade, he sliced the first throat. As the blood fountained forth, warm against his chest, he moved on, one circular motion of the sword, all the way around, oh yes, the cycle of being, the grand circle of creation, the cosmic egg, the navel of the earth, the womb, the earth, the universe . . . so much blood, so much blood, so warm, so healing . . . gushing now, spurting, spritzing his face, slick and slippery, hardening his penis . . . oh God yes, the blood, the blood, hotter than semen, wetter than a whore's cunt, oh he remembered the smell of his parents as they rutted on top of his helpless body, the blood streaming from his palms like the blood of the savior, oh God, he was rubbing himself up and down with the blood, and there was an eerie music, too, the air rushing past the slit syrinx, breaking the girls' silence at last, a weird, whistling sound, ethereal and penetrating . . . and now these gifts of love, he told himself, stuffing the eyeballs down his throat, feeling the jelly run down his tongue, just wolfing down those eyes and feeling them pop as his teeth bit down . . . chewing on the nipples.

Oh, I am reborn, he told himself, *I am bloody from the womb of time . . . I am the infant god in the baptismal font of blood, and these spewing throats are the source, the spigot, the river of life and death.*

He was ejaculating now, spilling his seed into the sluicing blood.

"Lift up the coffin lid," she told the boy. "What do you see?"

"A garbage bag," he said. "Is that—"

"Yes." Linda unstoppered the vase that held the liquefied remains of her grandson, and began to pour its contents over the plastic bag, telling herself over and over, *These mortal remains are but earth and water, external objects, not to be grieved over, not to be clung to.*

As she emptied the vase, she murmured a short mantra of making and unmaking. She told the boy to close the coffin lid, lit more incense and candles, chanted more mantras, all busy work, perhaps, for she was afraid to give in to her grief.

"They're really dead, aren't they?" said the boy at

last. "What does that really mean? What really happens when we die?"

"The wheel of karma turns, little one, and we move on."

"Then why are you saying those magic words?"

"Because, my child, you always have to beware of thinking too much in black and white. *Farangs* do that, you know. To them, life is always an 'either-or.' Man or woman? Dead or alive? Gay or straight? Good or evil? Truth is never that simple. Yes, they're dead. And when you die, you are reborn. But you see, between those two events, there is a doorway. Do you know what ceremony is designed to send you through that doorway?"

"Of course. It's the cremation. Big party, celebrating the new life . . . but I've never been to a cremation. I guess poor people don't get big parties at their cremation."

"Between the last breath of the old life and the first breath of the new, there can sometimes be . . . something else."

"Ghosts?"

"Perhaps. That's why we have a sacred cord, a *saisin*, to make a boundary for the lost *vinyaan*—to keep the spirits from coming back and reanimating their corpses. Sometimes they don't realize they are dead for quite some time, and they do try to get back in . . . as your soul does every morning when it returns to your body from the land of dreams."

"Is anyone going to come back?"

"I feel it," said Linda, and the feeling made her very bones ache. "They are *phii tai hong*, spirits who died violently, who may need to work out the trauma of their death before they are ready to pass into the next life. Usually, we'd call an exorcist, Duan, but we're not going to. Do you know why?"

"Because we miss them . . . and because they may have something to tell us?"

"My grandson and I had a number of visions . . . we've been seeing a lot of crows and ravens in those visions. And that can only mean one thing."

She was tired, so tired. Soon the dawn would come. Soon the shock would abate, and the numbness, and then, she knew, she'd fall apart, she'd be wracked by paroxysms of weeping. She wanted to make sure she was alone when that happened. She was too well brought up to be given to vulgar displays of grief. No. She had to concern herself with others, not give in to such consuming sorrow.

"Do you have a place to sleep?" she asked the boy. "And I know you haven't eaten."

Agony! Worse than death, this was an agony of atom bonding with atom, flesh knitting itself to flesh, the pain of giving birth to oneself. Bone to muscle, muscle to skin, skin to darkling feathers to the swirling tempest.

Why? he screamed. *Why me?*

And there came a voice from within—was it God who spoke?—and the voice said: *There is no why. There is only cause and effect, the unending cycle of karma. Certain conditions were met. A shattering trauma. An unfulfilled love, stronger than the boundary that divides the light from the shadow. Terrible crimes that demand a terrible vengeance. When all these things come together, it is time for you to be return to earth.*

Who am I?

*You are the one who is always alone. The disconso-
late one. The one who walks between the shadow and the
light. You are the instrument of retribution. You are the
fulfillment of the darkest love, the darkest death.*

Open your eyes!

He looked. There was the doorway. Had he not
passed through the doorway? No . . . it seemed to
have moved farther away. Had he not fallen into the
abyss of no return? What kind of trick was this?

*You feel it. You feel the urge to go through . . . to enter
the light . . . to begin your next incarnation. But you cannot.*

The world around him shimmered. It was coming into focus . . . in the minutes before the dawn.
There was a river. There was a temple . . . its pagodas
starting to catch the glint of dawnlight. There were
voices. Traffic, too. And the river *smelled* real: the rich
silt, the floating puddles of gasoline, the boats laden
with durian and mango and jackfruit and pomelo,
being ferried to the predawn markets.

*Look down. See yourself in the murky waters of the
River of Kings.*

He looked down. What did he expect to see?
Fragments of a man named Stephen. He could not
know that those fragments amounted to little more
than a small jar of viscous fluids with a few bloody
chunks of flesh.

The creature he saw in the waters of the Chao
Phraya River reminded him of a harlequin doll . . .
white as snow, black as death . . . divided between
light and shadow . . . a permanent chiaroscuro etched
into his face. The face was leaner, more angular than

Stephen's face . . . the lips more taut, the cheeks more hollow . . . and yet the eyes, the eyes were still all Stephen . . . his eyes were still human.

A flock of crows wheeled overhead.

And suddenly he realized that he was among those crows . . . his psyche was hovering in the air high above his corporeal self . . . that he could circle, he could swoop, he could plummet through the burning air.

I too am a crow! he thought.

More than a crow. I am the Crow, the Archraven. I am the darkness and the enigma of crows distilled . . . I have become an ancient archetype . . . I am something that has existed since time began. I am the inconsolable one . . . the heart that can never be healed . . . and I have power . . . power I could not even have dreamt of when I was living.

. . . and Dirk Temple rose from his baptism of blood, stood at the center of the flower that sprayed him with sizzling life force, watched calmly as the blood drained from those who had once been whores, whom he had now elevated to servants of the Most High . . . and he knew that his handiwork was good.

If blood could sing! he thought . . . *but what I am thinking? Of course it can sing! The world can do any-thing I tell it to do!*

The blood sang to him as it poured from a dozen slit throats: *Let everything that hath breath praise the Lord.*

Tomorrow night Dirk would plant another flower. Flower by flower, he would remake the world. Bangkok is the new Eden, he thought, and I am its Lord.

• • •

The sun was rising. The Crow felt a strange disorientation. *What's happening to me?* he thought. The light burned his eyes. He screamed. The light lanced him. He smelled burning feathers and sizzling skin. *Illusion, illusion,* he thought. *Nothing is real, why then this pain?*

Time for you to disappear now, said the voice within. *Not for you the kiss of the sun . . . not for you the warmth of the day.*

How can you say all this to me? he cried out. *Whose voice are you? Are you God?*

You know who I am.

How can I know that?

Listen. Listen.

The morning breeze over the rooftops . . . the tinkling of a million temple bells . . . yes. He knew the voice. And wept—his tears mingling with the waters of the great polluted river—for he knew that all was illusion, even God Himself—and the voice that he heard was his own.

He did not belong to the light, to the laughter. He belonged with the shadow and the nightmare. He must return to the land of shadows.

The wind on the water gusted.

Children playing by the riverbank looked up for a moment, wondered, went back to their games.

Except one child . . . a child with an amulet on a crude string around his neck.

That child knew *me!* the Crow thought as he spiraled into the wind and could be seen no more.

Nat did not think of himself as a child. He was fourteen years old, and an eight-year veteran of the streets. He and his friends were getting ready for Songkraan, which would be in full swing by mid-morning. The kids were filling their neon-colored Super Soakers with river water. Each one was good for a thorough hosing. But it paid to have a pile of the water guns ready; once Song-kraan got going, you rarely got a chance to reload.

He fingered the jade amulet he had found last night. Maybe he shouldn't have kept it, but Nat thought he deserved a little more than the five hundred baht he'd gotten for drenching that man in acid.

Well, it was a good evening's work, and maybe a little more honest than picking a pocket, or blowing some tourist in an alley. He and his friends did this kind of strong-arm work sometimes, when their boss needed to punish someone for welshing on a debt, or some other violation of the thieves' code of ethics. 'Course, they'd never actually *killed* anyone before.

Nat didn't want to think about it. How the man had looked. They'd actually melted the flesh off his bones, and dissolved a big chunk of the landing, too. He'd heard that acid eats concrete, but he hadn't been prepared for all the hissing and bubbling. That was scary.

Well, the man probably deserved it. According to the boss, he raped and killed a woman and her baby brother. Nailed the kid to the wall through his palms, then ripped him off the wall and stuck him in the mother's arms like a little Jesus . . . ripped out their eyes, too.

"Simple justice," the boss had told him.

Still, Nat couldn't forget the way he looked . . . he had laughed and joked for a moment . . . thinking it was just some early Songkraan revelers . . . and the way he'd sort of buckled over, his hands getting stripped to the bone as they grasped the banister, then the metal giving way and the man sailing south . . . down about fourteen, fifteen floors . . . shit, Nat thought, I deserve the amulet. Bring me luck.

His friends were all running around the dock in circles, spraying each other. Soon the river bus would arrive and they'd ride it, up and down the Chao Phraya, dousing the passengers with water—no one could get mad, the water of Songkraan is a benediction—and they'd ride the boat all day long, never getting off, paying one low fare for a whole day of pranks and laughs.

Nat decided not to be gloomy anymore . . . to forget last night . . . if he could.

"Gotcha!" he shouted, and aimed his water pistol at one of the others. They returned fire. The water was refreshing. Gleefully, Nat emptied one water gun at his attacker. He knew that the water of Songkraan was a sacred thing, blessed enough to wash away all the sins and misfortunes of the year gone by.

It was going to be a glorious day.

part three

The Vengeance That
Never Dies

Ten million acres is this earth,
And yet there is no place to berth
For him who sails the empty air.
Heart-piercing thorns grow everywhere,
He swoops, he soars; he finds no rest;
For he's a bird without a nest.
                    —Sunthorn Phu,
                    18th-century Thai poet

fourteen

THE AMULET

THE FIRST DAY OF THE FIRST YEAR OF DIRK TEMPLE THE
God was an uneventful one. It would not be good to
display his powers quite yet. After all, who knew, in 1
A.D. that a new two-thousand-year cycle had begun?
It wasn't a good idea to go around wildly changing
water into wine. No. It was a day of reflection.

April 13, the first day of Songkraan, fell on a Friday. He liked that—all the different magical numbers
and dates and days coming together in a grand conflu-
ence. It all added to the auspiciousness of his rebirth.

Although it was a holiday, he was surprised, on
returning to his apartment that morning, that there
was a message from the ambassador, demanding that
he come to a briefing at once.

Doesn't he know who I am? Dirk thought.

Well . . . on the other hand, of course he didn't,
he reminded himself. *I have not chosen to show forth
my true form; the light would blind ordinary mortals.*

Let him go on thinking I'm just some paper-
pushing, rubber-stamping GS–3, at His Excellency's
beck and call even on a national holiday.

He took a taxi to Wireless Road, breezed cockily through security, and was ushered into a room he'd never seen before, a music room with a grand piano. A portrait of George Washington hung on one wall—a signed photograph of President Clinton adorned the credenza, along with one of the ambassador and Congresswoman Lewin.

Ambassador Niewinski was seated at the piano. He was banging out a Chopin Étude—tolerably well, oddly enough. Dirk had never thought of the ambassador as a man of culture.

On the sofa sat a man Dirk knew only too well—it was Ai Tong himself. Well, well, well . . . quite a brave new world, wasn't it, where pimps could rub shoulders with ambassadors. In the overstuffed paisley armchair, puffing on a cigar, was a Thai whom Dirk had never seen—a rotund, bald man in an unpressed blue suit—clearly the sartorial inferior to everyone in the room.

Abruptly, the ambassador stopped playing in mid-phrase. It was amazing that none of them could see Dirk's radiance—surely his face was now as dazzling as the very sun. He constantly marveled at the gullibility of the mortal world—and at the brilliance of his own sleight of hand. Not one of these people could—in the words of the immortal bard—tell a hawk from a handsaw.

"Mr. Ambassador," he said, and was waved to a chair. It was a plain wooden stool—none of them realized that he should be accorded the place of honor; they all still assumed that he was at the bottom of the pecking order.

"Ah, Temple," said Niewinski. "There's well, an

awkward situation afoot. This is Minister Pratap."

"Sir," said Dirk. The ambassador silenced him.

"No, there hasn't been a change of government, or a coup, or anything like that . . . the reason you've never heard of Minister Pratap is that he's . . . well, a sort of minister-at-large."

"I handle many things," said Pratap, "but I am activated only when there is a threat to the economic or political status quo. Otherwise, I wait in the wings."

"Oh, I get it!" said Dirk. "You're sort of the KGB."

"Heavens, no! We are a liberal, pluralistic democracy. Our constitution says so. No secret police."

"If that is the case," said Dirk, "then what is this meeting about? There's nothing democratic about any of this. You got yourselves a hot potato of some kind."

"Some prostitutes are dead," said Niewinski. "Do you know anything about it?"

"No," Dirk said.

"A missing American journalist—what about that?"

"Beats me," said Dirk. He looked at the ambassador, the minister, and the pimp. Each one of them was hiding something. They knew . . . they *knew!* And yet they had summoned him to this grave and secret conference.

Tong spoke up. It was strange to see him without his opium pipe, in a western-style suit and diamond Rolex that undoubtedly outcost all the clothes everyone else was wearing put together. "Your Excellencies . . . it seems to me that the ultimate goal now is containment."

"Yes," said Minister Pratap. "No scandal. Nothing to compromise public relations during Songkraan, and nothing to lessen the flow of tourist dollars."

"And no Americans to be implicated," said Ambassador Niewinski, gazing intently at Dirk . . . with an almost coconspiratorial look. In fact . . . did he just *wink*? It was true, it was true . . . they *did* all know. "Especially Americans with diplomatic immunity. Temple . . . you'll be the point man on this."

"Why, Mr. Ambassador?" Dirk said. "I'm just a third-rate paper-pusher in a back room."

"Don't make me get specific," Niewinski said. "I'm not going to allow this kind of scandal on my watch."

"So it's true, then, sir . . . you *are* up for Secretary of State."

What a supreme irony, Dirk thought. This isn't about the lives of a few miserable whores. No one gives a shit about them. No one except me, that is . . . because I have the power to raise them out of the dust . . . to make them the handmaidens of the most high . . . I am the only one who truly appreciates what these women are . . . I have bathed in their blood . . . I have devoured their eyes . . . they are within me, each one a voice that cries out its paean of praise to me, who put her at the right hand of the most holy one. And what are these people concerned with? Limiting scandal. And money . . . most of all, money.

"I'll take care of things," Dirk said.

The day was wild . . . the evening even wilder . . . and crowd control was the overriding concern. Toward midnight, though, Detective Samreung was on duty, and the holding cell was crowded with the usual riffraff: pickpockets, whores that had strayed from their appointed turf, a heroin addict who'd had the bad luck to fall asleep in the driveway of a bank president's mansion. There were also a lot of ragamuffins: the mayor had ordered a sweep of street kids, who bothered the tourists and whose omnipresence tended to lower the tone of Bangkok's more upscale boulevards and shopping areas.

He would not have paid any attention to any of them; he had more serious concerns. But one of them was wearing a jade crow. It was obviously something he could not have come by legally. Even the dolt of an arresting officer had made a note of it. So now they faced each other across a table, in a windowless room with a single naked bulb, a boy of indeterminate age, skinny, in a tattered Polo shirt and cutoffs, and a young investigator who had rapidly been losing his faith in the system and in the principles of truth and justice . . . and Samreung was asking about the amulet.

"Like I said," the boy said, "I found it." He struggled. The cuffs were tight.

"Don't do that," Samreung said. "Sit still. They'll chafe your skin, and they're rusty. You don't want to get an infection."

"You're a weird sort of a cop," the boy said. "They don't usually pretend to show any concern . . . they get straight to the beating part."

And suddenly there sprang to Samreung's mind the conversation he'd had with a man now dead.

Oh . . . so you're a torturer.

Semantics! he had protested. *I'm one of the good guys.*

"Where did you get that amulet?"

"Get it over with. What's gonna be—electric shock? Or just a quick caning? Or you just gonna slap me around a bit? Come on, I have to get back on the street."

The kid was daring him. They were like that, always teasing you, taunting you. He felt a murderous rage spring up . . . but he held back.

"Chicken," the boy said.

"Don't make me do this," said the detective. Why was he feeling so defensive about roughing up some punk? To get the truth, a little pain was sometimes de rigueur. Everyone knew that.

"No one is making you do anything, Mr. Policeman," said the boy. It occurred to Samreung that he had not even bothered to find out the kid's name. "I was just minding my own business."

"You know it's illegal to sleep under that overpass. Besides, it's dangerous. Look, kid, I just want to know where you got it from."

"Hey, look. If I don't tell you, you'll beat me. But if I *do* tell you, they'll kill me. It ain't much of a choice, but it's the one I got."

"Where were you last night?"

"With my friends, playing with water pistols."

"Were those pistols by any chance filled with acid?"

"What are you getting at?"

He would stonewall all night . . . and then, perhaps, Samreung would be compelled to use a little . . . *mild* violence.

So you're a torturer.

Semantics, semantics, semantics!

Suddenly, Samreung realized that he just couldn't do that anymore. "I'm going to confiscate the amulet," he said, "and then I'm going to send you on your way."

"Such generosity! I suppose you want a blowjob now, you pervert."

"Don't push your luck," Samreung said mildly, and unlocked the cuffs. Quickly, before the kid could deliver another infuriating wisecrack, he slipped the red cord off the boy's throat and put the effigy on the desk. He stared at it for a while. Its primitive, angular style of carving reminded him of something American Indian . . . he'd seen such things in books, not Chinese at all. It was cool to the touch. In fact, it seemed to steal the very warmth from his fingers . . . and in this unventilated interrogation chamber, cooled only by a single, ineffectual overhead fan, it felt like a block of black ice.

"Go," he said to the boy.

"You don't want my name, even? You don't want to know which of the street gangs I'm affiliated with? Mr. Policeman, I appreciate not being beaten, but now you ain't doing your job. What about my paperwork?"

"You want your criminal record added to?"

"Paper's a point of pride among my kindred," said the boy. "You have to rack up a few arrests to get promoted. Even these can be a badge of pride." He stripped off his shirt to show the old white scars of a whipping. There were little round marks, too . . . cigarette burns, perhaps. Why did Samreung feel so sick to his stomach? He knew these people had it rough. For all he knew, the streets were less cruel than a factory job.

He pulled a blank triplicate report form from a drawer and began typing in the information The precinct had still not been computerized—in fact, the manual typewriter had been there for at least fifty years. Still, the thing was official enough, once he had stamped it in three places, and signed it, and scrawled a few longhand notes in the margins.

"Here, kid," he said, handing the boy his freedom—at least until the next bust.

The boy didn't quite comprehend the fact that he was being allowed to walk. But when the detective actually escorted him to the door of the station, the boy finally gave him a big smile—and seemed to mean it—and shouted "Happy Songkraan" as he sauntered out into the fray.

And it was quite a fray, too, even at this hour of night. The water cannon, water pistols, and super soakers were out in force. Trucks were moving through the alley at a crawl, their riders emptying pails of water onto the celebrants that crammed the sidewalks. An elephant was trying to squeeze its way through the bumper-to-bumper traffic, and the thick air thrummed with every kind of music from folk opera to hip-hop.

What was it about the events in the interrogation room that had made him let the kid go? I don't even have a kid of my own, he thought. I don't even have a woman. Every Saturday night, he and his colleagues went to the whorehouse for a beer and a massage, of course—that's what every red-blooded Thai guy does on the weekend—but Samreung was starting to wonder if things could be different.

So you're a torturer.

Maybe it wasn't about semantics.

At length he went back to the interrogation room. He saw the paperwork he'd filled out for that little criminal . . . and he scrunched it up and tossed it away. Then he picked up the phone, intending to call Linda Dusit to tell her that he had the amulet, so she could use whatever power she had to help him trace the perpetrator of these crimes.

As he was about to dial, a fax machine beeped; a paper, addressed to him, came sliding out. It was from a department he'd never heard of before, but it had the seal of the highest authority. They were orders, addressed to him:

> *Deputy Inspector Samreung Boonravi:*
>   *Prostitute murder case: Status is hereby changed to "Low Priority." Factors: low probability of solving the case; negative impact on foreign tourism; relative insignificance of victims.*

So this case was to be on his own time, then, he thought. *But I can't just let it go . . . my hands are bloody, too.*

He called me a torturer . . . and now he's dead.

Samreung picked up the phone. It was an ungodly hour, but you never knew with shamans; she could be up, and anyway, she probably had a servant on night duty.

The phone rang and rang and rang.

When someone finally picked it up, he noticed

that the amulet wasn't where he'd put it. In fact, it wasn't there at all.

The room had suddenly become very cold. As though a chill wind were blowing . . . though this was a room without windows.

The naked bulb had begun to swing.

Back and forth . . . back and forth . . .

. . . a shadow on the wall! Wings! Feathers! And a strange smell . . . putrefaction, mixed with an acrid stench of some chemical . . . perhaps an acid. The shadow-outline of a great bird . . . the slow flapping of its wings was the source of the wind.

. . . and then a plaintive screeching . . . as if the sound of shattering glass had been slowed down and given melody . . . *ka, ka, ka, ka* . . .

A creature that now swooped at him, aiming at his eyes—

Samreung picked up the first thing he saw. A truncheon. Lashed out. A sound like breaking glass. Obsidian shards scattering in the air . . . he drew his pistol.

The shards reformed. A bird-creature condensing out of the shadowed air. The lightbulb swaying now, swaying . . . the shadows spilling across the room. Something moving in the half-dark, something man-sized—

Samreung fired. Again and again. He was panicking—something that hadn't happened since he was a young officer. He emptied the contents of the revolver into that fibrillating shadow, which continued to shift, to dance, to advance toward him.

"What do you want?" he cried.

"The truth," said a voice. A voice he knew. The

voice had become harsher, more echoing, as though it came from somewhere far away.

A voice that belonged to a dead man.

"Have you come to kill me?" said the detective.

"Perhaps." The creature stepped out of the shadows. And perched on his shoulder was a crow—no earthly creature this, but a crow of black crystal—its feathers gleaming with a glasslike sheen, its eyes smoldering, volcanic.

The creature had once been Stephen Lelliott. He was sure of it. The eyes, the general outline of the features, were all the man he had last seen as a pile of liquefying flesh in a concrete stairwell. But there was something skeletal about the face now . . . a bleached, bone-white, chalky coloring . . . dark lines reminiscent of clown makeup . . . and the voice was hollow. Spirits are commonplace in Thailand, but such an encounter, not out of the corner of an eye, not just some quavering voice borne on the midnight breeze, this was unusual. Samreung was afraid, but he dared not show fear. Spirits feed on fear.

He should not have fired. Bullets don't hurt the dead.

"Did you have me killed?" said the spirit. "I have to know. I can forget about your little hysterical display just now . . . I'm invulnerable. But if you ordered me killed . . ."

"No," said Samreung. "Unless it was by inaction . . . or by my suspicions of you. I am so deeply sorry." He fell on his knees in front of the apparition, as was proper before any ghost or spirit, and lifted his palms in reverence. "I was wrong to blame you, *Khun* Stephen."

"I feel that," said the *vinyaan*. "Still, I hope your repentance is sincere. Have you any idea what it's like to have your face eaten away by acid . . . to feel your body melting, burning, being rent apart? I know you have inflicted pain before. You have been callous. And yet . . ."

"I apologize," said Samreung again, and made a humble obeisance at the apparition's feet.

"Get up," the spirit growled. "You must help me. I want to cross over to the other side . . . I want to go through the doorway of death . . . but something impels me . . . something keeps me here, in the half-world."

"Perhaps an exorcism will give you peace," said the detective. By Buddha, Dharma, and Sangkha, he was kneeling there dispensing advice to a ghost! Ironies within ironies.

"No . . . I have a mission to accomplish . . . a great battle that I must fight and win . . . but with whom? There was a woman. I loved her, though I never spoke those words to her, never even dared admit it to myself. Some things are crystal-clear now, you see. But others are murkier than ever. Who are my enemies? Who must I kill before I can cross the river of no return?"

"I wish I knew," Samreung said.

"Detective," said the ghost. "In my last days, many people put on masks of gentility . . . even obsequiousness. The ambassador . . . the owner of the brothel . . . the official I lunched with . . . all went out of their way to feign politeness. You alone despised me to my face . . . you told me that you thought me a murderer . . . and what you thought of me. I believe you have some culpability in my death . . . but your honesty has earned you your life."

"I'll help you," said Samreung. "But I'm not in the loop anymore. They've sent me my orders . . . this thing is to be wrapped up, ignored, thrown away."

"You let the boy go," said the apparition. "I watched. I can be everywhere, you know. I can be invisible. I can spy on these little moments of compassion."

"Something's happening to me. I'm changing. I'm no longer sure of anything."

"I know. That is why you still live. Not to change . . . that is truly death."

He laughed. It was a wheezing laughter tinged with bitterness. "Friends, then? Call me *Ka*," he said.

"Ka? Crow?"

"The Thai for crow . . . the Egyptian for soul," the Crow whispered.

Duan slept only for a couple of hours, in the hallway outside Linda's bedroom. It had wall-to-wall carpet and was more comfortable than the wooden plank bed he had used in the slum. The door to the bedroom was ajar; Duan saw that the old lady was sitting on her bed, watching something on a television just outside his field of vision. She was sobbing quietly to herself.

There was a small camera connected to the TV by cables. The sound was very faint, but Duan knew what she was watching. Perhaps she'd been watching it over and over since they got back to her house.

Duan waited at the door to Linda Dusit's room while she watched the video. He knew better than to intrude. He had experienced it all for real. Of course, he hadn't actually *seen* much. Hidden behind that counter, peering out now and then . . . but *hearing* it had been as bad as seeing . . . worse, maybe. He knew she'd have to be alone to watch it. A dignified woman like that . . . it was better to let them have their emotional moments in private.

The sounds coming from the room were faint, but he knew he was going to piss himself again if he stood there any longer. He was ashamed of that. He'd never watched the videotape. He didn't even really know how those little tapes worked . . . they didn't go in a regular VCR. That must have been why she had Stephen's miniature video camera connected to the TV.

He went to the landing and sat on the stairs, leaning against the cool marble wall.

It was long after noon when Linda emerged. She had the video in her hand, and she had put on makeup. Quite a lot of it . . . almost as though she was about to go on stage. She must have been crying, Duan thought . . . and now she's covering it up with foundation and blush. Dao used to do that. But Duan was struck by the woman's composure. She was an aristocrat to the core. "They have to see this tape," she said.

"Which *they* do you mean?" Duan said bitterly. "Whatever *they* you turn to, they're probably involved in this somehow."

"I know. That's why we need to make copies."

"Who for?"

"Well . . . one for our authorities . . . one for the Americans. I would think . . . and maybe one for my grandson's television station. One of those people must be willing to face the truth. Come on."

"You want me to go with you, ma'am?"

"Hurry. There's no use sitting around the house, getting more and more depressed . . . besides, you haven't eaten, have you? And with all this fuss, the cook hasn't been to market this morning. We'll go to the street emporium . . . there's an old Chinese shop for duplicating tapes, too. I'll get them copied onto VHS . . . easier for them to watch."

She had a kind of manic energy. Duan was a little frightened by it—he had never, in his short life, encountered an old woman who wanted to get up and go places in the middle of the night. Most old women he knew were professional beggars, working their street corners twelve hours a day, then gathering by night with their friends to play cards or chew betelnut. And this old woman actually cared about whether he was hungry. That was a strange feeling inside . . . even his sister had always assumed that Duan was going to feed himself.

He was even more amazed when the old lady commanded him to take a shower, and when a maid brought him "some of the *khunphuchai*'s kid clothes that haven't been given away to charity yet." *Farang*-style kids' clothes—Oshkosh and Benetton—each item probably worth a week's pay. It was strange to be wearing what *Khun Phii* wore as a child . . . especially knowing that now he was a few scraps of flesh inside a great wooden coffin.

"You look a little more human now," said the old lady, and told him to go and wait in the car.

He got into the car. He sat in the front with the driver. It was the first time he'd been out in the Mercedes in the daytime. He thought about his sister's fantasies of being rich and pampered. He was still numb from what had happened . . . could not bring himself to think of the awful scene that was on the tape.

The view of the street was so different from this vantage point: the garland-sellers like himself clamoring at the intersections . . . the vendors, the bright colors of the street stalls . . . all the colors seemed muted in here, cushioned by the soundproofing of the car, the soothing music on the stereo system, the soft upholstery.

Even the wildness of Songkraan seemed toned down. In this part of town, the splashing was a lot less boisterous. Big rainwater jars had been rolled up to the main street, and people were soberly dipping in little bowls and asperging the passersby, who turned, smiled, and walked on.

They turned down Sukhumvit, away from the tourist-ridden single-digit-numbered side streets . . . soon they were in the food markets of Soi 38, with dozens of carts packed together on the sidewalk, the owners frantically cooking under tattered canvas sun shades. The Mercedes parked in an impossibly tiny alley, and Duan and the old lady got out and walked around the corner to the food stalls.

She parked the boy on a stool by a *kuaitiao* stand and told him to order anything he wanted. Out of respect for the diners and the chefs, the water-splashers gave the area a wide berth; he could watch them in the streets without getting too wet himself. He ordered a bowl of steaming fat *senyai* with hot broth, meatballs, sliced pork, shredded beef, a couple of shrimp . . . in fact, once Duan started telling the cook what to put in it, he couldn't seem to stop, and just pointed at everything in the little glass cabinet of ingredients.

"Put some meat on those bones," said the old woman. "That's good. I approve."

Duan started eating.

"And you have to call me something," she went on. She must have noticed that he didn't say much . . . because he didn't know how to address her . . . whether she should be *khunpuying* or *khunying* or just *khun nai*. To use the wrong address would be a deadly insult, excess formality almost as bad as excess familiarity. "I suppose it will have to be Grandmother, mother of my mother."

"Thank you, *Khun Yai*," Duan said humbly, knowing that this lady did him honor beyond all measure by permitting him to address her as a relative. Then hunger claimed him again, and he returned to eating.

"There is a video store run by an old *thaokae* in that alley," said Linda, indicating with a look. "I'm going to go and order copies of this video now. This afternoon, you and the driver will come and pick them up; I'll give you the money. Now eat your fill, and wait for me."

He watched Linda shuffle into the alley. After a time, the noodle chef called out to ask if he wanted a second bowl. He nodded.

More time passed.

An entire hour now. He was starting to panic.

"That'll be forty baht," said the chef's assistant, a scruffy little kid of about nine.

Where was the old woman? He looked all around. No trace of her. But she had told him to call her Grandmother! Was she abandoning him now? Could she really be that cruel? Of course she could. The rich were cruel all the time—and most of the time they didn't even know they were being cruel. They just didn't think. They *never* thought about the people of the streets . . . everything just revolved around themselves.

So it was, and so it always would be.

He waited for a moment. The chef screamed the little boy's name—a customer's noodles were getting cold.

The chef's assistant turned his attention elsewhere. This was Duan's chance. He ducked down low, crawled past a couple of tables, then made a dash for the alley . . . where he was soon swallowed up in the celebrating crowd.

fifteen

THE MADMAN

THE *THAOKAE'S* VIDEO PLACE WAS AN UPSTAIRS cubbyhole-sized shop specializing in pirated videos—first-run American movies, often before they even opened. It catered to those who simply had to see every film before it came out. The owner was a brother-in-law of an old family retainer to Linda's cousin's, so she often made the detour to this place rather than patronizing the Blockbuster by her house. They promised her three copies by that afternoon—run off on their multicopy duplicator, they assured her, and no one would even so much as peep at it, oh, never a peep, some of the customers have privacy issues, if you catch my drift, *Khunpuying.*

As Linda walked down the narrow steps to the alley, she was greeted by a volley of water. She started to laugh—one had to accept the festivities gracefully—but the water kept on coming. It was forcing her back. She was getting soaked, and the steps were slippery.

She was losing her balance!

"No!" She tried to hold on to the wall, but the water kept coming. Suddenly, she was seized. A man's arms. The water was in her eyes, her face, she could see nothing at all. Something came crashing down on her face, and her *vinyaan*, easily separable from her body through years of practiced meditation, bolted quickly so that she lost consciousness before she could feel the pain . . . but not before she'd felt the presence of something terrible . . . something unconscionably evil.

The same presence she'd felt on the videotape . . . even though the killer's face was never in the shot. This presence was something more than human.

Duan was sure that the white Mercedes had been parked in a certain alley, but it wasn't there anymore. Instead there were several police cars, a crowd of curious gawkers, and a man lying in the gutter in a pool of blood.

Yom, the driver.

He couldn't get close. The sea of onlookers was getting thicker by the minute. Police were everywhere, ordering the crowd to stand back, asking people if they could identify the victim. Some people were snapping photographs.

So it was all over, then. Just my karma, Duan thought. I'll always be on the fringe of the real world, looking in. I'd better not stay. Next thing you know, they'll say *I* did it.

The world hates me, he thought.

He began running.

• • •

When Linda came to, she was in the backseat of her own car. She was tightly bound with duct tape, but not gagged. And she felt the presence.

"You can't move a muscle, can you?" said the voice. It was a small *farang*, an ineffectual-looking man. She was surprised at first that he'd been strong enough to bind her and carry her. But then she reflected that the man was a mere shell, a corporeal mask for something far more ancient than himself. That much was clear.

"What are you going to do to me?" she said. "I'm an old woman—as I understand it, you only dismember the young."

He laughed. "I haven't gagged you; as long as you can't move, I think it would be amusing to engage you in conversation . . . and, of course, the sound-proofing in this car is *so* effective. So tell me—you're the one who converses with spirits, correct? And what have you found out about me?"

"I have not gone on any spirit journeys," Linda said, "since I blacked out and found myself here."

"Good, good."

"Aren't you afraid you'll be pulled over? This is a stolen car."

"You must be joking. The police wouldn't dare stop a car that is so obviously owned by someone rich and important . . . and being driven by a *farang*, moreover. The cops around here are scared shitless that they'll accidentally insult some big shot and have to answer to their boss for losing face."

The logic was unassailable. "Who are you?" *Why am I even asking?* Linda thought. The evil *thing* that

permeated the videotape—the force behind the slashing knife—was in this car. Acting *through* this man.
This was not just any madman. This man had broken
through to the forces beyond the barrier that separates
the real from the metaphysical. Had Stephen really
ever known what he was dealing with?

Surely he had to by now.

"Where are you taking me?" she said.

"To hell," said the man, turning to her and leering.
"Oh, allow me to introduce myself. Dirk Temple,
embassy bureaucrat, geek, serial killer, god."

"You forgot madman," said Linda.

"You're lucky I have to concentrate on driving,"
he said, "or you'd get an advance display of my divine
powers."

Linda decided to be silent. She had braved the
forces of darkness many times . . . but the fear she felt
now was very different. She had never really experienced great physical pain. She had seen the video . . .
but video, however horrific, always seemed remote,
disengaged.

There was only one way to defeat this man—
by enlisting supernatural help. Linda tried to concentrate, to enter her state of *samadhi* so she
could send her soul flying out over the void. But
there was something blocking her. She turned to
turn her *vinyaan* loose, but it was as if a force
field enveloped the Mercedes and all its contents.
This man had the protection of darker forces, that
much was clear.

How was this man so powerful? Did he even
understand what he had tapped into?

Perhaps not. After all, the *farang* were virtually

blind when it came to spiritual matters. They were so confident of the absolute reality of the world—and the illusory quality of other worlds—that when other worlds impinged upon their own, they tended to deny, ignore, or possibly seek psychiatric help. Conversely, not having any grounding in Buddhist philosophy, they did not understand that the world on which they chose to anchor all their reality was just as illusory as any other world . . . that they themselves were as insubstantial as their own dreams.

"Where will you take me?" she said at last.

He hooted with laughter . . . the laughter of mad scientists and black villains throughout the world.

"I have had the baptism of blood," he said, "and my apotheosis. But you probably don't even know what that means, you two-bit heathen shamaness. I've been reborn as a god. Now . . . I'm getting ready for the great battle for the soul of the world . . . and my final ascent into the bosom of the Great Light."

So he was perverting the great ritual of Songkraan—the renewal of the world through the cleansing waters of heaven.

This was bigger than even this poor deluded madman knew.

This was about the creation and destruction of the world.

Duan had been walking all day. Around him the celebration raged. People were hosing down strangers from the backs of elephants that had been painted with mythological scenes. On some corners traffic was at a standstill while kids squirted each other from car windows. Transvestites were out in full force, dancing in the side streets and pelting each other with water balloons. Children were passing buckets up and down the sidewalk, indiscriminately dousing the young, the old, the high, the low.

Duan kept his head down, ducked from alley to alley, tried to blend in. He did not even know where he was going. He was far from the known routes, and he didn't have the couple of coins he needed for bus fare. He was too well-dressed to beg—no one would believe a freshly showered street kid in real American clothes. So he just walked and walked.

As evening fell he was so exhausted he had to find somewhere to lie down. He was walking alongside a *klong*, beautiful once, perhaps, before the highways were built, but now stagnant and piled high with refuse. Tall pylons rose up, unfinished, the beginnings of the new L-train system that one day, it was said, would do away with the congestion of Bangkok's road system. An unfinished train station in the sky, reachable by precarious metal footholds in the concrete pillars. Shelter . . . if he could only reach it.

Duan began to climb. There was a station platform—the track was not yet laid—and a roofed area that provided some protection from the dusty wind. There was a staggering view across the city . . . the futuristic towers streaked with neon, cheek by jowl with pagodas, the gilt eaves of temples, the twisty alleys that curved around each other, each one crammed with night-long partygoers. Some distance away a temple fair was in progress . . . the familiar sight of transvestites in bathing suits readying themselves for a beauty pageant . . . gigantic murals advertising the latest movies, illumined by searchlights . . . college students in their embroidered uniforms . . . and everywhere the bursting *dok mai fai*, the fireworks, filling the air with brilliance and gun smoke. Bangkok by night was electric, heady, disorienting . . . and Duan was alone for the first time in his young life, his stomach growling from hunger, terribly alone amid this city of myriad souls.

Sitting down, leaning against the concrete barricade, he drifted into slumber.

He was dreaming of food, almost smelling it, when someone kicked him awake. He realized that the smell was for real.

A bunch of kids was looking down at him. The oldest, a boy with long hair and a dozen white scars on his bare chest and back, said, "You're on our turf, little brother. Get lost."

Duan rubbed his eyes. "There was no one here. I thought—"

"Who you with? The general? The brothel? The *farang*?"

"I'm not *with* anyone."

"Then how'd you find out about this place?"

"I saw it. I climbed up here. What do you care? There's plenty of room."

Another kid—he had a harelip, his lisp was hard to understand—interjected, "The beggars guild sent him. They must be scouting out a new squat for their kids fresh in from the country."

"Don't be stupid," said the leader. "Look how he's dressed. And did you smell him? That ain't cheap soap."

"So who is he, then?"

"I dunno. Who are you?" The leader pulled Duan

up, looked him over thoroughly. "My guess . . . some *farang*'s kept fuck-boy, back on the street now because his owner went back across the great big ocean. Too bad, so sad. Thought you were better than the other kids. Thought he'd send money. You *loved* him."

"I don't love anyone," Duan said. "Not anymore." It was true. Everyone he'd loved was gone. Walked right out on him. That gnawing feeling in his stomach . . . it wasn't just hunger. It was *hate*.

"Good," said the leader. "There's hate in your eyes. I like that. Do you want to be one of us?"

"Us?"

"Yeah. We're bad boys. We do terrible things. We get paid. Sometimes the police take us in, but we can take anything they dish out. We'll work for anyone, but mostly we work for a guy we call the General. We'll even kill for him."

"There's someone *I* want to kill," said Duan.

"Then you'll need practice," said the leader. "My name's Nat."

"Duan."

"We wasted a man yesterday," said the guy with the lip, who introduced himself as Lek.

"Yeah. I guess he owed our employers money or something. It was cool. We got him in a stairwell."

"You kill people a lot?"

"Millions of 'em," said Lek.

Nat silenced Lek with a quick look. "Don't let him get to you," he said to Duan . . . he was not ungentle when he wanted to be, Duan noticed. "We've really only killed one person. And he was a bad man. And they paid us well—a thousand baht each."

If these kids only knew what a thousand baht was to the *farang*, Duan thought. Twenty-five dollars—you couldn't buy shit for that in America. They were just ignorant kids, for all their posturing.

"So *who* paid you?"

"Our *ajarn*," Lek said.

"You guys have a guru, then."

"We call him the Minister sometimes. That's because he sometimes has guys in uniforms with him . . . and they call him 'Minister,'" Nat said.

"He gets us gigs sometimes. Nothing big . . . a break-in, or purse-snatching. He says it's to punish people. Bad people," Lek said. "When someone high up does something really evil, you know the regular police won't do anything. 'Cause they *own* the police. So they ask us to help out."

Nat held out a couple of pork satés wrapped in a banana leaf. "C'mon . . . eat."

Duan ate. He couldn't help himself. He was starving. He demolished the two skewers, and a couple of *khanom sali* pastries that Lek produced from a paper bag.

"Full now, huh! Feeling better, then! Things aren't so bad, are they?"

"Maybe not," Duan said.

"Come on, then. We've work to do. We're not paid to laze around all night. We've got pockets to pick—alms to beg—and glue to sniff," said Nat. "Look around you! It's a big, beautiful city . . . it's a great mango orchard, and it's all ripe for the picking. Oh, it's okay to be on the streets and homeless—long as you got friends. It's gonna be another fine Songkraan."

The boys climbed down the pylon and ran into the night.

The white Mercedes pulled into a tiny alley in the back of a small hotel . . . it was somewhere on the Thonburi side of the river, not too far from the Temple of Dawn.

Although it was broad daylight, and the Songkraan festivities were going on only a few yards away, Temple had pulled the car up to a back entrance behind a huge Dumpster, and nobody saw them as he forced Linda out, duct-taped her mouth, and marched her up a back stairwell.

They entered a corridor.

This wasn't a very nice hotel. It was more of an apartment hotel—the kind you can book from a German sex tour for a week or a month, and it comes with a "vacation wife" that you can select from a catalog.

"Don't worry about us being discovered," he said. "This hotel owes me a favor. Plus, I got myself the whole floor."

He opened a door. "Nice, huh. This is where they bring the food."

A pleasant little suite. TV, wet bar, view of the river . . . and the Temple of Dawn.

"But now here—here is where the fun begins."

There was a walk-in closet. Temple flung the door open. Inside were a full-length mirror, a couple of dowdy suits and ties, and some Polo shirts.

"Nothing out of the ordinary, right? But remember, I have the whole floor to myself."

The mirrored wall was actually a sliding panel.

He pushed Linda through. The smell assailed her right away. Someone had sprayed perfume, and the air-conditioning was on full blast. But behind it was the stench of rotting meat. And the room was a spectacle of carnage.

Truncated torsos lined the floor. From the ceiling, four human heads had been strung together to make a chandelier. A necklace of human hands formed a valance over the four-poster bed.

"If I weren't a serial killer," said Temple, chuckling, "I'd have taken up interior decorating."

He waved to the window. Planks had been nailed across it. Here and there a withered penis had been nailed up. "I don't like those," he said, shrugging. "Well, they're all right, I suppose, but in this forsaken country you can never tell if a girl's going to have a dick."

Linda stood there. She was pretty thoroughly tied up, and the duct tape was making it hard to breathe.

"Say something, you old cow," said Temple. He was jabbing something into her back—a knife, perhaps. She did not speak. He caressed her, breathed down her neck, a sour, alcoholic odor.

"Oh. I forgot. The gag."

He ripped it off. She gasped from the pain as her skin tore. He pushed her onto the foot of the bed, cuffed her firmly to a bedpost, then was kind enough to loosen some of the ropes so she could breathe a little easier.

The bed was soaked in blood . . . Temple had killed. Recently. But there were no bodies on the bed. The sheets were dripping. She watched him dully as he removed his clothes and rolled about in the blood, anointing himself with blood, reaching up to the ceiling to yank on the human heads so they sprayed blood over him like grizzly shower heads.

As she watched him, she realized—to her own discomfiture—that there was a mythic resonance to what he was doing. Many of the Hindu gods bathed in human blood. The Mayans, the Aztecs, the Vikings all understood the meaning of these rituals, and as a shaman, Linda knew that the rituals actually worked . . . if one had the true conviction.

And this man did.

Maybe it was just insanity. But he was fingering the pulse of darkness.

People aren't evil, Linda thought. People go astray, they go insane, they suffer from delusions . . . true evil belongs only to the supernatural world. But she felt it here. As the blood ran down his face, his shoulders, he was being reborn. There was a dark god in him. Maybe *he* didn't even know it. But she was inclined to believe that he did.

Here, in this place where so many sundered souls screamed out in pain, her inner senses were on overload. If she had felt blocked before, now she was being assailed from every side. These people had died so recently that their *vinyaan* were still congregating here. Though they did not feel physical pain, their attachment to the corporeal was still intact. It was a phantom pain they felt, and now she felt it with them. It was unbearable. *I have to escape*, she thought. With her inner eye she saw Dirk Temple transform from man to demon.

He rose from his baptismal font of blood. He was

red from head to toe, and his eyes glowed. When he cackled, she could see fangs. "You're not human," she said.

"And you are the only one privileged to see that," said Temple. "You see, I had to reveal myself to someone capable of appreciating me."

"And when will you kill me?"

"Oh, I shall take my time," he said. "Don't worry, your turn will come. But now I'm going to take a shower, metamorphose back into human form, and go to work. You are my guest. There's food in the fridge. Oh . . . you can't reach the fridge, silly me. I think you can just about make it to the bathroom on that length of rope, so don't soil any of my handiwork. Oh . . . and tonight, we're moving to better digs . . . it's time for my lair to be discovered . . . slash and burn agriculture, you know. Use up one space, on to the next. I've got all of creation to play with. So many souls, so little time! Goodbye, old woman."

And he was gone. She heard many keys turning in many locks. She heard a shower running in the other room. There was no phone here, of course, and she had about four feet of slack. The bathroom was in fact out of reach.

She was glad she had learned meditation, that she could slow her bodily functions and still the raging of her emotions. She heard his footsteps . . . noticed the change from the confident, overbearing gait of the killer to the shuffling, shifty footsteps of the bureaucrat . . . and then she heard the door slam. Abruptly, the evil presence was gone. She was still surrounded by butchered corpses, by agonized souls, but there was no longer that suffocating dark cloud in the atmosphere.

She closed her eyes . . . this time it worked. She sent her soul soaring. There were dead people she needed to speak to, and no time to lose.

"Where to now?" Duan shouted, out of breath.

They'd been running all night, dodging random volleys of water, stealing the odd wallet, gorging themselves at the night markets on barbecued squid and chicken liver skewers.

Now they were somewhere in Chinatown . . . run-down city-within-a-city full of goldsmiths and food stalls and fabric vendors and antique stores . . . decaying mom-and-pop places with apartments above the shops . . . another stagnant *klong*, mosquitoes swarming. The back alley by the canal was empty, though again people were celebrating only a few yards away. It was understandable. The place reeked of decay. No one in their right mind would want to hang out there.

"We're here to meet someone," Nat said.

"Yeah," said Lek. "Our *ajarn*."

"The Minister?" said Duan.

It made sense that the street kids would have a guru. Not some big shot, not like a government minister! Probably some older guy—superannuated at twenty-five—or graduated to serious felonies. Passing a few jobs down the line, keeping the little brothers in food and petty cash. It was a good thing, Duan thought.

I've tried the rich, he thought, *and they're a bunch of hypocrites. I should stick with my own kind.*

"I hear a car—" said Nat. Indeed, there was a

sound. A whirring, churning sound. From the other end of the alley came the light from neon signs and traffic. It pooled over the *klong.*

"It's not a car," said Duan.

No. It was more like a helicopter. Blades thrumming. Setting your very teeth on edge. And then—

"It's coming from the *klong!*" Lek screamed. He pointed.

The water was erupting, whipping itself into a swirling tower of brackish, oily liquid. And inside the tower, burning crimson eyes—

The tower shattered into a hundred crows. Clamoring. Beating their wings. Circling. And now, in their center, standing on a raft formed from the living, levitating bodies of ravens, stood a man.

A man all in black. A man whose face was pale as death, except where it was etched with tattoolike patterns in black. A man who was supposed to be dead. And the birds wheeled about his head, screaming their endless refrain of *ka, ka, ka.*

"You!" Nat shrieked. "Aren't you dead yet?"

"I'm neither dead nor alive," he said. "I am the Crow."

"How'd you find us?" said Lek.

"The amulet has a kind of memory," the Crow said. "Even though it was taken from you . . . it led me to you." His voice was like liquefied night. He spread his arms. His hands were pale as moonlight.

"You're evil. We were told to execute you," said Nat.

Duan suddenly realized who it was those boys had killed the night before. How could his benefactors have done that to someone they didn't even know—who hadn't done them any harm? "Don't you know who that is?" he shouted. "That's my *khun phii!* You killed him!"

"Who's side are you on?" Lek said. "Don't you know better than to trust rich people?"

Duan didn't listen to them. "You fucking murderers!" he screamed, and threw himself at Nat. Knocked him down. Nat crumpled to the pavement—to his own surprise. Duan leaped on top of him. He felt the hate welling up. These boys had taken everything from him. For a thousand baht a head. He just kept punching and punching.

Other boys piled on top of him, pulling him away.

"Stay out of this, Duan," Lek said.

The gang of boys pushed Duan against the wall. He heard switchblades clicking. The platform of living birds, like a flying carpet, moved away from the *klong* toward the army of children. The Crow descended to the ground.

Nat charged, a knife in each hand. The other boys followed. They screamed a primal war cry. Duan saw them stabbing, thrusting, over and over. *Khun Phii* just stood there, his arms outstretched in an invitation to an embrace. His hands, his face, were riddled with stab wounds. Blood poured from him as if through a sieve.

The Crow didn't seem perturbed. He closed his eyes and seemed to draw on some inner force. The wounds began to close up. Duan stared, transfixed. The boys backed away.

"Please . . ." said Nat hoarsely.

"Why did you kill me?"

"They were paid, *Khun Phii*." Duan stepped forward. He knew that this spirit would not—could never—hurt him. "I'm not afraid of him," he said to Nat and the others. "He's my brother."

The boys fell on their knees. They placed their palms together in an attitude of prayer. That was how you placated a vengeful spirit.

"Don't kill us," Nat said softly. "They told us you were an evil man. They told us we were carrying out justice."

"Then tell me who," said the Crow.

"They were good to me," said Duan. "But that can't take away what they did to you."

The spirit moved toward the prostrate boys, still backed by the carpet of birds. They were shivering. Some murmured a prayer to the Lord Buddha. As they watched, the birds shifted position.

The Crow walked among the boys. "Don't be angry at them, Duan," he was saying. "They were only the instruments of my karma. I will not harm them. I only want to know who sent them . . . and who took the life of my star, my Dao."

"I was hiding behind the counter . . . I couldn't see a face . . . but there was a videotape, *Khun Phii*. I gave it to your grandmother, but now . . . she's gone." Duan began weeping. The pale apparition came to him. Duan held out his arms. They embraced. But there was no substance to the Crow. He was half in, half out of the world, and Duan was hugging the insubstantial air, cold and passionless. He was sobbing as he tried to rest his head on *Khun Phii*'s chest . . . encountering only a gelatinous quasinothing. "But you've come back to me. And maybe my sister and brother will come back, too."

"No, Duan," said the one who had been Stephen Lelliott. "They are waiting for the flames that will carry them to the next life."

"Then why have you come back?"

"I'm part of an ancient war," said the Crow. "I have to walk the narrow path between the light and the shadow." He turned to the frightened street kids. "Get up. My quarrel is not with you. Someone used you. Tell me who sent you. I won't hurt you."

"We don't know his name," said Lek.

"But we call him the Minister."

Shakily, the boys rose to their feet. The Crow put his arm on Duan's shoulder. The boy could feel a little substance now, as though *Khun Phii* was struggling to put on flesh. The flock of ravens gathered around them, cloaking them in a tangled darkness.

"Where is this Minister?" said the Crow.

Before the boys could answer, there was a burst of gunfire. A limousine had pulled up, blocking the alley. Uniformed men were charging them. They had AK–47s. The boys were crumpling to the ground now. It was fast. They barely had time to scream. The crows circled around Stephen and Duan. They were weaving, darting back and forth, encasing them in a protective bubble. Duan watched in disbelief. Nat was clutching his stomach as his guts spilled out. The armed men kept advancing, firing. The kids were in a heap, shot full of bullets, and still the men came forward.

"Hold on tight," the Crow whispered. He grabbed Duan under one arm and backflipped over the advancing gunmen onto the roof of the limousine. "Stay put," he whispered, and let go. "They're not gonna fire on this car." Duan hunched down and watched.

The Crow spread his arms as if to fly. Cart-wheeled over their heads. Stood over the pile of dead and dying kids. The gunmen kept coming. He stood his ground. They were right on top of him, surrounding him, bludgeoning him with their weapons. He stood, impassive, just taking it. Then he gave a terrible cry, *Ka, ka, ka* . . .

The crows regrouped. Streamed down from the sky. They tore at the assailants' eyes. The men were scattering now, clutching at their faces, trying to rip the birds loose from their cheeks. The men were firing at phantoms. The Crow ripped off one man's head, flung it against the wall. Duan winced at the cracking sound. The birds were pecking out eyeballs and sipping the jelly. Others were tearing off ear-lobes, lips, noses, cheeks. Maddened, the men ran in circles, braining themselves against the walls, falling into the putrid canal.

Duan felt the thrum of the limo's engine. They were starting up. Where was *Khun Phii*? What was he to do now? Suddenly, Stephen materialized on the car roof alongside him.

The car was swiftly backing out, abandoning the carnage.

"What do I do now?" Duan said. The car was hav-ing a difficult time navigating the narrow street. It turned a corner. A Chinese parade was in progress. Lion dancers were leaping, drums were banging, fifes shrilling, fireworks popping, and always the splashing water.

"Stay very still. No one will see you. And I am with you always."

And *Khun Phii* was gone in a puff of blood-tinged smoke. In his place, there was something hard and shiny in Duan's clenched fist. It was the amulet.

What does he mean, no one will see me? the boy thought. They zigzagged through the snail-like traffic. There were people everywhere. He lay down on the roof of the limo, and presently a crow descended and perched on his arm . . . then another . . . and another . . . camouflaging him in a jet-black feather cloak.

sixteen

THE UNDERWORLD

EYES. EYES. EYES.

This was no underworld she'd ever visited. Trussed up, in pain, surrounded by eyeless dead, Linda had sent out her *vinyaan* to explore the world of shadows. But this was an unfamiliar place. It was like an alien city. Eyes stared from behind old trash heaps and entrance-ways. Cars raced by. Always the eyes, the eyes. And something stalking her. Footsteps. Always the foot-steps. And the fear. The pounding fear.

I'm trapped!

She energized her *vinyaan*, sent it flying through the desolate streets. Fire and brimstone through open windows. Blood dripping from rusted drainpipes. The streets went round and round in circles. No way out. Suddenly she understood what had happened.

I'm a prisoner.

This was worse than the ropes and the cuffs. Con-finement was supposed to be liberating, freeing the soul to soar to greater heights. But no. There was no escape.

Somehow, Dirk Temple had caged Linda inside his own nightmares.

This was a higher order of power than she had
known. It proved that Temple was more than human.

She had to get out. She had to warn her grandson, who must even now be wandering the space
between spaces. But how? With this psychic barrier
around her, how could she contact Stephen?

It was then that she saw the woman.

She was standing in a doorway. She was suffused
with an eerie incandescence. She was waiting for
something, someone. Twin stars shone in her eyes,
and she wore the white robes of a Christian angel.

"Dao," said Linda softly.

"Oh, Grandmother whom I never met in life."

"Nor would have," Linda said ruefully. "I would
have been against such a friendship. You and Stephen
could not have been meant for each other. Your karma
caused you to be born on opposite sides of a great
divide. In life, it was not to be. And yet . . . in death, the
rules can change."

Dao said, "I keep on running up these steps . . .
endlessly I run . . . the staircase spirals and spirals . . .
the doorway is always out of reach . . . this isn't
supposed to be where you go when you die . . .
what's happening to me?"

The spectral woman took Linda's hand. Together
they flitted from landing to landing. The walls wept
blood. Everywhere there were pieces of human bodies. Intestines, strung out and stitched together, were
the water pipes. Blood vessels were the power con-
duits, and they exfoliated along the walls. Here and
there a severed hand beckoned them upward. Beams
of light spilled from empty sockets of decapitated
heads.

In a room, an ancient man with white hair that swirled down to the floor and out the door and down the balustrade was puffing on a hookah that filled the air with suffocating fumes of frankincense and copal. In another room, a man in a shabby suit barked orders into a telephone made from a human femur. These were not dead people . . . Linda knew that; they were reflections from the land of the living, caught up in the madman's magic.

The landings widened until at last they were in a vast L-shaped room. At one end of the L, a light storm raged. Whorls, sparks, shimmering veils of color. A wind whipped through the room, sighing, sending Dao's hair flying.

"It's the way to your next life," said Linda.

"I can't get through—"

The wind howled. Linda tried to step toward the light. A surge of power thrust her back. She fell into Dao's arms.

"I'm trapped here . . . at the edge of the tunnel," said Dao. The other side of the L was a chamber of horrors. A hundred stone crows, tall as men, stood guard. The dungeonlike walls were hung with writhing corpses. The headless ones dribbled blood. Bell jars full of human eyes adorned the mantelpiece. The stone floor was slick with blood and rheum. Blood welled from the cracks in the stone.

A child was weeping . . . and Linda saw that it was a toddler, playing among the rubble and the corpses . . . a glimmering outline of a child, sometimes barely visible, as though his very soul were clinging tenuously to a quasihuman shape. This had to be Din, the young one. Young ones dart more eas-

ily from world to world . . . their sense of reality isn't
fully formed yet, Linda thought. We may lose him
completely.

"Only one thing can free you," Linda said. "But
now he's a prisoner, too, he's in his own hell, fettered
by love and vengeance."

"Stephen. Yes."

"But first there is something he must know . . .
something we have to tell him."

"Only we can't reach him," said Dao. "If only I
could see him . . . if only I could show him who did
these terrible things to us."

"Perhaps we *can* see him," Linda said, "even if we
can't speak to him."

She took Dao's hand. Both women were *vinyaan*,
insubstantial; their hands blended into each other . . .
their souls melded a little. "Let's try to see him," she
said. "Call your little brother."

"Din," said Dao. "Din, Din." The name sounded
like the tolling of a funeral bell. The child crawled to
them out of the heap of body parts.

"He's not quite as imprisoned as you," said Linda,
"because his soul is less complete . . . let's try to see
through his eyes."

The boy came to Dao's arms.

At once, Linda saw a vision—

Night. A long black vehicle in the traffic . . . like an
eel wriggling through a school of fish.

A glowing amulet—

The limo moved more swiftly now, inching its way
toward one of the bridges over the Chao Phraya. It
was hard to hold on. The great ravens were every-

where. Was *Khun Phii* inside the amulet now? What was Duan to do? What would happen if they discovered him clinging to the roof of their car? He was scared. He tried not to think of all those kids, convulsing as they collapsed in a heap beside the filthy canal.

Halfway across the bridge. The smell of the Chao Phraya in his nostrils . . . the silhouette of the Temple of Dawn in the neon-tinged moonlight . . . the hot, foul wind blowing in his face . . . he was afraid, terribly afraid. On the other side of the bridge, he could see several police cars pulled up, their lights flashing. They were obviously going to rendezvous with this limo. Which meant that they were allies somehow. The police and the murderers.

The he heard *Khun Phii*'s voice.

"Duan, Duan . . ."

Where was it coming from? He held the amulet to his ear. "Are you in there, respected brother?" he whispered.

The voice was inside his own head. It spoke tenderly to him, calming his terror a little. "Listen . . . when this limo pulls over, when the door opens, I want you to get this amulet inside somehow. Do you hear me?"

"Yes, *Khun Phii*."

"When you've done that, go as quickly as you can to my family's funeral pavilion at the temple—wait for me there. No one will profane a temple . . . you'll be safe there."

The limo pulled into a parking lot. There were police cars on either side now, and several officers standing at attention. The limo stopped. "When you let go of the amulet," said *Khun Phii*'s voice, "you will become visible . . . so get away as soon as you can."

The door of the limousine opened. Swiftly, Duan leaned over, tossed the amulet in, then rolled down the rear of the car onto the pavement. The policemen did not notice; they were conferring with a man in a suit who had stepped out, and who in a moment returned to the limo accompanied by a plainclothes-man.

Songkraan revelers stood nearby. He joined them. One of them doused him. He laughed, although inside he felt ready to die.

Detective Samreung felt distinctly uncomfortable when the Minister asked him to ride with him toward the latest crime scene. In the limo, the Minister poured them both a glass of Black Label.

"The containment is not working," the Minister said simply.

The Minister drained his whiskey in one gulp. Something glinted at Samreung's feet. He picked it up. It was the amulet. He looked over at the Minister, who seemed distracted. He slipped the amulet into his pocket.

"I've been forced to eliminate a few people," the Minister said. "It's for the best. We have to dig out every piece of the contagion. It's for the future of our country, you know."

"Yes, Minister," Samreung said.

"When panic spreads, Samreung, it's cancer. What we do is not bad. It is necessary."

Where were they going? Samreung had received a call at home, had been told it was of the utmost importance, had come to this rendezvous to find other police already present . . . and the Minister-at-large ordering him to ride in his private limousine. This ought to have been an honor, yet Samreung had immediately felt that something sinister was afoot.

And what was the amulet doing on the floor of the limousine?

Off the main road, down a few tiny *sois*, a plaza with a run-down hotel, maybe four or five stories tall, with a neon sign that read simply HOTEL. Several police cars were already there. There was a team of special unit men with flame throwers. Samreung had a sinking feeling.

"Are we destroying more evidence?" he asked Minister Pratap.

"Yes," said the Minister. "But first I thought you might like to peruse it. It is, in its grisly way, quite a work of art."

They exited.

The lobby: The receptionist was a human head on a pole. A forked stick held two hands, impaled like marshmallows. The rest of her was protruding from a trashcan. The registry was open. There was only one recent entry—from three days before—and it read simply: *Mr. Deus X. Machina.*

The rest of the lobby was immaculate. A guest sat on a sofa with a cup of coffee in his hand. Only on close examination was it apparent that the cup was literally *in* the hand; a hole had been carved out of the palm to make it into a fleshy cup holder. What looked at first like a reddish baseball cap was in fact the man's blood-gorged brain, exposed; the top of the skull, with the scalp still on it, rested on the coffee table.

One of the officers started to take pictures. Angrily, the Minister whirled around, grabbed the camera, and pulled out the film. "We're here to destroy, not to commemorate!"

They went up to the top floor.

The bodies, the whimsical arrangements of the body parts, the chandeliers of human heads, the penises pinned to the wall . . . Samreung's gorge rose. He couldn't hold it in. He ran to the bathroom of the suite, started to barf into the toilet before realizing that it contained a human heart. *Professionalism!* he told himself. Get a fucking grip! Then he lost it totally and just vomited his guts out, right there, right over the gore-drenched evidence.

He washed his face. Straightened his clothes a little.

He pulled out the amulet and stared at it.

The black crystal began to shimmer . . . to vaporize . . . all at once, the bathroom was filled with a black fog. An animal smell . . . the smell of feather dusters, laced with carrion.

A man condensed out of the mist.

"I've come back," said the man who had once been Stephen Lelliott.

Linda had been here. The Crow could sense her in the air . . . knew she was already gone. As he materialized, his familiars began to shimmer into being . . . crows oozed out of dripping faucets, poured out of the bathroom mirror, squeezed themselves out from the cracks between marble tiles.

"How did you get here?" said the police detective.

"I chartered an amulet," said the Crow. "Let's go."

Samreung opened the door of the bathroom.

There was a pistol pointed at his head. It was wielded by a chubby man in a shabby suit. *So this was the man who ordered my death*, the Crow thought. He remained concealed within the shroud of fog. Drinking in the atmosphere of the room—the despair of lost souls, the stench of putrefying flesh. He put a comforting hand on Samreung's shoulder. Two crows flew in from the bathroom and perched on either side of Stephen's hand, camouflaging Stephen from view.

"Who let in the birds?" said the Minister.

"I . . . don't know," Samreung said. "The bathroom is full of them."

"Curious things," said the Minister. "I don't like their eyes."

"Are you going to kill me?"

"I'm glad you've had your last vomit," the Minister said softly. "It's always good to have one's affairs in order."

"Why?" said Samreung.

"It's regrettable. You're a good man, with a good heart. But you ask too many questions. I'm sorry that you will be dead, but rest assured—you die a hero, tragically killed in a mutual shootout between yourself and this appalling serial killer."

"Who you haven't even caught."

"Oh, he will tire of it—they always do. He's just some crazy *farang*—and every one of them is crazy, you know that perfectly well. Perhaps he'll wander on to Malaysia, or the Philippines, or even back to *farang*-land into the hands of the FBI. Meanwhile, I have to protect the economic well-being of this country. I'm sorry, Samreung. Best of luck in another life."

"So you orchestrated the destruction of all this evidence," said Samreung. "But who pulls *your* puppet strings?"

Pratap stood for a while. He seemed to be fuming. Finally, he whispered harshly, "My puppet strings? *My* puppet strings?" and cocked his revolver.

The Crow emerged and pushed Samreung to the ground as the Minister fired. He fired. He fired. The Crow could feel the bullets tear into him . . . one into his stomach . . . one into his groin . . . one whistling through his cheek. The pain was distant . . . an echo of a memory of pain. He stepped forward. He could feel the capillaries weaving back together, the flesh knitting itself, nerve to nerve, muscle to muscle. He reached out and caught the next bullet through the hand. Slowly held up his hand to show the bullet hole closing itself up. "Do you know me, Minister?" he said.

The Minister fired three more times. He was out of ammunition. The Crow seized the gun from his hand and tossed it aside. The Minister reached for something—a cell phone, perhaps. But the Crow grabbed him by the wrist and yanked.

The hand tore free. Wristbones clattered to the floor like a handful of marbles. Pratap screamed. He waved his arm about. Blood spattered the walls, the ceiling. The Crow tossed away the hand.

"So who, Your Excellency," he said, "who *does* pull your puppet strings?"

"It's not my fault," the Minister croaked.

"It never is," said the Crow. He flicked his head. The birds were streaming from the bathroom now. They

descended on Pratap's hand stump . . . began to feed.
Shred by shred they took him apart. The Crow did not
want to watch. This was the working out of karma . . .
he took no joy in it. There was nothing in this act of
vengeance for him. Only the emptiness . . . emptiness
inside of emptiness . . . oh, if he could only weep . . .
but no. He could not do so until the cycle had run its
course.

Fire now. He could feel the heat.

"Get up," he said to Samreung. "They are torching
the building, and we have more work to do."

"Work?" Samreung gasped. The Crow could tell
that the man was at the very limits of his power to
believe. He had been allied with these forces, had
never questioned them before—and now he was
being bludgeoned into a brand new, topsy-turvy
world view, where good and evil were blending into a
featureless ambiguity.

"Come." The Crow listened. His attenuated
senses could detect the footsteps of men as they
stalked about the perimeter of the hotel with their
flamethrowers. "We're about to have one of those
Bangkok fires . . . the ones that flare up for no reason,
and then die away without ever appearing in the
news."

As he spoke, smoke was filtering into the room.
"Come," he said. "I don't want you to die of inhala-
tion . . . now that you've become one of the good guys."

He cried out: "*Ka, ka, ka.*"

The flock of crows moved away from the body
of the Minister. He was picked clean now, a skele-
ton adorned with tatters from an old suit. The
crows gathered around Stephen and Samreung.

Other crows stormed the window, which was boarded over, and began pulling out the nails with their beaks. As the planks clattered to the floor— the nailed-up body parts scattering along with them—the birds began smashing against the glass. They were breaking out the window. A blast of hot air. They could see flames now. Black fumes were streaming into the room. Samreung coughed and spluttered.

There was a banging on the door. "Your Excellency!" voices were shouting. "We must get you out now—before the entire building catches fire!" The pounding came harder now. He could hear them forcing the door. Samreung murmured something. He was barely coherent.

"Hold on to me," said the Crow. Samreung clasped his waist. The Crow climbed up onto the sill. The birds were clustering around them. The room was black with birds now—crows clambering over the bloody bed sheet, ravens ripping out of dead women's stomachs. The birds began to gather around the two of them. Their wings fanned away the fumes from Samreung's face. He breathed easier.

"It's over," whispered the Crow.

The police were storming into the room now, riddling the corpses with more bullets.

"Don't be afraid," Stephen said. "Just hold on tight."

And leaped.

seventeen

THE RIVERBOAT

IT WAS A SEVERAL-STORY DROP, BUT SAMREUNG'S FALL was broken by a carpet of crows. They flocked beneath him, buoying him against the searing wind. But Lelliott was gone . . . instead, there was the amulet, on a red string around his neck. And there was the limousine.

The firetrucks were moving into position now. They would let the building burn a while, then put it out . . . all very efficient. Some policemen were saluting him. He realized that it had been necessary for Minister Pratap to shoot him in secret . . . that the different divisions of the establishment could not have been seen to be at odds with each other in public. That was, after all, the entire basis of Thai interaction. Never, never, never break the veneer of artifice. Never, never, never lose face.

Samreung fingered the amulet around his neck. It was cool to the touch . . . while everything around him was blazing. Get a grip, he told himself. He walked over to the limousine. The driver came out and stood at attention. He beckoned to a police sergeant and gave him what would, he was sure, become the official story: "Regretfully, the Minister died heroically in a gunfight with the killer, who also died. The case, I think, will soon be closed."

What to say next? Where did the trail lead?

He was going to have to bluff. "Take me to His Excellency's next appointment," he said to the driver. "I will take care of the rest of the evening's business, and announce the sad news myself."

"Very good, sir," the limo driver said. He bowed and opened the door. An assertion of authority went a long way . . . especially when no one wanted to risk their neck . . . or face the responsibility for Pratap's death.

He was taking a gamble by assuming that the Minister *had* another appointment that night . . . considering the lateness of the hour. But it was Songkraan. Doubtless there were still parties. Besides, it was clear that the Minister had business to wrap up . . . and needed to get it all done as quickly as possible.

They pulled away. Sirens screamed and firehoses were being turned on the burning hotel now. Thank God the limo had air-conditioning. And a well-stocked bar, he thought, as he helped himself to a Mekong on the rocks . . . a working-class whisky, but Samreung didn't really appreciate Black Label. . . .

The two women, trapped in the nightmare of Temple's mind, saw glimpses of what was happening . . . the hotel on fire . . . the incandescent air suddenly black with congregating crows . . . and now the limo inching its way along the riverfront.

"Look, look . . . ," Dao said. "My brother. . . ."

A little boy, slender as shadow, slipping through the labyrinthine back streets. . . .

"He's lost," said the shamaness. "We must try to send him help."

The night of festivities was a night of terror for Duan . . . he did not know what he was fleeing, or why . . . all he knew was that he had to get back to his sister's coffin. He walked in a daze . . . past temple fairs and midnight markets . . . never looking back . . . ducking the volleys of water where he could, where he couldn't trying to force a smile out . . . one street had become an impromptu parade of Mercedeses, elephants, and traditional dancers in cloth-of-gold costumes and pagoda hats . . . another street was a virtual river, with all the fire hydrants gushing, with naked children leaping up and down in the cooling water . . . Duan went on walking. His mind reeled with images of amputation and decapitation. He didn't know where he was. Had he been walking around in circles? The streets all looked the same.

Suddenly, out of nowhere—

A crow perching on his shoulder.

Whispering in his ear: *Ka, ka, ka, ka, ka.*

Then taking off again, weaving through the throng. Someone's sent me a guide, thought Duan. Quickly, he elbowed his way through the crowd, and now the crow was always a little way ahead, its beak a citrine beacon in the darkness.

The limousine went alongside the river until it stopped beside a pier. From his vantage point in the other world, the Crow watched. This was the pier beside the old Christian graveyard. A wave of desolation assailed him. The heartache was so intense as to make him feel almost alive again. He imagined Dao standing there, in the gloom, as she had once waited in the dazzling sun.

A motorboat was waiting, manned by a paramilitary with a turban and a rifle.

The Crow reentered the jade amulet and eavesdropped as Samreung talked with the chauffeur.

"Sir, you will be escorted to the rendezvous point," the chauffeur said. "And I'll be waiting here at dawn."

Samreung did not ask what the rendezvous point was; to show ignorance might well be the kiss of death. He trusted that the supernatural force within the amulet would come to the rescue.

The chauffeur said to the guard: "The master has passed over. This man comes as his emissary, to complete his activities for the evening."

He returned the Sikh paramilitary's salute, and sat down in the boat, which sputtered to life. They started to move across the Chao Phraya.

Moonswept, the river was a mystery. The Temple of Dawn, its fantastical spires occasionally lit up by distant fireworks. Farther along, unfinished skyscrapers, huge condo developments started during the boom, abandoned during the bust. Where were they going? The river widened . . . and at length a riverboat hove into view.

It was like something in a historical epic. Something like one of those gambling boats that used to ply the Mississippi—he had seen many old movies that showed them—and something like Cleopatra's golden barge—he had seen *that* movie, too. And also something out of Thai mythology. The prow of the vessel was a *kinari*, a half-woman, half-bird out of ancient legends, completely covered in gold paint. As the motorboat pulled alongside it, steps were lowered. Above the waterline, they were carpeted in red, and the wood was gilt, and carved into representations of garudas, messengers of the gods. He saw no one, although the cabins seemed brightly lit, and there was laughter and soft music.

At last, the Sikh said something to Samreung. "Sir," he said, "you should go straight to the dressing rooms. You should find something appropriate there."

The paramilitary went up first. More Sikhs stood guard by the prow. The first guard whispered to them; the others saluted and helped him over. Then they escorted him to a small room—more a walk-in closet than a room—and left him.

The racks were full of costumes. There were dinner jackets in every size. There were harlequin masks, powdered perouks, even a Roman centurion's uniform.

"A costume party," said the Crow, suddenly shimmering in out of the shadows. "This is where it ends. In a world of illusions, a boat of illusions; charades within charades."

The crow with the glowing eyes led Duan through the maze to a familiar place . . . the cemetery by the bank of the Chao Phraya. By moonlight it was full of people . . . there were even stalls set up, with pork skewers barbecuing. Young boys hawked lottery tickets.

"What's going on?" he asked one of the boys.

A Brahmin ascetic walked past, intoning strange Sanskrit verses while piercing his cheeks with metal rods.

"The word is," said the boy, "this graveyard is very lucky tonight. It's a good place to watch the pre-dawn fireworks . . . and there's a rumor that one of the spirits here is going to appear in someone's dream with a winning lottery number."

An elderly Chinese couple were picnicking over his father's grave.

"Excuse me, aunt and uncle," said Duan politely, "but I'd like to pray to my father's spirit."

"How quaint," said the old lady. "A Christian father for a little street boy. Would you care for some *salapao*?"

Duan gratefully bit into the bun he was offered, with its juicy filling of roast pork and Chinese sausage, and leaned against the gravemarker. The crow with the citrine beak settled above his head, and Duan dozed. Although there was a loud party atmosphere in the cemetery, and Thai, Chinese, and American pop music playing from several boom boxes, Duan felt more secure than he had felt in several days, and he drifted into sleep.

"A fine idea of the Minister's," said Ambassador Niewinski, "this little gathering on his private riverboat. But where's the host?"

Dirk Temple said, "He's late. We'll have to start without him." Insufferable, the way these mortals ignored the strictures of time and space! The ambassador didn't even seem to realize that the cosmos was coming to an end—that by dawn they would be in a brave new world. And how rude this Minister Pratap was, to proffer his private riverboat and not even show up for the premiere of his show!

"I'm glad they put you on the entertainment committee, Temple," said the ambassador. "Since you seem to know a great deal about Bangkok's more . . . unusual entertainments."

Dirk smiled. "I'm a god, Mr. Ambassador," Dirk said, and smiled wickedly. A clown costume! he thought. His Excellency the representive of We the People—and he plays the fool. Typical.

The ambassador laughed and fiddled with his big red plastic nose. "Such a delicious idea . . . to watch the predawn fireworks from the river . . . it will be quite a spectacle."

Dirk was, indeed, God—at least, his costume was. He wore the robes of a Greek god, and had a thunderbolt or two tucked into his tunic. He was basically playing himself, he noted with grave satisfaction.

Dirk walked about the room, fussing over details. The main ballroom of the riverboat had a proscenium at one end; behind was a green room where performers prepared. The proscenium arch had a heavy purple velvet curtain; the show, painstakingly prepared by Dirk earlier, was to be a surprise. *And it certainly will be*, Dirk thought grimly.

There weren't that many guests—but they were all special. Ai Tong was there—along with four young virgins who were due to be auctioned next month. Most of the guests were notorious voluptuaries, people from the ambassador's private circle of friends (his wife, as usual, was conspicuously absent) and there was even a Hollywood personality or two—of course, they were always slipping off to Thailand to enjoy the you-know-what. The guests were all male—with the exception of an uncharacteristically butch U.S. congresswoman in a tux—it was Cassandra Hathaway of New Jersey, who on C-Span never wore anything but the most becoming navy blue Chanel suits. She had two playthings—drag queens in elaborate Cleopatra costumes.

Indeed, the playthings were of many genders and even, if one looked carefully, species. All were draped over the guests, and the affair was in danger of descending to the orgy stage even before the serving of the cheese fondue. There was Devin Motz, the infamous artist who had daisychained a string of naked Playboy bunny-types across the ceiling of Grand Central Station as a metaphor for corruption in government. Motz had two whores on leashes, and was painting a watercolor on a young man's buttocks. And . . . was that some Arab prince? Dirk could not tell.

Hateful, hateful, hateful, Dirk thought. But what can I do? They are my audience. For now.

The ambassador had gone over to the piano—a big white grand—and was tossing off showtunes. Now was as good a time as any to begin the show. Dirk clapped his hands for order.

"Ladies and gentlemen—"

"Wait," said Motz, "this is ruining my light."

"Just a cotton-picking moment," said the ambassador suddenly, slamming the piano lid down in mid-"Oklahoma." "I want to put in this last-minute addition."

"Not *another* addition, darling," said the Congresswoman. "You're *aggravating* my PMS!"

Niewinski turned to one of the impassive Sikh guards, who turned to another, and another, and presently a large-screen television was being wheeled in. In front of the curtain, luckily. None of the surprise would be ruined.

A dozen leather couches had been arranged in a semicircle for the delectation of the guests, with little side tables of hors d'oeuvres. The ambassador, as befit his station, sat in haughty solitude in the front row. Ai Tong occupied a sofa by himself as well . . . with room for his hookah on a leather ottoman next to him.

"Since our host hasn't seen fit to show up to his own party—I understand he's been held up somewhere, fighting crime or some such nonsense—," the ambassador announced, "I wanted to share with you all this video. Apparently it's the hottest thing in Bangkok. It hit all the bootleg shops this morning. I haven't seen it, but I'm told it's pretty damn shocking. Not the kind of thing we're going be able to enjoy once we get back to Ponca City, Oklahoma, so—dim the lights—roll it!"

The room went dark.

How like the ambassador to try to sabotage the evening by putting on his own show, Dirk thought. Oh well—I'll just have to put up with it.

It was at that point that two new guests slipped unnoticed into the ballroom.

He stood there, behind the ambassador's sofa, a raven perched on one shoulder, the only one in the room not in some kind of fancy dress. Yet he blended in perfectly. The detective waited in the back of the room.

The Crow, the inconsolable, the eater of souls, watched the video monitor. He was transfixed. At first he could hear the audience murmuring, sentiments like, "Is it true? Are these real? . . . the things those effects people do nowadays . . . oh, sick, sick . . . I saw a snuff film once, in Guatemala City, but nothing like this . . ." Then, after a time, the voices fell silent. The videotape was utterly, horribly engrossing.

It was Dao.

Ah, love, the Crow thought, my love and my pain are one.

Dao in the doorway, Dao in the shaft of light, Dao the innocent.

The video camera did not move at all . . . an eerie sense of voyeurism . . . of entrapment.

A knife descending into the shot. Dao's eyes, wide. Struggling. Hands, arms of a stranger. The knife slashing down.

And in the ballroom . . . in the darkness . . . nothing but eyes. Eyes. Eyes. Riveted. Watching.

Faint and scratchy now . . . a scream . . . not the throaty scream that you'd hear from a B-movie queen but . . . an ugly scream, a cat-in-heat scream . . . you could not dream that such a scream could come from a dainty throat . . . the knife plunging into flesh now. Zigging, zagging, swerving, slicing. The scream ending in a gurgle as the knife slit clean through the throat . . . a whistling through the sundered trachea as it flopped out, oozing dark blood and mucus . . . the slow gouging of the eyeballs . . . the carving open of the breast . . . the hard sternum hung with globules of glistening fat . . . and behind it all the soft warm light of the doorway . . .

He remembered how she had stood there . . . how he was thinking . . . *great television such great television.* . . .

Ambassador Niewinski sat on the front sofa, never looking away from the screen. His face glinted in reflected video light. He looked like a zombie. His hands were hidden under a silken cushion on his lap; he was sweating.

The Crow whispered in his ear. He started.

"Enjoying the show? You find it interesting . . . arousing, even?"

The ambassador gulped. The Crow reached out and touched the nape of the ambassador's neck . . . Niewinski's skin crawled. The Crow could tell. The fear beneath the skin, like a mass of wriggling worms.

"You're not . . . masturbating, are you?"

The ambassador's lip quivered a little. Oh, the despair that seethed beneath the Crow's impassive exterior! That his love's passion and death should be reduced to this . . . a peep show for jaded men . . . lost in the trappings of their own power.

"Of course not!" said Niewinski.

"But you are . . . entertained. By these . . . visions of torture and death."

"It's nothing," the ambassador murmured. "It's just illusion, sleight of hand." But the Crow could see that he believed . . . and was inflamed. And the other guests! An artist was languidly painting someone's bare skin—and barely paying attention to the spectacle of love and death on the monitor. A woman in a tux was panting heavily and guzzling champagne.

An armchair was being moved into the shot. The convulsing body of Dao was being arranged . . . so artfully arranged, the neck tilted just so, so that the slit throat seemed knit once more, with only a telltale slice of crimson . . . the lips carved into an artificial smile . . . and then . . . one could only see the killer's back . . . placing the young boy in her arms, one arm cradling, the other caressing his pierced hands. Then—for a fleeting moment—one could see the killer's face.

"Temple!" the ambassador whispered. "So that psychiatrist's personnel report was . . . prophetic."

The ambassador sighed. Perhaps this artful butchery had actually given him a sexual climax.

From deep within the Crow came an anger, a pitiless anger. The blind rage built up inside him. He could feel it coursing through his tendons . . . breaking through the graveyard stillness of his soul. He snapped the ambassador's neck with a single flick of his wrist. A gasp, a wheeze, and the man was gone. But no one noticed. They were sucked in, ensorcelled by the madman's world . . . shackled to their seats by their own morbid lust and curiosity.

There came a horrible cackling sound on the tape. The unholy laughter of the mad.

The camera dwelled, unmoving, on the obscene Madonna and child. The rest of the audience continued to stare. Most, the Crow thought, must be in denial. He sat beside the ambassador, arranging his body carefully so that he appeared to be in a natural state of slumber—as though anyone could doze off at the sight of Dao's murder. The laughter continued.

Yes. The dead watching the dead. Even the

undead Stephen could appreciate the irony.

No one knew or cared.

Except Temple, apparently. Temple, who abruptly stormed the stage and switched off the television, who started ranting at the audience, "Enough, enough . . . you don't even know what you're looking at . . . you don't know reality when it's right there on the screen. Well—have a look at *this* little spectacle, then!"

He yanked down the curtain. The stage was dark except for a few spotlights, each one trained on a beautiful woman. But there was something wrong. Their heads rotated all the way round. They were mounted on servos. Their lips began to move in sync to an out-of-tune rendition of "Cabaret" from off-stage loudspeakers. Their breasts heaved left, right, left, right, in a grimly well-synchronized choreography. There was blood everywhere.

"Vanity," said Temple, "all is vanity. Oh, you are all skin-deep. That's why I've had to turn you all inside out. You think you have free will, don't you? But you're all a bunch of simplistic machines. Well, there's a new owner now, and the world will dance to a different tune."

Center stage was a bizarre array of rotating knives. The whole thing was powered by some kind of outboard motor. There were several semicircles of knives: They pointed in, out, up. It was a little like one of those medieval models of the Ptolemaic universe, circles within circles all turning madly, the crystal spheres that comprised the cosmos.

He has created the universe in his own image, the Crow thought.

Temple casually removed one of the heads from the lip-synching prostitutes and threw it at the machine, which shredded it instantly, spraying the audience with bone shards, brain tissue, and blood.

"Applaud, you imbeciles!" Temple cried. "This is high art. A few trips to the junkyard . . . the junkyard of cars, the junkyard of souls, the immense heap of decay on which this entire city is built . . . a few choice engines . . . a few kitchen utensils . . . and heads will turn, I tell you!"

Appallingly, the audience did begin to applaud. There were scattered cries of "Encore!" This crowd was still trying to be sophisticated, still trying to believe that the whole thing was some kind of artistic statement, all effects, all illusion.

And Temple began to laugh.

It had been Temple in the video. Temple had killed Dao . . . and many others . . . knew that he had always known it, almost before it happened . . . knew that all his dreams and premonitions in life had pointed to this confrontation.

Ai Tong got up now. "This is outrageous," he shouted. "I gave no permission to neutralize my most precious merchandise!"

"Perhaps you want to be paid," said Temple. "Oh, look. Ambassador Niewinski is an example to us all . . . he has dozed off."

It's time, thought the Crow.

He stood up. His face shone with a phosphorescent pallor. As he stretched out his arms, he summoned up the thousand thousand ravens of the underworld. They were clamoring as they flocked about the vessel. He could hear gunshots . . . perhaps the guards were trying to fend them off. It would be useless. He heard the squishy thud of bodies slamming against walls. The guests betrayed surprisingly little panic. Perhaps they thought this was all still part of the show. Certainly they were not the type to think that anything bad could happen to them in this life.

"Do you know me?" the Crow said softly.

"Lelliott," said Temple scornfully.

Ai Tong said, "I was given to understand that you had been taken care of."

"I have been," said the Crow. "I am dead. There is nothing more you can do to me."

"Guards! Guards!" Ai Tong shouted. One guard staggered into the ballroom. His skull had been cracked open, and a crow was feasting on his brain. He moved erratically, his eyes rolled up into the sockets, his arms flailing. He landed on top of Ambassador Niewinski. Crows began streaming in from the open doors. One sipped at the ambassador's eye.

The Crow could feel the dread in the room now . . . nobody moved. The crows flitted from guest to guest. There was fear. Every guest, the Crow knew, had some dark secret that cried out for vengeance. He could feel their minds working feverishly to figure out who was here to call them to account for their misdeeds. The crows kept their distance from Ai Tong. Somehow the smoke from his bong had drawn a protective circle around him.

"You're all under arrest," said Detective Samreung, popping up from the shadows.

"I don't think so!" said Temple. "Ever heard of diplomatic immunity? Look it up, pal. I can do anything I want in this fucking country."

"And should you decide to arrest me," Ai Tong said smoothly, "you will, I am sure, have to answer to Minister Pratap."

"Minister Pratap," said the Crow, "is already dead."

With a gesture, he sent the crows flurrying toward the feast of corpses. Like a black cloud, they settled on the stage, screeching, rending flesh, carpeting Temple's tableau. Those that flew into the diabolical knife device were hacked to smithereens. The dead birds piled up in a circle.

"You're not going to touch me," said Dirk Temple. He waved his hand at the ceiling. "Not until you've seen the pièce de résistance." Slowly, something was being lowered from the flies. It was a shriveled creature, trussed up with robes and chains, bloody, barely alive . . . and it was slowly descending toward the whirling apparatus of knives.

"The good witch," said Temple. "I have her."

Linda spoke—her gasping barely audible above the clamor of the crows. "Let me die, Stephen," she said. "I have many more lives in my journey toward nirvana."

The rage exploded now. Dark powers stirred within the Crow. Black flames spewed from his eyes. Lightning danced about his hands. He opened his mouth to speak, but only a crow's raucous cry escaped his throat.

"An interesting display," said Dirk Temple.

Linda was being lowered . . . a centimeter at a time . . . toward the machinery of death.

"You may be some supernatural creature," said Temple, "but that doesn't make you invincible. You're a puppet of your own instincts, your so-called karma."

"And who pulls *your* strings, Temple?" said the Crow.

"I am a god," said Temple.

Detective Samreung ran toward the stage now, firing. Bullets ricocheted off the whirling knifeblades. Shrapnel pelted the audience. A piece went through the artist's eye. He screamed and jabbed his paintbrush hard into his subject's anus. Crows threw themselves against his head, sucking out the juice from his shattered eyeball.

As Samreung reached the proscenium, Ai Tong blew a blast of smoke at him. The smoke enveloped him. He spluttered. He tottered. Where the smoke touched him there were pinpricks of flame. He was on fire! He was falling toward the knives!

The Crow leaped onto the proscenium. He snatched the detective away. There was a crunch of bone. Samreung's hand, still clutching the pistol, was catapulting through the air. More bullets went off at random. The artist and the tuxedoed woman fell dead into a bloody, necrophilic embrace.

Ai Tong caught the hand, still clawing the emptiness, and regarded it with disdain. "You were right to ask who pulls the puppet strings," he said to the Crow. "Above the gods . . . there are even higher gods . . . there are the ultimate powers of light and darkness."

He sat back and puffed.

"No!" Temple screamed.

He ran backstage and yanked on a cord. Counterweights shot up to the flies. Linda Dusit plummeted. She was only an inch or so above the spinning knives. Stephen called out to the crows in his mind.

The crows rushed in to break her fall. They clustered beneath Linda, flapping crazily, trying to force her into suspension. There was a buffer of crows between her and the blades . . . a suicide buffer as one by one the knives minced their living bodies and spun a whirlwind of feathers out over the ballroom.

Can't hold her forever, he thought. She's going to die—

And Linda . . . whose mind was still in the L-shaped room, watching her own imminent demise next to the *vinyaan* of Dao, said: "Now, my little star . . . how great is your love for him? . . . show him . . . reach out to him from this imprisonment . . . it's your own terrors that have caged you, your own pain . . ."

—and Dao gathered up all the force within her into a pulsating ball of light and—

—the barrier broke! In the air above Linda's bound and spinning body was a starburst and through that pinwheel of radiance came the specter of a woman, glowing, the soft lines of her limbs bathed in a rich white radiance.

Time stood still. Linda was suspended above the churning blades. The light crackled as it shot through the room. It forked and forked again. It played over the woman's head like a halo. She was nude, and she held a nude child in her arms; yet it was a vision of sublimest chastity.

"Yes!" Linda cried. "Your love for each other has torn down the wall between the living and the dead!"

In that moment in time yet outside time, the battle between the Crow and Dirk Temple took on the proportions of myth. As crows stormed the riverboat,

dismantling it, as the surviving guests leaped into the
river, clinging to driftwood, as the corpses began sliding down decks and into the river of kings—the sewer
of kings—Dirk Temple began to glow. He was greater
than human. He was a force that drew its potency
from the bowels of Narok itself.

He flung himself at the Crow. The Crow plucked
ravens from the air and set them on fire with the heat of
his anger—threw them at Dirk's eyes. The Dirk-creature
breathed fire. As he spun around and around, he himself
became a machine with a thousand blades. A thousand
crows immolated themselves against him. A corrosive
ectoplasm streamed like vomit from his mouth.

"I am a god!" Temple shrieked. "They thought I
was just another serial killer, another madman—but I
am a god!"

They fought. Their bodies flamed. Like giants of
old, they leaped from shore to shore. They heaved great
boulders at one another. The crows blackened the
moon. By the banks of the river, people were already
gathering, waiting for the pre-dawn fireworks.

A hand tapped Duan's shoulder. He started. The old
Chinese couple seemed frozen in time. He looked
around. The loud music was gone; instead there was a
tinkling, sourceless music, sensuous and sweet. Everyone was either asleep or in some kind of suspended
animation.

The hand again.

It was a child . . . a dead child.

The child laughed.

"Come on, come on," the child said, and seized
him by the hand.

They ran toward the river. Everyone they saw was in the magical sleep. Even people who were in the midst of hurling water at each other . . . the water was a streak of wetness hanging in the dark air. Across the river, the only light came from distant condo sky-scrapers . . . the Temple of Dawn loomed, black and huge, and the moon was blocked by a flurry of crows.

"Where is our sister?" Duan said softly.

And there she was, clad only in her silken hair, bathed in a silvery radiance that seemed to come from within. Duan's heart was beating fast. Song-kraan is a time of ghosts, of souls renewed and cross-ing over to their next existences. He wondered if he was going to die now, whether his brother and sister had come to fetch him. . . .

Dao said, "Don't be afraid. Your brother and I will soon be gone. But we wanted to wake you . . . for this special moment . . . so that you will see . . . and remember."

Crows filled the sky. They blackened it. Blocked out the light from the skyscrapers. Concealed the moon. These were no earthly crows. They had come from another world. Their eyes began to glow, and soon the world was lit by an eerie light, a million red pinpricks, a million red stars that glowered on the surface of the water.

Two demons were battling on the farthest shore. Uprooting trees and slamming them into each other. One bestrode the highest pagoda of the Temple of Dawn—

"*Khun phii!*" cried Duan.

And in the sky, on opposite sides of the river, sat two gods . . . each one enthroned . . . each one with a hundred arms . . . and Duan saw their faces, and knew that one had the face of Ai Tong, and that god sat on a pillar of smoke, blowing his foul breath over the world . . . and the other god, who was wreathed in light, from whose throne wafted this celestial music, had the face of Linda Dusit.

"It's an eternal battle," said Dao, "and the gods work through humans, sometimes without their knowledge."

They fought on. For hours they fought, upending boats, plucking pylons from the ground, lassoing each other with electric power lines. Fireballs careened through the air. Ravens swooped from the sky to stab at Temple's eyes. A burning wind howled about them as they struggled.

A terrible, timeless rage consumed the Crow. How could this worm of a man have transformed himself into a god? The Crow leaped through the air, his fingers clenched like talons, as Temple clawed his way along the footholds at the base of the pagoda. Temple held on to the heads of the gargoylelike *yaksha* statues, thousands upon thousands of stucco demons circling, spiralling the perimeter of the building. The Crow flew on a magic carpet of ravens. "Stop running!" he cried out in the language of night, the rasping, screeching clamor of a million birds. "Do you not know that I must finally kill you . . . that this struggle and your death are part of the wheel of karma?"

The Crow was swooping down on his quarry now. Temple was panting as he made his way up the narrow steps of the great pagoda. Many dimensions inter-

sected here. They were titans, smashing mountains
with their fists. They were constellations, battering
each other with comets and meteor showers. They
were mortals, out of breath, gasping as the hot wind
whipped them, as they struggled to retain their balance. They were wind and water, earth and fire, yin and
yang. They were the energy trapped in the cosmic egg,
the force that danced creation and destruction.

The central pagoda of the Temple of Dawn
stretched up toward the stars. Each flight of stairs was
narrower, steeper than the first. Dirk was slipping and
sliding in his own blood. The Crow was gaining. Perhaps the outcome of the battle was inevitable . . .
preordained from the beginning of time. As they
raced toward the top, the Crow gained in power. His
feet felt lighter, his heart less troubled. There was a
crazy joy in him . . . knowing that the moment for
which he had been created was coming to pass.

Temple was gasping for breath. The anger was
leaving the Crow. Instead there came a desolate sense
of inevitability. There was almost compassion . . .
almost, for a fleeting moment, a kind of love.

Finally they were at the summit of the pagoda.
And now the crows that had blanketed the sky
parted . . . a shaft of moonlight fell on the Crow . . .
battered, Temple lay at his feet . . . still clawing at the
empty air . . . his cracked lips still proclaiming his
abortive godhead . . . the creature who had once been
Stephen Lelliott roared out the last dregs of his rage
to the unlistening wind. Why this unending pain?
Why this restless, relentless anguish? There came no
answer from the heavens. Karma is cause and effect,
beyond compassion, beyond pity.

I loved her! You killed her!

He looked into the monster's eyes . . . and he saw the same question that tormented his own mind.

Why must this war go on, from age to age, from eternity to eternity?

"I do not know," he whispered. "I haven't come to answer questions, but to fulfill what must be fulfilled. I am the Crow."

A sadness filled him as he pounded the man into a pulp. Beat his brains out against the porcelain-studded stucco. Lifted the shattered corpse high above his head, and hurled it at the sky—

Temple exploded! Blood, flesh, phlegm, and bone scattered all over the pagoda. As the fragments blew upward, the wind caught them, toyed with them. They detonated further . . . into fireworks that festooned the dark sky . . . the crows too were bursting into flame, each one a fiery splash in a sea of black . . . and more crows were smashing themselves against the sides of the pagodas . . . rushing toward certain death with open wings . . . each becoming a fireburst . . . feathers were raining from the sky . . . the birds popped, sizzled, plummeted in streamers of white light . . . came a sound like distant rain.

Rain? In the height of the dry season? But when the Crow gazed over at the far shore of the river, he saw that the pattering raindrop sound was the crowd gathered along the bank . . . applauding the fireworks.

He felt Dao's presence. The air that buoyed him up was scented with her sweet breath. She stood by the doorway to the next world, and though her lips were solemn and unsmiling, her eyes held a transcendent radiance that touched even the coldness of the Crow's dark heart.

"Now you know," said the Crow to the *vinyaan* that permeated the air about him, "now you know how much I have loved you."

And the wind was stilled, and the spell was broken, and the portals of the sun flew open.

The dawn was almost upon them. Police boats had been dispatched to rescue the survivors of the Minister's riverboat. In the twilight, Duan stood with his brother and sister. No one else saw Dao and Din, or if they did, saw them only as tricks of the light.

Fireworks cascaded in the pre-dawn light. Behind the Temple of Dawn, little boys hawked lottery tickets up and down the riverbank in the last hours before the winning numbers would be announced, while would-be millionaires poured out of the cemetery, each one having dreamed of a possible winning number. Waterhoses, buckets, and waterpistols were already out and ready. It was going to be a long wet day, this final cleansing of last year's bad luck.

Duan watched the river anxiously. A line of ambulances was forming in the parking lot of the old Catholic church. One police boat was docking . . . and, tottering, leaning on the shoulders of an officer, was Linda Dusit.

"Khun yai!" Duan cried, and ran to her side.

The policeman tried to brush past him. "Get out of the way," he said. "I'm sorry, *Khunpuying*, but these kids—"

Linda smiled. "That's all right," she said. "I know this one."

"Oh, your houseboy," said the policeman. "Excuse me."

"No," Linda said, "my grandson."

The officer stared at her, thinking perhaps that the capsizing of the riverboat had addled her wits.

"Look!" People were pointing at the sky. It was moments before sunrise . . . the horizon was already streaked with red and purple and magenta, the lurid hues of a polluted dawn. There came a crack, like the splitting of the sky. And then, for a moment—

Through the torn curtain of twilight, they could see—

A many-headed demon, taller than the Temple of Dawn, wielding a glittering club, enveloped in twists of firework light, exploding, showering the river with a million shards of fire, and—

Wheeling above the demon, a raven drawn in a thousand points of fire, bursting, the lines of light cascading across the clouds, and—

Duan felt a wave of love sweep over him from the exploding sky.

"*Khun Phii*," he said softly. And he began to weep.

"I go now, little brother," said Dao's *vinyaan*. And embraced him, and slipped through his embrace like a chill wind, and then—

In the sky, intertwined with the outline of the burning crow—

The incandescent outline of a woman—

The laughter of a child—

Soon lost, all lost . . . as the sunlight stole up from the horizon . . . as the throng cheered and clapped and chattered about the pyrotechnic display, more

thrilling, more elaborate than any previous year . . .
yet this was to be expected . . . for was this not the
New Year in the city of illusion and enchantment, the
city of excess and magic, the city of spectacle and
bewilderment? Duan clutched his new grandmother's hand . . . he wept with bitterness and joy.

Water washed over them . . . sacred water, water
scented with jasmine and blessed by monks in an
ancient ritual of rebirth.

Duan helped Linda as paramedics moved in, lift-
ing her up and laying her down gently in the waiting
ambulance. No one stopped him as he climbed in
beside her. She moaned . . . she smiled a little.

"I'm sorry for crying," he said. "I should be
happy . . . you're alive . . . and the nightmare is ending . . ." It was an embarrassing thing, to weep like
this; I'm a *luukphuchai*, Duan thought, a man now,
the only man in my family.

"Weep all you want," Linda said. "Even tears are
water, and on this day even this water is a blessing."
She squeezed his hand, closed her eyes, and fell into a
deep slumber.

eighteen

THE OVERWORLD

IN THE TEMPLE, IN THE COURTYARD NEXT TO THE FAMILY'S pavilion, the funeral pyre had been set, and the coffin laid on top of the bundles of fragrant wood. It was June, monsoon season. Clouds lowered. It was proper for a decent interval to pass before sending the souls of Dao and Stephen off on their journey; cremations, in Thailand, are a time of celebration, not of mourning.

There weren't many people at the *phao sop* ceremony. Nine monks for the chanting, some of the girls from Cleo's, which had been taken over by Ai Tong's nephew since his body washed up on the riverbank in the wreckage of the Minister's riverboat, and a contingent of garland vending boys from the slums. Not the most normal clientele in this most upscale of Bangkok temples. Linda was amused at that. None of her friends had deigned to come—well, except for Father Santini, who, not being Thai, was not offended at the affront to the class system.

And then there was Detective Samreung. For now, he was not working for the police force. He had sought retreat and renewal in the monastery, and was

on indefinite leave while he satisfied the obligation of
every Thai male to *buat phra*, to become a Buddhist
monk for a time.

The detective was one of the chanting monks. As
an apprentice, he was mouthing the words; he didn't
seem to have them memorized yet. But he clutched
his prayer fan with his good hand, and seemed at
peace.

Dressed in black, Linda sat in front of the flames,
thinking of that day only two months ago when she
had been drawn to buy this coffin in the alley of the
coffinmakers. The boy, enrolled in a private school,
was developing an upmarket accent, and had a few
friends now; they were playing with yo-yos behind
one of the pagodas. It was a little awkward with the
street kids there too . . . but somehow Duan managed
to be both gracious and a little standoffish. He had a
new life now. A calm life. But his innocence . . . that,
Linda knew, was lost the night his sister was mur-
dered.

Her new chauffeur, Krit, came up to her with a
box of videotapes. "I think we got most of them," he
said.

The notorious murder video had circulated
briefly, but Linda had been diligently trying to sweep
them off the market. With a symbolic gesture of tri-
umph, she tossed a few more copies into the flames.
Of course she had not found them all. Who could? But
this was sympathetic magic. As the fire consumes these
duplicates, she thought, so may any other tapes, wherever they are, charged with the magic that sends souls
forth from universe to universe, also crumble into the
empty air. . . .

The burning plastic seared her nostrils, made her weep with its acrid odor. All at once, her *vinyaan* left her body, and she found herself skimming the territory of dream.

A thousand crows traversed the ruddy sky.

Enthroned at the edge of the abyss, his neck hung with skulls, a three-headed hound growling at his feet, sat Yama, the death-god, the immortal men fear most. Clouds of smoke billowed about him. At his feet, fissures in the rock glowed with lava.

The death-god had the face of Ai Tong.

"I see you've come to see your little ones off," he said. "They've done well . . . they are moving ever closer to nirvana."

He gestured at the heavens. A single star hung in the dark sky, like a crystal teardrop. About the star, a lone crow hovered, mournfully flapping his wings and crying out, *Ka, ka, ka, ka, ka*.

Linda said, "When will it end? When will we lay down our arms and declare a truce?"

"I don't know," said the god of death. "The world dances to the rhythm of this war. The dance of life and death is the force that keeps the wheel of karma in motion. It's neither good nor evil, my dear shamaness; it's simply the thing that is. Look . . . my servant, Dirk Temple . . . see the new employment I've found for him . . . the shepherd of the despairing."

Linda turned and looked into the face of the man who had tormented her . . . who had concocted machineries of torture . . . and used the corpses of women as interior decoration. The madman.

"He *was* a god, in his own way," said Yama. "But

not the god he thought he was. He was not the god that creates the world in his own image—that honor goes only to Four-faced Brahma, architect of the cosmos—he was the god who becomes god for a day, so that his divine blood can be spilled and sacrificed for the world's pain. And your grandson . . . ah, yes . . . for a time, he too was a god. He is free now. Now he has learned that godhood is a curse . . . a terrible burden to be endured in solitary anguish."

The madman danced across the hellish landscape. Behind him was a legion of the undead . . . humans with mutilated limbs, decapitated torsos whose neck stumps gushed forth blood, men and women whose bodies were rotting as they shambled.

"The *phii tai hong*," said the god of death. "The spirits of those who have died violently, and who cannot quite extricate themselves from the tainted soil of life . . . they remain behind, stuck in a karmic stasis . . . until their moment of redemption . . ."

And then she looked skyward, and gazed for a long time at the star and the crow . . . the fixed point and the wanderer . . . the light and the dark.

"They love each other," she said. "I am content."

And, back in the real world, the fire consumed what remained of the lovers' bodies. Smoke, fragrant with jasmine and attar of roses, ascended to the skies, pleasing to the nostrils of the gods. The deep chanting of the monks stirred her. Soon children would play in the ashes of the departed. And soon—or not so soon, for the wheel of karma has a million million years to turn before enlightenment can free our souls—the souls of Stephen and Dao would come back into the world. In time, after an eternity of torment in the fires of Narok, even Dirk Temple would be reborn . . . and continue his journey toward nirvana.

Linda Dusit braced herself for a new grandson, new lives and attitudes . . . a new year and a renewed world.

epilogue

Ancient Wisdom

All sentient souls must fall into the dark
Only their deeds survive them.
Good and evil are the shadows that men cast
Through all eternity.

> —Phra Law,
> ancient Thai epic poem

S. P. Somtow
Bangkok, Los Angeles, 1998–99

about the author

CALLED BY THE *BANGKOK POST* "THE THAI PERSON
known by name to the most people in the world," S. P.
Somtow is an author, composer, filmmaker, and
international media personality whose multitudinous
talents and acerbic wit have entertained and enlightened fans the world over.

He was Somtow Papinian Sucharitkul in Bangkok.
His grandfather's sister was a queen of Siam; his father
is a well-known international lawyer and vice-presi-
dent of the International Academy of Human Rights.
Somtow was educated at Eton and Cambridge, and his
first career was in music. In the 1970s (while he was
still in college) his works were being performed on
four continents and he was named representative of
Thailand to the Asian Composers' League and to the
International Music Commission of UNESCO. His
avant-garde compositions caused controversy and
scandal in his native country, though, and a severe case
of musical burnout in the late 1970s precipitated his
entry into a second career—that of author.

He began in science fiction but soon started to

invade other fields of writing, with some forty books out now, including the classic horror novel *Vampire Junction*, which defined the "rock and roll vampire" concept for the eighties, the *Riverrun Trilogy* ("the finest new series of the 90s"—*Locus*), and the semiautobiographical memoir *Jasmine Nights*, which prompted George Axelrod to call him "the J. D. Salinger of Siam." He has won or been nominated for dozens of major awards, including the Bram Stoker Award, the John W. Campbell Award, the Hugo Award, and the World Fantasy Award. He now holds the post of president of the Horror Writers' Association. His most recent books are *Dragon's Fin Soup—Eight Modern Siamese Fables, Tagging the Moon—Fairy Tales from Los Angeles,* and *The Vampire's Beautiful Daughter.*

A media personality in his native Thailand, he has, in the U.S., been a frequent guest commentator on Sci-Fi Channel talk shows, as well as the occasional "talking head" on documentaries for the Learning Channel and the History Channel. He has returned to music in a big way, composing *Kaki,* a ballet, for a Royal Command gala in Bangkok, as well as a number of film scores. He has just conducted the Bangkok Symphony Orchestra in a new symphony commissioned in honor of the king of Thailand's birthday.

He has also made some incursions into filmmaking, directing the cult classic *The Laughing Dead* and the award-winning art film *Ill Met By Moonlight.* His website may be found at **http://www.primenet.com/~somtow/**